T0245977

WOMEN'S HOTEL

WOMEN'S HOTEL

a novel

DANIEL M. LAVERY

HarperVia

An Imprint of HarperCollins*Publishers*

WOMEN'S HOTEL. Copyright © 2024 by Daniel Lavery. All rights reserved. Printed in the United States of America. No part of this book may be used or reproduced in any manner whatsoever without written permission except in the case of brief quotations embodied in critical articles and reviews. For information, address HarperCollins Publishers, 195 Broadway, New York, NY 10007.

HarperCollins books may be purchased for educational, business, or sales promotional use. For information, please email the Special Markets Department at SPsales@harpercollins.com.

FIRST EDITION

Designed by Yvonne Chan
Illustrations © Natalya Levish/Shutterstock

Library of Congress Cataloging-in-Publication Data has been applied for.

ISBN 978-0-06-334353-5

24 25 26 27 28 LBC 8 7 6 5 4

To Grace and Lily
"Better a dinner of herbs where love is"

AUTHOR'S NOTE

The women's hotel left no lasting mark on the American city. It was born in the nineteenth century, then briefly prospered and died within the compass of the twentieth. In the 1930s, perhaps two or three such hotels could be found in Denver, Seattle, and Dallas, with a few more each in Philadelphia, New York City, and Washington, DC, but they never became either popular or reliable. Most residents did not stay longer than two or three years, and those who did stay longer usually suffered from straitened circumstances. None of them held a unified definition of collective living. Few of them shared ideals. There were no Oneidans among them. Their heyday was briefer than that of the Shakers, and their legacy weaker. It is possible that the nineteenth century had seen such a supersaturation of utopian societies spring up and wither along the river valleys of the eastern states that no desire for perfection survived into the next.

Whatever the cause, the abbreviated popularity of women's hotels sparked no consequent movement and left behind no organized legacy. They served as short-term stand-ins to replace those now-lost, sometime-consecrated institutions for feminine maintenance that had once served as catchments for the middle class and superfluous: religious houses, country schoolrooms, the ever-retreating frontier, ladies' seminaries. They were made obsolete by the credit card, by hippies and the New Age movement, by lesbianism and feminism, by the increase in affordable apartment stock and the increased acceptance of premarital cohabitation. The residents of these hotels did not *rent* in quite the same way we use the term today. Almost anyone who rents an apartment today expects, and is legally entitled to, not just a private bedroom but a bathroom and a kitchen too; these women paid at the end of every other week for a single room, a shared bath at the end of each hallway, and half their board. They were neither short-term guests as at a standard hotel, nor quite independent bachelor girls responsible for their own housekeeping either. And of course they could do no entertaining. There was nowhere to put guests and nothing to refresh them with had there been room. Their socializing was either cloistered inside with their fellow residents or somewhere else out in the world. Today almost all these buildings have been bulldozed and replaced with something more useful or gutted and refurbished and converted into condominiums, often very expensive ones, with unlisted rates.

Why live in this way? Had these women no family or friends in the city who might rightly be expected to take an interest in them on arrival, no private homes that might have admitted them, that they should live in a hotel? So wondered the acquaintance of the first Biedermeier residents upon learning of their intention to "take rooms" in the early days, when residential hotels, except for the most palatial, were seen as a poor substitute for family living. The acquaintance of latter-day residents, who considered residential hotels at worst an encumbrance and at best an oddity that ought to have died with the speakeasy, wondered why they didn't go all the way and enter a convent. Few of the women would have given the same answer to the question, and possibly none of those answers came near the truth: to live somewhere that was socially and professionally accepted by everyone, and yet was decidedly, categorically not a home. Not being prepared to commit themselves to a mode of living that might have excited comment (there were, of course, women living together privately in twos and threes all over New York during this same period, but informal arrangements between women had a habit of falling apart under even mild external disruption), they nonetheless sought to establish themselves in the city with the fewest possible number of social ties, keeping acquaintance and expectation at bay. To disappear in a large city is no especially difficult task, but to disappear without ever exciting remark, without compelling a flurry of letters and telegrams or visits from the home folk, requires careful accounting and economy of movement. Such ties cannot be cut abruptly or all at once; it jars an entire network of invisible interests and prompts others to repair the rupture in angry determination. Ties must instead be slackened gently and at long intervals, and not dropped before some other node has been built up over the abandoned junction.

Let this book be taken for no more than what it is: a diffuse sketch of a short-lived, patchwork commonwealth, a few impressions of a manner of living that was briefly possible for a small group of women in the middle decades of the last century. It is a story of provisional, often unwilling, cooperation between people with no real allegiance to one another, the diary of some women, and a few men, who occasionally found themselves sharing the cells of unheaded and deconsecrated abbeys, and were sometimes glad of it.

Chapter One

THE END OF BREAKFAST

I t was the end of the continental breakfast, and therefore the beginning of the end of everything else. For thirty-five years, every Biedermeier girl whose rent for the coming week had found its way to Mrs. Mossler's crocheted lantern-bag could go to sleep secure in the knowledge that she would wake up with a breakfast tray slid into the recess of her door, delivered just as advertised, "silently and gratuitously, no waiting—no waiter!" During the war the fourteen-dollar rent was raised to eighteen dollars, then again to twenty-five dollars after Carmine DeSapio replaced Hugo Rogers as the head of Tammany, Mrs. Mossler certain that a non-Irish Tammany boss was a harbinger of the rising prices, social upheaval, and general chaos soon to come. But the Biedermeier's daily rendezvous between tray and door never failed, not even on Sundays, and aside from a wartime substitution of Postum for coffee, the menu had remained implacably untouched by time. One's choice of either sliced grapefruit or tomato, a Vienna roll or brown buttered toast, a shirred egg, and a cluster of grapes sustained plenty until dinner (new girls learned quickly not to speak of supper within the walls), as lunch was not included in the weekly rate, and fewer than half the inmates were so reliably employed as to be able to comfortably commission a week's worth in advance.

Possibly by way of consolation, lunch had become a slightly un-fashionable meal at the Biedermeier. The girl who paid for hers some-times discovered that she had hung an albatross around her neck. It was a daily custom for residents who considered themselves "at home" enough to receive visitors to leave their doors ajar between the hours of ten and two. Since no more than twenty of the Biedermeier's more than two hundred rooms were larger than the original ten-by-fourteen-foot floor plan, only visitors of supreme or long-standing intimacy were entertained all the way inside the room, usually given pride of place upon the bed while their hostess perched against the desk. Ordinary callers were received in the doorway, sometimes sev-eral at once, depending on the attractions of the inmate, but the girl who received her lunch from the hotel often found that her floormates treated the sight of the tray as a NO VISITORS sign. Then, no matter how charming her conversation, no matter how ingenious her tricks of arranging hair or repairing handbags that might have otherwise endeared her to them, no matter how invitingly open she propped her door, she could not tempt a single straggler to her threshold. The girls whose jobs occupied an entire working day took their lunches, if they had any, at their desk or in company cafeterias, luncheonettes, or at a coffee stand, but as they ate them properly in public and therefore out of sight, no one held it against them. (The Biedermeier had a caf-eteria, but for six years had not been able to support the staff required to prepare and serve lunch.) To eat in conspicuous privacy, in full view of your fellows, was generally understood as selfish, antisocial behavior that required immediate checking, lest it spread and infect the whole population. The record holdout, a girl named Sylvie who had possessed an immaculate brow, had endured six weeks of freezing out in 1958 and ultimately resigned her tenancy rather than give up her lunch, her loss regretted by none.

The rest were happily won over to the great and delicate game of scrounging, whereby every girl cadged food—whether a box of chocolates from a date or covered plates from church suppers, bingo hall refreshment tables, gallery openings, employers, women's City Club lectures, or high school cafeterias (a sweater set, in either tan or navy, and an innocent expression being sufficient for entry in many of the public schools downtown, though any interloper who tried the same institution two days in a row or more often than once a month did so at her own risk)—then laid out the spoils of war for general consumption during visiting hours. Anything short of fishing out of the garbage was considered legitimate, and special acts of brazenness or ingenuity were a sure route to long-term popularity. This cooperative and piratical approach was nowise countenanced for either breakfast or dinner, only the midday meal. Biedermeier residents took great social pride in belonging to that class which considered certain types of theft as fair play and even a mark of distinction, while regarding thefts of desperation, or hitting the same target too many times in a row, as a humiliating admission of ineptitude. To score an elaborate sampler of chocolates off an inept date was a triumph, especially when he might otherwise make his own score off you. To meddle with the boss's punch clock or secretly rig an attendance system to add fifteen minutes to the employee lunch hour, to feign the loss of a token in front of a soft-eyed subway station clerk, to scrounge among friends and relatives when necessary, to abuse honor systems, to capitalize on an idling delivery truck or lodge an invented consumer complaint, to recycle a nickel on a long-distance call—all fell under the perfectly appropriate remit of getting one's own back in an unfair world. Even to steal from a high-traffic newsstand or drugstore, once in a while, was no more than a good woman's fault. But there were inviolable limits to such broad-mindedness. Breakfast and dinner were bailiffs to the rule of law. No self-respecting Biedermeier girl stole before eleven or after dark.

One eighth-floor resident, Elizabeth Watson Perkins, had set the record in the summer of 1955 when, in a single week, she was able to serve visitors to her room brown bread and baked beans from a Friends Meeting House, noodle pudding from the Eldridge Street Synagogue, cheese-and-butter sandwiches from St. George's Episcopal Church, little toast-brown pasties from St. George's Ukrainian Catholic Church, potted shrimps from the Fourth Universalist Society, pancakes from the Jan Hus Presbyterians, a nearly full carafe of coffee from St. Mark's relief house, and an entire platter of Baptist ham from the Mariner's Temple. She had invented three absent-yet-devout fiancés and enrolled in just as many conversion classes in order to secure the eatables, and became a local hero in the process. Her name was spoken in awed accents for three residential generations longer than anyone else's, before or after.

Mrs. Mossler had personally arranged the breakfast menu in 1929, and remained passionately evangelical on the subject of culinary conveniences, for no woman setting foot into an office thinking about the breakfast dishes in the sink or the dinner yet to be planned could be expected to keep her mind on the job, "or indeed to keep the job itself!" Mrs. Mossler's belief that every Biedermeier girl was at once the ideal employee and within a hair's breadth of being fired was unwavering. As being fired was the worst disaster she could imagine, worse than hatlessness or moral degradation, she imagined it fairly often and in vivid detail. She encouraged the girls to imagine the same, impressing upon them the closeness of mealtime to catastrophe and assigning a maximum of evils to the dinner bell, "for it has cut short many a promising career."

This was more generally than particularly true for residents of the Biedermeier, which even in the grand old Art Deco days had failed to come out on the right side of the glamour line. Of course Biedermeier girls worked, some of them even regularly. But they rarely found employment in those promising industries that facilitated being addressed by their surname or riding in elevators with ambitious young men. Residents who worked as switchboard operators, bookkeepers, and assistant dressmakers in their first year could be reliably found among the ranks of switchboard operators, bookkeepers, and assistant dressmakers in their third, and usually back in Duluth or Essex County by their fifth.

This dismayed Mrs. Mossler not at all. She had been born alongside the century and in every subsequent decade seen a wave of New Women descending on Manhattan to make good on the promises of the last. It was an article of unquestioning faith for her that each generation would be the one to finally make that grand push over the top. So each new year saw her as cheerful and vigilant as she had been in the last, once again bringing together mediocrities and their breakfast, first in day suits and on bicycles, then streetcar- and khaki-crazy, with unbuttoned overcoats and marcelled hair, and later as disciples of Schiaparelli carrying Pernod-colored gloves, as certain of the current crop's success as she had been of their grandmothers'.

The first three decades of the twentieth century had seen an out-and-out scramble among developers to build hotels for every sort of working women, boardinghouses being now as hopelessly old-fashioned for the office-girl generation as horsehair sofas had been for their mothers. The working woman's moment required publicly available monuments to efficiency and reproducibility—part icebox for preserving virtue until such time as its usage might be lawfully required, part beehive for concentrating the secretarial pool, and part sorority. The few built before 1916 were massive hulks, relentlessly absorbing all the fresh air and daylight and casting all their neighbors in perpetual secondhand shade. Eventually their neighbors got together and demanded that the city safeguard the public's access to the sun, which resulted in the 1916 Zoning Resolution. The hotels built in afteryears, including the Biedermeier, were forced to withdraw from the level of the street through progressive setbacks in what came to be known as wedding-cake style, as if each successive floor were being slowly eaten away. Venerable old firms, from the Allerton House Company to Murgatroyd & Ogden, all took a joint interest in producing neat little refrigerators for storing career-minded girls from just-good-enough families against spoilage, when root cellars and iceboxes would no longer do, or salt curing wouldn't take; right up until October 1929, after which point they had enough problems of their own and left the hotels to fend for themselves.

For the truly down-and-out there was the House of Detention on Greenwich Avenue, which willingly accommodated all comers, even on short notice. Only slightly more discriminating was the Young Women's Christian Association on East Sixteenth Street, rich in piety and poor in electricity, where management forbade the keeping of even a single dish in one's room, lest residents might be tempted into the sin of washing up for themselves. French unfortunates hoping to transmute their suffering into employment as *femmes de chambre* might beg sanctuary at the Jeanne D'Arc Home on Eighth and Twenty-Fourth Streets, courtesy of the Fathers of Mercy, where it was not unheard of for boldhearted Yankees with barely passable schoolgirl French to try their luck anyhow.

The Martha Washington Women's Hotel on Twenty-Ninth Street between Park and Madison could boast nearly five hundred bedrooms, many of them en suite, and had a Renaissance Revival facade to boot, swathed in dressed stone, with a red belt of brick running between each floor. So far from denying residents the odd dish, the Martha Washington even applied for a license to serve wine, granted by the State Alcoholic Beverage Control Board in 1933 and approvingly noted by the paper of record as an appropriate *result* of the change in women's drinking habits over the past decade, rather than an unsavory *cause*. The Barbizon on Sixty-Third was a sort of public curio cabinet, where celebrities and oilmen might park their most promising daughters for a few years to the benefit and beautification of the neighborhood, but rooms were available along the strictest of Calvinist terms. Only the elect might enter, and God had already made the whole of the elect known to one another.

If the Biedermeier had never been among the first-rate of women's hotels, Mrs. Mossler would never admit it. She believed in the unrelenting swell of feminine progress as only a child of the century could. Any woman who could with a straight face claim to occupy that fortunate bracket of age between eighteen and thirty-four, who could supply the real or merely plausible name of an employer, as well as two weeks' rent, could safely appeal to Mrs. Mossler's justice.

The first-rate hotels were assembled in light brick or rusticated masonry, asked for three letters of reference, and boarded models, actresses, the best-looking stenographers and social workers, art students, choreographers, and magazine editors, who dutifully waited out their ambitions in an assortment of skyscrapers for three to five years before they could depart for their father's or husband's home without a conscious sense of failure. In the meanwhile there were any number of short-term careers to attempt, rehearsal studios to occupy, novels to begin concerning the peccadilloes of fellow residents, shows, restaurants, public and private libraries, conservatories, dates to meet at their clubs, museums, botanical gardens, abortions, dances, Daughters of the American Revolution, and public hearings at the halls of justice. By the end of this period, any of them might honestly say to herself that she had really done something with her time in the city, that she had, if anything, realized her aspirations sooner than she ever expected, that she had never intended to stay any longer than five years to begin with, and that her family really had gotten their money's worth out of the whole thing. Those years, which in less expert hands might have grown shabby, acquired a retroactive patina of distinction that would only deepen with time, gracefully framed by stonework and iron sculpted into cursive flourishes. A little interlude all her own, with no shared landmarks or memories that anyone else at home might claim a stake in or contradict, a wholly private history to refine and elaborate over the course of another lifetime, was a fine bargain for half a decade.

The third-rate places asked for no references at all, but made up for it with a florid, pious overfamiliarity, where floor managers were addressed as "mothers" and residents as "daughters" or even "our girls," and no meal could be set upon before chanting in unison some shockingly abbreviated prayer of thanksgiving, one that more often than not attempted to rhyme "food" with "good."

Rounding out the middle of the pack was the Trowmart Inn at the northwest corner of Abingdon Square, the Allerton Hotel at East Fifty-Seventh Street, the Evangeline opposite Gramercy Park, which looked reasonable enough on the outside but was secretly run by the Salvation Army. There was the increasingly shabby East End on Seventy-Eighth Street and FDR Drive, the Rutledge on Lexington, and near Union Square, the Margaret Louisa Home, initially "for Protestant Women," then later, simply, "for Women," Protestantism either having become negotiable or merely implied. For the literary-minded and well-to-do there was also the Hroswitha Club, convened by the frightening-sounding Sarah Gildersleeve Fife in an act of social dominance in the last year of the war. But as there were precious few new arrivals to the city confident enough to say "Hroswitha" aloud for the very first time to a taxi driver, this hardly entered Mrs. Mossler's thoughts.

Mrs. Mossler had arrived at the Biedermeier within three years of the grand opening, and had so far outlasted her contemporaries that no one within living memory had any sense of how the building might have been run before her. She had joined her fortune to the Biedermeier after the collapse of her first quiet little dream of operating a tearoom. The combination of Prohibition and the proliferation of the genteel lady motorist had produced a short-lived boom in light lunch. The larger and cruder the vehicle, the greater the demand grew for thin, tender half meals on dainty china. Working women who had a generation earlier been earmarked for nursing or teaching school began to set aside their little, all in hopes of renting a garden storefront or cottage to serve sandwiches from, and Mrs. Mossler (Emmie then) dreamed of nothing but hooked rugs, wicker furniture, chipped chicken on toast, trained wisteria on latticework, paper-shaded lanterns, blue-and-white lacquered dishes, painted tables, floors of glazed faience tile, potted ferns and catbriers, and rehabilitated hearths snapping efficiently through the afternoon. Of course there would have to be lemonade, and fussy miniature cakes to reel drivers in from the dusty pleasures of the open road, but she did not trouble herself overmuch with an occasional, unavoidable compromise with bad taste. Some of the furniture itself might be for sale, unmarked of course, with a preference for hickory and Colonial patterns, to the discerning customer eager to clear her own parlor of heavy Victorian furniture and thick draperies. It was a dazzling vision of homeyness and tempting little morsels on toast. She had resolved never to stoop to the level of chintz exhibited by those mushrooming roadside deformities with winking names like Dew Drop

Inn or Roll-E Poll-E. Hers would be a quiet monument to discerning taste and modest, never urgent appetite. The mental cultivation of such modesty acted as a sort of protective charm. "*Only* a little, only a little" became the silent watchword of her industry as she made her preparations. The tearoom had the advantage of improving the countryside with a dose of urbanity and improving the city with a touch of country charm, had neither alcohol nor chef's salaries to trouble its owner, and had the happy knack of bringing together operators and customers in a shared home away from home. Nothing Arthurian, she decided firmly, having herself endured too many indifferent meals in out-of-the-way places run by grandmotherly types called Tintagel or Joyous Gard, and certainly no Xanadus or El Dorados. Nothing overly familiar, like Emmie's, and nothing literary like House Beautiful. No alliteration—no Polly's Pantry, no Whistling Waitress, no Chimney Corners—nothing celestial like Seventh Heaven or Silver Lining. No false sense of the pastoral, no The Willows on East Twenty-Third Street. The Carriage House or the Copper Kettle she considered acceptably prosaic.

Having secured a lease on West Forty-Sixth Street as well as a hired Hungarian girl named Nadin to clear tea trays and churn the ice cream, Emmie was briefly deflated to learn there was already a Carriage House and a Copper Kettle in operation within ten blocks. She soon resigned herself to the White Quill after rejecting the Samovar as too open an overture to the bohemians, who were sure to come but unlikely to settle their bills either at the conventional time or in the customary mode of exchange.

What she had failed to take into account while pleasantly contemplating the modesty of her compromise was the prevalence of that very same modesty among other women of her breeding and background. By the end of 1927 there were thirty tearooms on a single block of Twenty-Ninth Street alone. The bohemians stopped in for a saucer of tea and cake in all of them. There was an Old Mill just opposite the White Quill, with a blue-and-gilt awning and the most luscious spherical paper lanterns that blinked dreamily awake shortly after sunset every summer's evening. In addition to chipped chicken on toast and peach ice cream, it also served Hungarian delicacies like chicken Paprikás and sour cherry soup, which Emmie unexpectedly discovered from observing Nadin's brilliantly violet-stained mouth one afternoon.

Nadin, disappointingly, could only appreciate such national dishes, but could not re-create them, in spite of Emmie's most encouraging attempts to incite her to try. "It was as red as pink, and as pink as red," Nadin said, shaking her head. "I cannot describe it more. So beautiful, beautiful, and I cannot cook it for you." She was neat and punctual, was fastidious with a tea tray, smoked cigarettes beautifully, and was otherwise entirely useless. Emmie, who considered this particular type of incompetence as a promising indicator of potential, liked her enormously.

Almost every other lady proprietor in the teahouse boom had Colonial-pattern furniture for sale, and rattan-and-wicker porch sets in the summer, potted ferns and glazed tile flooring, homemade strawberry preserves, and scarlet runners just outside their charming wooden front doors. A few had French menus and charged ninety cents for chicken salad. The city was seemingly overflowing with lady motorists with a restrained yen for a small dish of cold curried lobster and stylish hostesses eager to accommodate them. The dreamworld grew too crowded, and the whole city seemed a sea of tastefully appointed living rooms. The White Quill sputtered along for a year and a half before expiring gently and without protest. Nadin wiped her hands decisively on the tea towel folded into her waistband, trotted across the street into the Old Mill, and never emerged again.

Emmie walked home slowly, stopping to inquire about open positions at every hotel, cafeteria, and department store between the Quill and her apartment in Kips Bay, having decided the problem with the tearoom was one of scale, and resolving from now on to deal with mealtime as a shared public prospect rather than as a private enterprise. This process took rather longer than expected, since in each new building she had to size up the various employees on the floor before deciding on the likeliest candidate to be the hiring manager, wait until he was no longer engaged in conversation or stock-taking, adjust the strap on her left shoe that slid further off her ankle the longer she walked, work up the courage to address him without introduction, arrange her face in a neutral expression when he left to consult with some remote authority, and so on, with each rejection feeling a rising sense of panic as well as of rudeness.

By the time she reached the Biedermeier she had acquired and then lost a wholly imaginary Mr. Mossler, hoping his name would confer an aura of matronly dignity to her inquiries they might otherwise have lacked after a year of brewing lemonade and molding salmon pâté. Whether it was that intimation of reputable widowhood or a more practiced and careless air, having already struck out dozens of times, she could not say, but she considered the name a good-luck token thereafter. It had been a long and unpleasant walk, chafing her sense of reserve as well as her feet, and in time it took on the same dimensions of the Stations of the Cross in her memory: here the penultimate humiliation; there the final broken strap of shoe.

The Biedermeier was a tidy fifteen-story structure set back on an irregular lot, running for 126 feet or eleven window bays north-south and 120 feet or ten window bays east-west, receding into a horseshoe wrapped about a slender, airy courtyard beyond the fifth floor, with wrought iron balconies installed at the tenth and fifteenth. Inside, it had not a single hooked rug, nor a stitch of Colonial furniture, only deep pile carpeting, a scattershot assortment of plush green-and-yellow two-seaters, and a mirrored sideboard pushed against the far wall from the entrance. There was only one clerk at the front desk, who handily answered the question of whom to approach, and he was not busy in the least, was in fact delighted to field her inquiry, and by unlikely coincidence, *could use* a resourceful young person with a little experience, not *too* young of course—a young widow would suit their purposes admirably—she had scarcely removed her gloves before she was putting them back on again to run home to pack an overnight bag. Her loyalty, first to the Biedermeier and second to communal dining, was sealed from that day on.

While little outside the building ever claimed her attention, she could be counted on to have a fairly up-to-the-minute sense of what the other women's hotels were doing, the size of their enrollment and staff, the gradual repurposing of servants' quarters and the citywide postwar drop in occupancies; who was cutting back on their milk order; who was making the switch from weekly to monthly rent; and who was considering going coed. Within the Biedermeier her dominion extended to all the residential floors, including the mezzanine, the former palm court, and the front desk. The mechanical floor, the garage, and the basement were the province of Mr. Gantz and his seemingly inexhaustible supply of nephews who served as porters and errand boys. There were rumors of an off-site owner who outranked even Mrs. Mossler, but hardly anyone believed in him.

The ground-floor restaurant ran along self-service lines and required only a skeleton crew to arrange and monitor the dinner buffet, although had anyone wished to adhere strictly to the letter of the law, only Mrs. Mossler was entitled to manage the front-house dining staff. By that same law, she was technically entitled to fillet any and all fish entrées in need of boning tableside, as well as mixing salads, although it had been years since she had felt the need to lend that kind of prestige to a meal. The lounge steward had been easily replaced by a key on Mrs. Mossler's chatelaine during the Depression. The former palm court was now a makeshift library, meeting space, and studio, and the rooftop garden on the sixth floor was jealously guarded by its proprietor, who interrogated would-be visitors so ferociously that most of them abandoned the idea of lunch al fresco. In addition to restaurant staff, the Biedermeier employed an elevator operator, Stephen, whose rule was confined to the daylight hours. After sunset he was not permitted to hold doors, to press buttons, or to ascend any higher than the lobby level. Stephen was a sort of perpetual student who worked toward his degree after the manner of the fairy bird in the Brothers Grimm story about eternity, who every hundred years flew to the top of a distant mountain and sharpened his beak on it. Strictly speaking, Stephen was also responsible for enforcing curfew against any non-Gantz males in the building, but Stephen was not a strict person, and did not go out of his way to look for them.

There were also two day maids, both of whom declined to live in the building themselves, and five semiprofessional floor managers, who were really only glorified residents themselves. There really ought to have been fifteen managers, one for each floor, but most had been struck with a simultaneous case of patriotic wanderlust in 1941, gave notice to join the war effort, and never returned. In subsequent years, as the remaining few peeled off, Mrs. Mossler found it increasingly difficult to convince the older tenants that they required the same daily supervision that they had submitted to placidly enough as ingenues of 1939. Like many champions of progress, she was quick to declare a cause lost and was therefore as perfectly happy to abandon the question of residential directors as she had been the question of who held the right to carve fish and mix a vinaigrette tableside. Besides which, most of the girls preferred Catalina dressing from a bottle nowadays, and so the remaining managers saw their territories expand even as their responsibilities dwindled.

It was really only the first-floor director, Katherine Heap, who still held any regular duties worth noting—minding the library, which in practice meant knocking on doors every month or so and repossessing any books left out on the nightstand; manning the reception desk during Mrs. Mossler's rounds and taking down any telephone messages that came through in her absence; supervising maintenance requests and their subsequent denials; handling whatever other little odds or ends that might arise in the course of daily life that did not fall within the remit of the kitchen, which like all kitchens ignored any outside interference; and discouraging men from using the elevators, since Stephen could not be counted on to stop them.

"Well, just do what you can," Mrs. Mossler said abstractedly when Katherine had asked just how strenuously she was expected to discourage them, whether it was forbidden outright or merely disapproved of when done too conspicuously. "Plenty of them will still get in, of course, so don't wear yourself out trying to stop them from closing the doors or anything. But if you happen to be nearby, you can frown or hang up a note. Of course there's no need to bother the reliable ones."

Whether Katherine had a particularly discouraging frown, or whether the kind of men likely to try breaching the inviolability of the Biedermeier were an especially easily dismayed bunch, she could never be quite sure. There was something slightly thrilling about the possibility that she might possess a forbidding aspect. Men so rarely told her anything about herself, and it was wonderful to think this might not be the result of unremarkable features but rather attributable to certain grim and austere offices of her scowl. But she could hardly chase after the men who wandered nearly into the elevator bay before catching sight of her, conspicuously looking at their watches, then turning around to ask, "Did you really forget you were due somewhere else before just this minute, or were you really afraid of me just now?" This was too bad, as Katherine very much wanted to ask them.

And, she had thought, *I think I could be happy with any answer they might give me, even if it were a conspicuously gallant lie. Because if on the one hand a man had been frightened of me, I would be enormously pleased with myself, and if on the other hand he hadn't been frightened of me, he might have found my desire to be found frightening (which is not the same thing as being frightening, I think) charming, and that would be its own kind of pleasure. Or, if he had found me frightening to begin with, but had easily recovered by the time I stopped him, then I would still be formidable without his having to be a coward, and that might be best of all.*

As Katherine did not bother wondering whether women found her intimidating, and did not dare ask men, she remained in a constant state of necessary ignorance of her own ferocity, a condition that seemed likely to persist indefinitely.

Not minding outside interference herself, Katherine had managed to achieve an exceptional Biedermeier tenure of nine years, most other floor directors averaging three. The first floor was her only official charge, but unofficially, floors two, three, and eight through eleven also fell under her bailiwick, making her Mrs. Mossler's deputy in almost all things. She did not resent the incidental accumulation of duties that accompanied seniority. Neither did she mind killing insects (of reasonable size), giving directions, smoothing out hangovers, impersonating a professional reference for girls looking for jobs, impersonating Mrs. Mossler on the telephone (only when unavoidable), inquiring after lost laundry, or performing any other by-the-way tasks that fell within her sphere of influence. New girls, once acquainted with the full sweep of functions Katherine did not mind, saw to it that theirs landed within that sphere as swiftly as possible. This was, she had decided, more charming than irritating, and she enjoyed their obvious sense of triumph at "getting one over," many of them for the first time in their lives, almost as much as they did.

The better part of the morning had been given over to the recovery of the various managerial odds and ends that Mrs. Mossler had lent to residents over the course of the previous year in anticipation of Moving Day. Since Mrs. Mossler only ever lent her things on the spur of the moment (if given the chance to consider whether she could spare it, she would always shrink from making a decision) and never wrote anything down, the process of reclaiming Biedermeier equipment was a long and piecemeal affair. Every year it involved a great many "just saying hello" knocks and meandering conversations designed to lead up to, "By the way, I don't suppose you've seen that little gray glue pot of Mr. Gantz's?" or "Mrs. Mossler's cabbage-rose pincushion?" or "That jar of varnish I had on the desk in the lobby last Monday?"

There were several possible acceptable responses to such questions: "I don't think so . . . but I'll keep an eye out for it. You said it was gray?" thereby giving the impression that the girl considered herself formally deputized to complete the task on Katherine's behalf, taking up the banner as her own, even confirming a detail as proof she'd been listening, or else, "No, I don't think I have. You might try Corinne's room. I think she's been taking piecework home from the dresser's," thereby giving Katherine a consequent and face-saving clue, prolonging the chase and lending it the dignity of an official investigation, complete with suspects and witnesses. It was not strictly "on" to provide Katherine with the object she was looking for on the spot, since everyone benefited from an atmosphere of vagueness around private contraband, nor (for the same reason) to announce *positively* who presently had it. Their traffic was in narrowing down possibilities rather than establishing definitive answers, which would have benefited no one but the house.

The Biedermeier still observed the old Dutch custom of Moving Day, whereby all annual leases expired simultaneously and at once, on the first stroke of midnight, May first. Every girl hoping to improve her situation, whether desirous of more light in the mornings, trying to avoid a new construction project or to move closer to the telephone at the end of the hall, was in a mad dash to disgorge all her belongings from her room before her juniors, who might then descend as a single body into her castoff, to pick it over inch by inch and fight for a lesser prize. Since fewer girls petitioned for admission at the Biedermeier every year, the minute differences between cells (*cells* really was the only word for them) carried increasingly consequential weight, such that an extra half inch of space along one wall might make the difference between squalid impossibility and paradise.

Katherine had timed her visits so that the last before lunch would take her to Lucianne's room on the third floor. Lucianne, having received an honorable discharge from Ma Bell that winter, now lived off her union severance and claimed to be training for stenotype via correspondence at LaSalle Extension University. She even displayed, as proof of her seriousness, a clipped advertisement of a woman with an optimistic bob-and-fringe saying, "Look who's smiling now! Why shouldn't a woman be happy when she proves she can make big money doing work she really enjoys?" As usual, Lucianne's door was wide open and the interior respectfully mobbed with visitors. Her room was conveniently situated neither too close to nor too far from the elevator, received excellent sun in the afternoon while still facing away from the street, and had the additional attraction of real rosewood furniture, which Lucianne had arranged to be shipped directly from her ancestral home in Delaware. Compared to the other rooms in the hotel, which came outfitted only with a chipboard desk and chair, a camp bed, a ceramic washstand, and a low dresser of indeterminate provenance, Lucianne's rosewood bureau, daybed with scrolled footboard and linen coverlet, and real writing table with pigeonholes might as well have come from the Amber Room. But they came from Delaware, no less, which sounded as exotic as Prussia to everyone else in the building, most of them hailing from somewhere on Long Island or the Midwest.

Lucianne had draped herself onto the floor against the side of her bed, irritatingly tasteful in an oatmeal-colored Shetland sweater, snug trousers the color of claret, neat little moccasins, and a man's watch with a plain leather band. Katherine's own skirt suit, not yet a season old, and which the salesgirl had taken great pains to assure her was garnet, proved by comparison to be decidedly and dispiritingly grape in color.

There had really been no reason to buy the suit, especially with that soft-bloused, muffled neck that threatened to utterly obliterate the line of her jaw, which was not always as definite as Katherine might have wished it to be. The suit had not even the virtue of being particularly inexpensive, such that she might have been able to console herself by having come out ahead on the deal. Its only real recommendation was that it had been the last thing she tried on after a number of even worse eyesores, mostly sleeveless and drawn unfortunately high and tight across the chest.

"They're almost all like that this year, worse luck for us," the girl had said by way of apology, which was worse still.

After trying a few of them Katherine had been overcome with

such a panicked, relentless sense of being encased that she stole only the briefest of glimpses at herself in the mirror in the suit before beginning to take it off and saying, "Yes, yes, I see what you mean, it really is garnet. Now that I can see it properly under the light, I see exactly what you mean," dizzy with the relief of being able to comply.

She had, at least, traded an immeasurable problem for a solvable one. An indifferent suit could be amended, accounted for, reworked, even treated with a compensatory overcoat or reserved for an unpleasant occasion. Katherine might safely imagine herself about to stumble upon something lush and unexpectedly becoming, if not for the existence of the faulty suit, rather than daily confront the question of where to find a new one, why she had not secured one already, which shops to choose between, the measurements to determine, whether to go now, or *now*, or now. The grape suit had real hope of claiming her attention and drive to useful ends. It might never look really nice, but it could still be the target of a worthwhile campaign of improvement, and the defensiveness with which she wore it slackened.

Seated at the writing table was Carol Lipscomb, ordinarily of the eleventh floor, in pink tights, coral slippers, and black and blond everywhere else. In the doorway stood Pauline Carter (second floor) and Kitty Milham (first). Pauline had taken to dressing like a country squire after seeing Albert Finney in *Tom Jones* at Cinema 1 the summer before, which suited her no end, with her high forehead and smoothed-back dark hair. She alternated between severe, almost chaste necklines with borrowed handkerchiefs refashioned into cravats or else billowing silk shirts plucked open at the throat. Today Pauline wore a mustard-and-cream waistcoat with breech-cut trousers, and yet somehow she did not look even remotely like a pirate, which Katherine certainly would have in her place. Kitty, in a blessedly nondescript pastel shift and house slippers, was the first to catch Katherine's approach, drawing slightly back from the threshold to accommodate her.

The subject of the afternoon's discussion was Stephen, the daytime elevator operator, and what ought to be done about him. Stephen, it was generally agreed, was a sympathetic person, and for fifty-one weeks out of the year hardly anyone found in him any cause for complaint. He was neither inquiring nor meddlesome, seemed to understand with silent intuition which dates ought to be kept out of the elevators and which should be permitted to ride up, and could largely be counted on for assistance straightening a bureau or running out for cigarettes. But the first week of May found him every year without fail a wholly changed creature, offensively conscious of his increased value and determined to profit by it, and as dangerous as a landlord, requiring great caution in handling.

The hallways were jumbled with boxes and ashtrays and books, collapsible wardrobes, broken dressers, and various other unsteady hills of movables, and Stephen had not one but *two* hand trolleys in his possession, besides which he also had a key to the service elevator. During Moving Day week no ordinary tip could move him. No resident who considered herself his particular friend the rest of the year would think to lean upon that friendship in order to secure a Moving Day appointment in advance, nor to hurry him beyond the limits of his own recondite schedule. On Moving Day itself Stephen was patient and pitiless. Next week would see a return to form, but until then no law could constrain him, no ordinance hasten him, and Stephen would recognize no authority besides the law of coin.

"Carol thinks we should kill him, like the King of the Wood," Lucianne said before Katherine had the chance to speak. Carol was a classical studies student at Hunter College. She had switched majors in her sophomore year after coming to the realization that if she studied hard enough, and long enough, she might become fairly good at translating Latin, but the same could not be said for understanding Hegel, so she was subsequently more or less seriously treated by the other residents as if she were the Oracle at Delphi. This was not to say that anyone followed her advice any more than they did anyone else's, since no one did, but it was fashionable to consult her before doing whatever one wanted. "*The priest who slew the slayer, and shall himself be slain*—Does Mrs. Mossler have any pinking shears? We could shroud his body in linen and bury it underneath the foundations of the building, for good luck. Do you know what he did when I offered him a half-dollar to help wrap my dresser?"

"I expect he laughed at you," Katherine said, slipping into the space Kit had made for her, "and as a matter of fact I believe the shears are missing. As are her plaster-of-Paris kit and trowel. And wouldn't you have to take over Stephen's work, if you killed him like the King of the Wood?"

"Yes," Carol said, "besides which, immurement doesn't do any good if you do it after the building is already put together. You have to bury someone underneath the foundation before the cornerstone is laid."

Lucianne gestured blandly around the room—though in reference to which question Katherine couldn't be sure—then returned to the discussion of how best to secure Stephen's cooperation for the next day. For some reason or another Katherine had failed to secure general interest in her point, although she could not have said whether she had offended or merely bored Lucianne. This was very often the case with Lucianne, although of course it was also possible that she had simply failed to hear her. Lucianne would often listen very carefully and with a great show of attention to the first half of almost any statement or question, then, python-like, break it off and digest it directly, without bothering to attend whatever else might be said afterward.

During the whole of the greater conversation, Kitty had at various points begun to open her mouth, look pointedly at Katherine, then just as pointedly look elsewhere, and cross and recross her hands over her waist. Katherine recognized immediately the signs that a trapping invitation was forthcoming. Kitty took advantage of a momentary lull at last to ask, in an offhand way, "What are you doing in the afternoon a couple of Thursdays from now, Katherine?"

Hideous question! And no way out of it that Katherine could see. To answer, "Why do you ask?" would be to admit she doubted Kitty's motives and, worse, make it obvious that she planned to lie in the event of an unappealing answer. And yet not to ask would be worse still—to commit anywhere from a quarter of an hour to a half day on some project of Kitty's, sight unseen and with no chance of escape, was unbearable. Would Kitty accept a deferral and a promise to check her diary? (But Kitty always kept track of other people's deferrals.)

"I might have borrowed those shears, Kat," Carol said. "I'm supposed to be heading back upstairs anyway."

A reprieve, at least. "I'll go with you," Katherine said gratefully, then to Kitty: "I'll stop by your room later, shall I? And you can tell me more about it then." Kitty only stared at her with wider eyes than usual, and Katherine felt a brief flash of doubt before the more familiar irritation settled down over it. Perhaps something really was urgently important with Kitty?

But nothing had ever been urgently important with Kitty, Katherine reassured herself on the ride up to Carol's room. Kitty was not a person whose life was ever touched by importance. Besides which, Kitty had borrowed the better part of three dollars from Katherine in the last month alone, and unless she had chosen that Thursday to repay her, which Katherine very much doubted, whatever might be on her mind would have to wait.

"We could of course throw him out the window," Carol said, once on the elevator. Stephen turned around, and she smiled at him reassuringly. "Lucianne wanted to bury you under the building, since your wickedness and avarice have grown so great this time of year, but I thought we should just push you out of a window."

"That wouldn't do you much good," Stephen said, turning back around. "You still wouldn't know where I keep the keys." Then, to Katherine: "Lucianne's dresser is bigger than her doorway. Wrap it as much as you like, it's not coming out of that room unless it's cut into pieces first and reconstituted afterward. I'm not going to slice up a family heirloom for less than a dollar, and you can tell her I said so."

"I'll make sure she gets the idea," Katherine said.

The elevator stopped and Stephen winched open the gate. "Eleventh floor, assassins and vipers," he called out. "Everybody clear out, and see if I do anything for you again."

"How much for you to chop Lucianne's dresser up and hide the pieces from her?" Carol asked, seized with a sudden inspiration, but he had already closed the gate again. She caught only a momentary glimpse of Stephen shaking his descending head before the doors closed after him.

A muffled voice drifted up: "The price of violence keeps pace with inflation," Stephen shouted. "It goes up every Moving Day."

Chapter Two

A PROMISE TO KITTY

Carol did not have Mrs. Mossler's shears after all. Katherine had initially understood the suggestion of going upstairs as a face-saving opportunity to retreat from Kitty, but she soon discovered it was in fact an opportunity for Carol and her roommates to ambush Katherine about breakfast.

The eleventh floor held five of the Biedermeier's largest apartments and as a result was home to many of the long-term residents. The suite tower began at the sixth floor but was given over to laundry, maintenance, and meeting rooms until the eleventh. Here residents had only to share bathrooms between every three bedrooms, instead of the solitary sink-and-shower cubicles at the end of each hall on the first ten floors. Carol had gone in with two other girls for the last several years and together they formed a sort of makeshift art collective.

Carol was the only of the three with any academic credentials, although aside from one painting she exhibited briefly under the title *Rex Nemorensis* (which she later changed to *Bugs Bunny Confronts His Adversaries*), there appeared to be almost no overlap between her research and her artistic output. Carol guarded her paintings jealously, and sold illustrations to the *Saturday Review* and *Harper's Magazine* to cover her expenses in the meantime.

Patricia De Boer, whose Old New York surname belied an amalgamated descent and Midwestern origin, had a real job at the New York City Transit Authority headquarters on Jay Street. She had trafficked primarily in sketches of elderly women playing bridge in unusual locations like railroad tracks or during the Paris Peace Accords until the No!art Doom Show appeared at the March Gallery. She had returned stricken to the heart, produced nothing at all for the next six months, then started leaving nude baby dolls, made up to look like victims of an exploding cigar, on the express train. The third member, Sadie Waldvogel, worked occasionally for a few dressmakers in the Garment District. Carol lent the collective an air of legitimacy, Patricia a sense of danger, and Sadie (who produced nothing at all, as far as Katherine could tell) a regular supply of mannequins. The trio had three or four jobs at least among them, but no more than a single income, and on the subject of breakfast, Mrs. Mossler's penny-pinching, and the overall plight of the working girl, they rose to new heights of eloquence.

"She doesn't *mean* it, surely?" said Patricia. "Does she realize this means we're going to have to think about breakfast every day?"

"You have to have one every day, you realize," Carol said. "You can't just get it out of the way early in the week. And we're all used to breakfast now. It's like smoking. You can't just ask people to give it up once they've made a habit of it."

"She doesn't like it any more than we do," Katherine said.

"Objection," said Patricia, "to the improper use of a collective pronoun. You're the one telling us there's not going to be any more breakfast. You can't say *we* while you're doing it."

"All right, Mrs. Mossler doesn't like it any more than you do," Katherine said, "and while we're on the subject, speaking only for myself, I don't like it either."

"That's better," Patricia said. "I don't object to your feeling the same way, but you can dislike it on your own time."

"But she says she can either cut out breakfast or raise the rent," Katherine said.

"I've already thought about it," said Carol, ignoring Katherine's last remark, "and I can't possibly steal any more cold cuts from the faculty dining room than I already do. I smell like a butcher shop half the year. I've stretched all my begging and borrowing powers to the absolute limit. It's ridiculous to call yourself a residential hotel while expecting your residents to live off one meal a day."

"Of course, it mightn't be so bad if we could keep a toaster and an electric kettle in our rooms," Sadie said. "But she's going to have to give in on one front or the other, Katherine. We put up with a lot around here, but—" Here she trailed off, being unable to think of a convincing-sounding threat. "We put up with a lot, but we don't like it."

"What it is," Patricia added, "is an outrage on civic virtue. It is also a perfect example of moral turpitude. I'd write to my father to complain about it in an instant, if I only had his address." She considered for another moment, then said: "I'll write to him anyway. I'll just keep writing in new addresses until one of them pays off. Which is going to cost me a fortune in stamps."

"We're not unreasonable," said Sadie. "We'll give up the egg. Wouldn't that solve most of Mrs. Mossler's problems? Nothing else on the menu is cooked, except for the toast. And we're willing to give up the toast, too, if it comes to that. But the Biedermeier can surely spare a few grapes and a roll and a cup of coffee without strain."

"And we're very willing to *become* unreasonable," Patricia said. "Tell Mrs. Mossler that. Tell her that we're very reasonable, but that if she doesn't give in to our demands, we'll become as unreasonable as we have been reasonable, and she'll never see her shears again. And I'll—I'll get a chafing dish, and start cooking in my room, and attract mice, and overload the circuit breakers."

Katherine reminded Patricia that chafing dishes were usually heated by Sterno cans, and didn't plug in, to which she replied: "I'll find something that *does* plug in, then."

"You're thinking of a hot plate," Sadie said.

"Just so," Patricia said. "Hot plates. I'll get ten of them. And I'll fry eggs on the curling iron. And I'll start stealing everything that isn't nailed down. And I'll start beating Stephen."

"Why Stephen?" Katherine asked. "What's he got to do with it?"

"Because everybody likes him. *I* like him. Everyone would feel sorry for him, including me. It would produce a wave of moral outrage so decisive and single purposed that they'd have no choice but to bring back breakfast. It's half a grapefruit and some toast, Kat. It's not going to break the bank, and don't let Mrs. Mossler tell you any different."

Katherine promised to bring their recommendations, if not their threats, to Mrs. Mossler's attention at the earliest opportunity. This was enough to satisfy Carol, at least for the time being, but Patricia insisted on being given daily updates, and strongly intimated that Stephen's fate hung in the balance.

"I'm sure I already know the answer," Katherine said, "but before I go, are any of you planning on switching rooms this Moving Day?" None of them were.

"Then would you consider moving your mattresses back onto their frames, where they're supposed to be?" None of them would. Katherine considered this a sufficient discharge of duty, and made her departure.

"Does Mrs. Mossler have a father?" Patricia stepped out into the hallway to call after her as she waited for the elevator. Privately, Katherine could not bring herself to believe that anything as implausible as a father could have had a hand in producing Mrs. Mossler. "I can write to him, too, if you think it'll help." She waved briefly but significantly at Stephen as he held open the door.

The errand to the eleventh floor had not even been effective as a distraction. Kitty was waiting on the first floor just outside the elevator bay, wearing a hopeful, hangdog expression that immediately put Katherine's back up. She had told Kitty she would stop by her room later, so there was no reason to lie in wait in the hallway unless she knew herself to be in the wrong somehow, or wanted by her presence to indirectly accuse Katherine of being unreliable.

"Hello, Kitty," she said, as steadily as she could. "You wanted to speak to me about Thursday?" Now it was Kitty's responsibility to explain before she could ask whether Katherine was free. That was better; there would be no getting out of it for her.

"You *are* free Thursday after next, aren't you?" Kitty said. "I don't mean this Thursday, or the next Thursday, but the Thursday after that. I know that's usually your day off, and I asked Mrs. Mossler, and she said it was true, that you weren't working Thursday, and that you hadn't said anything about any engagements—so you *are* free on that Thursday?"

The trap was undeniably sprung, and there was no getting out of it. Had Katherine made plans for Thursday? Not quite, not precisely, but still she felt sulkily attached to the as-yet-unplanned day, and reluctant to hand it over. There had been the vague question of a hat that was now, she supposed, settled: She would not buy a hat this season. Plenty of other girls were no longer buying them. It wasn't as if her most recent experience shopping for clothes had been so riotously pleasurable that she would miss a second opportunity, but

Katherine felt an irrational resentment toward Kitty just the same. It was not simply a question of the summer season, but of the grape suit, which she had hoped might be rendered significantly less offensive if paired with the right hat. But if she did not go shopping for one on that particular Thursday, there would hardly be time. Then there would be new girls to get settled into the building, and plans to meet a friend with a new baby, and then it would be well and truly summer, and then they would be halfway to fall. It was not the sort of errand that could be sandwiched into a workday morning, not when Katherine hardly even knew what she hoped for in a new hat, other than the redemption of the grape suit. And one needed *time* to shop properly, time to rest between snatched looks in mirrors, time to recover from the sight of one's face and neck at an unguarded, unexpected angle.

This certainly settled the question. There would be no new hat this year. Had she come to the decision on her own, Katherine might have experienced a sense of novelty or relief, but as it was, she felt as though she had been shoved awkwardly through an open door, and annoyed as a result.

"I *think* so," Katherine said. "Only I really can't promise you anything until I know a little more about what you'd like me to do, you know."

Kitty nearly folded in half with relief, and Katherine began to think it really might be something important after all. Kitty poured out a half-comprehensible story about getting a letter from the Southern District of New York, about sharing shifts with another girl at the telephone company (Kitty had been unexpectedly spared by the round of firings that had ejected Lucianne from the working world), and a vague-yet-definite engagement requiring Kitty's presence, and the long and short of it was: Would Katherine be willing to appear at the district court in Manhattan that Thursday in her place, giving Kitty's name instead of her own? It was not at all clear what the original letter had been about; Kitty made it sound as though it were something minor and mundane, like jury duty, although she had been careful to explain that it *wasn't* jury duty, only something very much *like* it.

"You almost certainly wouldn't be called upon to stay longer than an hour," Kitty continued, "and I'd never ask, only I've deferred so many times, and ignored so many letters, that they're saying if I *don't* appear on this *particular* Thursday they're going to find me in contempt, and might even sue me, and I don't know what they think they can get out of me when I haven't even been able to pay *you* back three dollars—and you've been awfully kind, not mentioning it, but don't think it hasn't been on my mind, because it *has*, and if I can only get that Thursday back, I'll have the money for you the instant you *are* back—"

"Kitty," Katherine said, "I haven't been knocking on your door in the middle of the night for it, have I?"

Kitty shook her head miserably.

"Is all this panic over three dollars? I'd certainly like to see it again someday, but I'm not going to repossess your front door."

Kitty reassured her that no, of course not, the hurry had nothing to do with Katherine.

"And you're not in any real trouble?"

No, of course not, again, it was all a matter of urgency, not trouble, and it would hardly even be lying because after all it would only involve giving her name, waiting around a bit, and then being dismissed, and this minimal dispensing of effort would have besides the happy effect of saving Kitty's life.

"All right," Katherine said after a moment's consideration. Kitty gave the impression of melting with relief, although how anyone could melt after so much folding and buckling was beyond

Katherine's understanding. Somehow Kitty managed to make the slightest inconveniences seem like a ruinous series of disasters. *And she never asks anyone for help until something reaches the level of crisis*, Katherine thought, *so a lot of things that were scarcely problems in the first place turn into emergencies.*

Kitty was never comfortable approaching people as anything other than a supplicant, and probably would have been horrified to learn that anyone thought of her as difficult, instead of frequently made desperate through a series of unforeseeable events entirely outside her control. But she never offered small, manageable problems that could be swapped for others along a fair system of exchange, only present catastrophes and the promise of future gratitude, which nobody, least of all Katherine, wanted from her. Gratitude from Kitty meant only that she was likelier to ask you again the next time she needed something. It really was remarkable to think of a company choosing to keep Kitty and firing Lucianne. One hundred years ago, maybe, it would be possible to picture Kitty safely stashed away in a convent somewhere, which would have limited the number of possible crises available to her. But of course it was easy to envision Kitty's anxious face framed in a wimple as she confessed to venerating the wrong saint on a particular feast day, or dampening the incense by mistake.

She was, Katherine thought, the kind of person who felt most secure on the debtor's side of the ledger, and who grew itchy at the prospect of a balanced social scale, preferring to maintain a mild deficit of favors with anyone she considered more powerful than herself. In Kitty's case this meant pretty much everyone. At least in a convent one might recuperate one's irritation in the service of spiritual growth. Katherine considered the possibility of praying for Kitty, then dismissed it on the grounds that God would recognize the insincerity straight off.

She left Kitty and her dubious promise of repayment in the hallway and went to her own room. Katherine had first come to the Biedermeier nine years earlier, after seeing an advertisement in the *New York Journal-American*: "Home away from home, complete with floor-length mirror, no-draft ventilators, a three-channel radio, and convenient electrical outlets. Modern living for working women. Convenient to both park and river. À la carte cafeteria and in-room breakfast *gratis*. Inquire E. 49th Street."

The other hotels to which Katherine had applied either wanted letters of reference, which she didn't have and were surely only required to drive an unspoken point home, or else made her wait to be seen for half an hour in a lounge strewn with ferns, sitting on a red plush couch and listening to an inexpert young violinist try to shove a bit of Schubert through her instrument. They had wanted to know when she would be coming and when she would be going, whether she had any boyfriends, whether she had any friends whose surnames were difficult to pronounce, what sort of jobs she planned to apply for, at what time she planned to eat dinner each evening. Fireproof maple furniture, stiff wing chairs, lamps of false pewter, narrow Murphy beds—the beds folded, the girls didn't—schedules arranged in cast iron, and mandatory group lectures on physical and moral hygiene held in the lobby on Tuesday nights.

All that Katherine wanted was a comfortable room that was easy to keep clean, reasonable conveniences, a plausible excuse not to entertain from home when she couldn't afford it, and to not have to do the washing up herself. The letters-of-reference places wanted ninety dollars a week in exchange for the privilege of making appointments to use the swimming pool or play deck tennis with a junior copy editor whose mother cherished certain social pretensions. The red-plush-lobby houses would take cash directly, but would have exercised the right to inspect her nail beds and her men friends, if she ever made any, on a regular basis. The Biedermeier came as a Goldilocks surprise when she finally found it. The lobby was blessedly free of plant life. No supervisory staff of proxy maiden aunts watched the doors for one's comings and goings. It was affordable, reasonably tidy, and blessedly without complex. Better still, Mrs. Mossler had said at the outset that Katherine was welcome to change the curtains in her room if she wished, at her own expense.

"I assume you don't sew," Mrs. Mossler had said. "So few girls do nowadays." There was no judgment that Katherine could hear in this statement; she merely observed the change without censure, remaining open to the possibility that it was sewing that had failed the modern girl, rather than the other way around. "I don't suppose the girls who do want to live in New York. And yet you would think sewing would be all the more valuable here, since a little carries you such a long way. If you've only got a few square feet to call your own, you ought to make them as homelike as possible. Anyhow, if you *do* sew, and you *would* rather make them yourself, I know a marvelous little place on Broome Street that takes fabric seriously."

This was a characteristic sort of offer, Katherine would come to learn. Mrs. Mossler trafficked in regional secrets. She delighted in uncovering out-of-the-way suppliers and on her rare days off scoured the rest of the city for the sort of outfitters a tourist's guide might call "a hidden gem." Then as soon as she uncovered them, she rushed to tell everybody she knew about them, deeply conscious of her native duty to keep the best places open. Mrs. Mossler was at her most splendid in these little outbursts of generosity; they saved her from becoming an entirely comic figure.

"I sew only a little," Katherine admitted, "but I did bring my mother's Singer Featherweight with me," and Mrs. Mossler went into sincere raptures over the sleek little hornet-shaped machine.

"Eleven pounds! Is *that* all," she exclaimed, holding it up admiringly. "I used to have one of those so-called portables machines, with the terrible tweed handle case, you know?—Took two people to lift it, and I was stronger in those days, too. But this is nothing! It might have been made for hotel living. You seem to have come prepared, I *will* say," and she turned the Featherweight over in delight, exclaiming again, "It's smaller than a cat!—It puts one in mind of a cat, I think, with that nipped-in little waist."

Katherine agreed that she was likely to find it very handy. Her own mother was not an especially demonstrative person, and she could not help but preen a little under Mrs. Mossler's obvious appreciation, who might have been willing to discard sewing as an essential accomplishment of young womanhood, but still appreciated talent where she found it.

It was an excellent room, and Katherine had gone to fairly extensive lengths over the years to stay put and avoid Moving Day altogether, like the Society of Friends upstairs. (This was how Katherine privately thought of Carol, Patricia, and Sadie. They had the same pleasing yet disquieting effect as the Quakers had—undoubtedly Protestants in good standing and yet something in the final tally did not quite add up.) Though set at street level, her room faced a shared rear courtyard that blunted the sounds of local traffic. Through the windows one could see part of the green tangle of the yard, set back in a frame of brick, with a lot of iron-grille period pieces and black window trim in remembrance of its former life as a coach house.

The marvelous little place on Broome Street did, as it turned out, take fabric very seriously indeed, as Katherine discovered on a subsequent trip under Mrs. Mossler's seasoned chaperonage. She was able to exchange the Biedermeier's heavy old draperies for a set of peacock-blue café curtains, tied back with a violently green cord tassel. She had pushed the head of the bed into the farthest corner from the door, facing the entrance, and arranged her chairs in conversation-style behind the dresser.

This arrangement had two distinct advantages: first, that it further subdivided the privacy of her room into separate areas where visitors might be restricted or admitted further on the basis of intimacy, and second, that it hid from common view what Katherine privately thought of as her cupboard kitchen. Behind the dresser, on top of the washstand, Katherine kept an extension cord, an electric water boiler, a cup-and-saucer set, a bread box, and her own hot plate. She did not consider this to be a violation of either the Biedermeier's standards or her own, although the memory of it had weighed on her conscience during her recent conversation on the eleventh floor. She could hardly have produced a proper meal with these implements if she had wanted to. They were for fixing a dull, comfortable little bite of something or other when the composition of a meal mattered less to her than the fact of its privacy—toasted cheese to be taken to bed at midnight, or a cup of cocoa on a winter's morning, drunk in her house slippers. She prized them with a mixture of guilt and creaturely possessiveness, and smuggled the saucer set, wound carefully inside a terry cloth robe, into the shower at the end of the hall twice a week for cleaning.

The light in the room was excellent three-quarters of the year, the bed sufficiently wide for sprawling, the chairs homely, the desk at just the right height for comfortable letter writing. It was a well-appointed room, the pleasures of which she was especially well suited to appreciate, and it sweetened all other accidents of life. Katherine was hardly alone in the building for being secretly romance bitten by domestic details. It was small rooms that bred cozy habits, rather than the other way round. It was not at all unusual for residents to begin to cultivate a sudden appreciation for the minute. Girls who could never in former life have been accused of a taste for snugness would begin to offer their own furnishings, once entirely necessary to homely comfort, to newer girls not yet won over to the cult of simplicity: "It's yours, if you like it. Really there's no reason for one person to have two nightstands *and* a chest of drawers. I don't know what I could have been thinking." And the new girl, who first thought of herself as having struck the better end of the deal, would gradually come around to the Biedermeier mindset and realize that she was now encumbered by a great ugliness.

Whether it was a result of natural contrariness or simply from a habit of egging one another on to the height of intensity in whatever direction, Patricia and Carol's tastes (Sadie seemed hardly to care either way) ran in perverse contradiction to the general consensus. They stuffed their suite with half-finished projects, lines for drying laundry, and superfluous furniture picked up from retrenching residents, former employers, and even on occasion hauled up from the sidewalk. Patricia had seen an exhibition of women surrealists at the Museum of Modern Art in the summer of 1958, which had concluded in a whitewashed room with a single table set with Méret Oppenheim's *Breakfast in Fur*, which was an inexpensive department store bone china set of teacup, saucer, and spoon, all covered in gazelle fur. This had deeply divided the room and struck Patricia like a thunderclap to the teeth. Immediately upon returning home, she set to work tearing her winter hat into strips, heating up pots of glue, and enfurring the doorknob, an ottoman, and Carol's sketchbook, at which point she ran out of hat and had to start begging the other girls for use of theirs. It had given Katherine a dry mouth just to see Patricia at work at what she called "the eternal feminine grotesque, lovely to feel and horrible to touch," and she refused point-blank to donate hers to the cause, even though it was only civet fur anyway and she hardly wore it. Perhaps she might offer it to Patricia now, if she was going to give up hats altogether. The fur craze had mostly passed, but every once in a while the mood descended on Patricia again, and she could be seen stapling bits of peeled muff to the elevator buttons.

Before Katherine could make up her mind on the question of the hat, Mrs. Mossler poked her head around the door, knocking belatedly as she did so. "All right, Katherine?" she inquired. Her hair was drawn slightly forward and gathered in bunches around the ears, in that old-fashioned style Katherine's mother used to call "cootie garages," and she wore a rose-colored head wrap low and tight across the forehead to secure them.

"All right," Katherine said, and at this Mrs. Mossler ventured a little farther into the room.

"It's not very good news, I'm afraid. There's only two new Moving Day girls, and neither of them want to pay for lunch," Mrs. Mossler said. "I thought I would give them both to you, since there will hardly be work enough for one between them."

"That's fine," said Katherine. "I'm sorry there weren't more, of course, but it's all right by me."

"That's just what I mean," Mrs. Mossler said. "I can't understand where they're all going. Don't girls still work? Don't they still have to live somewhere? They can't *all* be going to the suburbs," she added in amazement. "Suburbs don't even have streetcars anymore. You can't hardly get around, except by car."

"I think quite a lot of them do. Go to the suburbs and drive, I mean."

"Well, if they were, then wouldn't the suburbs all be as big as cities by now? If everyone's going there, how can they still be suburbs? It seems to me like it was just a few years ago that the whole world was living in New York, or wanted to. The suburbs were like a ring of waiting rooms for everyone who was trying to get in. They weren't a destination in their own right. I can't imagine where everybody has gone to. Besides which," Mrs. Mossler concluded triumphantly, having arrived in a roundabout way to a sense of conclusion, "there's never been a generation yet that's married 'em *all* off. At least not all of 'em at the same time. Even if this were the marryingest generation in seven, there still ought to be a few leftovers. Where are they going, if not here?"

"Where did the milkmen go?" Katherine asked. "Where did the icemen go, or goeth? *Ubi sunt reges, ubi sunt principes?* And I hear they're closing the Automat on Seventy-Second."

"*No,*" said Mrs. Mossler, stricken. She took openings and closings very seriously. "When? Why? Where will the people go for lunch?" Mrs. Mossler often worried about what "the people" would do whenever someplace closed, or a new freeway went up, or certain habits went in or out of fashion. It made her sound a bit like Cicero, and lent a certain weight to her anxiety, which might otherwise have seemed insubstantial.

"The lease was up," Katherine said. "I guess they couldn't afford to renew it. I feel a little guilty, when I think about all the afternoons I've spent there without buying more than a cup of coffee and a slice of cake."

"But there's still the Automat on Fifty-Eighth, of course," Mrs. Mossler said with sudden relief. "And that's closer to us, anyways, so that's all right."

"On the subject of meals," Katherine said, "you should know everyone's kicking about breakfast, and I'm inclined to agree with them. The Quakers want to know if they can't persuade you to change your mind if we all promise to give up eggs."

"But I'm *longing* to change my mind about it, Katherine," said Mrs. Mossler. She wore an abstracted air of industrious misery, which suited her. "I've certainly thought about giving up eggs. It would help, of course, there's no doubt that it would help, but then there's still the question of service. I can't afford to keep anyone serving meals in the morning. There's no way to square it. I've already cut every corner I possibly can with dinner." This last sentence was delivered with an unspoken but clear reproof, since it had only been at Katherine's urging, three years previous, that Mrs. Mossler had finally consented to a buffet dinner, where each girl fixed her own plate, and the loss of dignity still rankled. A cafeteria breakfast might finish her.

"What if Mrs. Chase sets the trays out by everyone's doors, last thing at night?" Katherine suggested. "Of course, there's the coffee to keep hot, and fruit to keep cold . . . and then there's mice to think about."

"I'll think about it," said Mrs. Mossler, "and you'll think about it, and between us maybe we'll come up with something. Although I very much doubt it. And next year no one will apply to come live here at all, and soon enough nobody will live here, and they'll tear it down to make room for something else, and then we won't have to worry about breakfast anymore," and by the end of the sentence she had made herself quite cheerful again.

"Here are the new girls' applications," she said, handing a sheaf of papers over to Katherine and returning to her original purpose, as if no time at all had passed since she entered the room. "The first is Gia Kassab—I don't know how you say her second name—do you think it might rhyme with *corn on the cob?*—twenty-two, a dancer, I think in the ballet, something of the conservatory rather than taxi dancing, I got the impression of chicness—she's Syrian, and very religious, something like Greek Orthodox—she might do well near Lucianne but then again Lucianne might find it amusing to tease her—and Ruth Morton Carpenter, twenty-six. Careful where you put her. Nothing too high."

Death by jumping was not common in the hotel business, but neither was it unheard of. Mrs. Mossler was not morbid, and did not dwell on the subject, but just the same she thought it worth assessing each new arrival, and kept them low to the ground if necessary.

"Do you think she's that badly off?" Katherine asked.

Mrs. Mossler considered the question. "I'm not sure. Time will tell. She's a bit unfocused, seems cheerful but I suspect without much in the way of inner reserves. Overall the effect is one of brittleness, and I think she's probably highly suggestible, so we wouldn't want to give her any ideas. And while we're on the subject, do you have any idea who's got my pinking shears?"

"Lucianne, but she's lying about it," Katherine said without thinking.

"Whatever would she lie about that for?" Mrs. Mossler said. "Can I leave that with you, too? I haven't time to try to discern the workings of her mind today. I'm behind enough as it is—Can you deal with her? And find rooms for Ruth and—I almost said Ruth and Naomi," and she took herself out of the room on a bubble of laughter, not waiting for Katherine's answer. There was something reassuring, even satisfying, in Mrs. Mossler's sudden bursts of whimsical abstraction. It was just what one wanted out of the curious mix of offices she held—part innkeeper, part guardian and guide, part quartermaster—especially since, not being their landlord, she could move freely and without resentment among the residents on a fairly reciprocal basis. If the Biedermeier's residents had come across a near-abandoned ship and boarded it to find only its captain still remaining, the rest of the crew being lost or having struck off in search of rescue long before, his condition might have been the same as hers, as grateful and dependent in rescue as he had formerly been venerable in power and purpose.

The question of how to manage breakfast still troubled Katherine, however. Mrs. Mossler *might* be persuaded to allow them to set out trays the night before if they conceded the egg (although now the dishes would all have to be covered, and there could be no question of choice between toast or rolls), but what to do about the coffee? Setting out an urn and china cups in the library would defeat the purpose of in-room breakfast altogether. A cafeteria approach seemed the only solution, even if it would break Mrs. Mossler's heart and spell the end of morning privacy.

Then there was the additional problem over where to place the newcomers. Gia was straightforward enough. There were at least three rooms spare near Lucianne, who had gotten a plum selection last year and had no intention of switching again. This was assuming Lucianne took to Gia rather than against her, but there were good reasons for thinking that she would: Gia's youth was likelier to arouse a protective big-sister instinct in her rather than one of resentment.

Like many vain women, Lucianne was an instinctively nice judge of character and remarkably practical. She did not admit the possibility of a rivalry with anyone much younger than herself, considering them almost an entirely different class of person and therefore outside her jurisdiction, and wore her own age proudly, as a mark of honor, considering even the appearance of vagueness on the subject to be beneath her. Besides which, the likelihood of Lucianne's whims proving difficult was a problem for another day, and they were better dealt with in the moment, hardly worth the trouble of trying to forestall in advance. Stephen might not yet have been enriched past the point of appeal, in which case Katherine might possibly be able to bribe him into helping move Gia's things.

But where was she to put Ruth? Not on Katherine's own floor, not until she'd had a chance to discover just what kind of fragility possessed her, and certainly not with Kitty living there already. It occurred to Katherine, not for the first time, that it *was* her job to help the girls with any and all domestic problems, and therefore she might be a little less hard on Kitty simply for calling on that help, and she filed away a reminder to spend some time in self-examination, entertaining the possibility of amendment at some later date when she had solved the more pressing logistical questions before her. One problem at a time. There was no telling how Ruth might react to the sight of Dolly and Nicola, both on the fourth floor, and at twenty-six she might be too old for J.D.'s mothering tendencies. She might rightly consider them interfering, even intrusive, but then anyone under forty seemed young to J.D., who could no more be persuaded that young women did not want mothering than they did not want water or air. She could not even be offended, considering any rebuff merely an indicator that the time was not yet right or the recipient was out of sorts, through no fault of her own, and would try again, as certain and unselfconscious as noon.

"Some girls, not many," is how Mrs. Mossler had put it when Katherine received charge of floors eight through eleven, "but some girls do come to the city in order to jump from tall buildings. It's almost a natural consequence of the skyline, like how sailors have to go down to the sea if they want to board a ship, only of course one is perfectly all right and the other needs to be discouraged. Other girls only get the idea after a few years of living in tall buildings. It gives them a new sense of scale. You'll come to recognize the signs in a while. In the meanwhile, if you're not sure about someone, don't for heaven's sake put her any higher than the third floor." Mrs. Mossler had a barbarian tolerance for suicide. If she could prevent one, so much the better, but she never expected to prevent them all, and as her primary allegiance always rested with generations rather than with individuals, she did not allow them to trouble her fundamental peace for long. Certainly there were still subway trains and taxis to step in front of, still taller buildings one could ascend, but it was not her vocation to make a haven of the whole world. Mrs.

Mossler was convinced that anyone who chose jumping over other methods was looking first for gracefulness and second for certainty, and that there were too many variables in a second-story fall to secure either. Also—although for whatever reason she could not say—she had come to find that people simply didn't jump as often if they had to leave the floor their own room was on in order to do it. Some people who would readily jump out of their own window were suddenly shy about jumping out of someone else's, possibly because this violated their sense of the essential privacy of the act. There are those who are made irrationally angry by suicides, who experience the discovery of a body that has made itself into a corpse as a personal, even a direct, insult, but Mrs. Mossler was not one of them. She felt that a suicide was hemmed in by an acute sensitivity to public notice, was only ever very briefly alone with itself, and she took it no more to heart than she would being accidentally jostled on a crowded train. In both cases she would have been aware of her own social obligations as a member of the public and nothing more. As always she preferred to deal with generations, with tendencies, with demographics, rather than with exceptions and edge cases. The minority interested her, as all people basically interested her, but it was the majority that mattered to her.

While her matter-of-fact tone had not suited Katherine's sensibilities at the time, on reflection it struck her as a fairly humane policy, one that sought to gently reroute destructive impulses wherever possible instead of getting into the business of directing souls in the direction she thought they ought to go. It also might have been that only the very grand and the very down-at-heel hotels provided a very great inducement to jump, and the Biedermeier simply failed to arouse any reaction powerful enough to overwhelm life in all but the most morbid. Of course Katherine could never be sure, one way or another, which or even *whether* any one of the women's hotels was home to more suicides than the rest, but without having any serious tendencies in that direction herself, she thought she might be slightly more inclined to jump from a French curb roof with cast-iron scroll-work than a plain roof of box concrete, to scrawl one final, decisive mark across the face of beauty on the way down.

She put Ruth as high as she dared, on the second floor, next to Josephine Marbury. Katherine herself had never gone for any room higher than the third floor. She had a healthy instinct for self-preservation and a strong, active desire to live even in the face of great trouble, but there was no telling what kind of ideas might present themselves in a sane aspect with a window at lethal distance over Manhattan every day. She saw no reason to push her luck.

Chapter Three

"HE SAITH AMONG THE TRUMPETS, HA HA"

That Sunday morning was Altheah Meachem's turn at the lectern. The pleasant buzz of the Psalter recitation had been succeeded by the booming announcement, "Hear the Holy Scripture as it is written in the such-a-chapter of such-a-book," in penetrating tones designed to return wandering minds to their appropriate attitude and to wake the dozing. Katherine was in no need of shepherding, but she valued the direction just the same; the Presbyterians knew how to manage shared time and attention.

This week's Old Testament reading came from Job. It was not one of the consoling passages, either, but came from the more obscure digressions about beasts and hooks found near to the end of the book. It included the section, "He saith among the trumpets, Ha, ha; and he smelleth the battle afar off, the thunder of the captains, and the shouting," to which "Amen" hardly seemed like an appropriate reply.

Altheah briefly hesitated over "Ha, ha," anxious to avoid the most obvious reading, which would have sounded like she was reading from the funny papers, before deciding on a declarative "Ha," followed by a distinct pause, before the second, slightly more solemn, "Ha." Then she hurried through the rest of the verse, as though she were slightly ashamed of God for resorting to such idiomatic dialogue, before sitting down and being replaced by the choir.

("Although, of course it wouldn't have *sounded* like a joke," Altheah said later to Katherine, during the reception hour, "not at the time they wrote it down. It's only an accident that it sounds that way now."

"It is a tricky matter of interpretation," said Katherine, by way of consolation. "I've often thought it must be very difficult for anyone putting on a Shakespeare play, too—all those *Ha ha*s, *there*s, and *Ho-ho*s, which don't sound right at all.")

It was not every Sunday that Katherine could be found at the First Presbyterian Church—"Old First" to such residents of Greenwich Village who made a habit of attending holy services, which had for decades formed a shrinking but still prominent part of the population. She felt that any professionally minded person younger than middle age who chose to attend services was choosing to do something in the way of bestowing a patronage, and ought to be received with gratitude and careful attention when she did attend, since she might have just as easily taken herself to the movies or out to lunch. As it happened, Katherine very rarely spent her Sundays at the movies, but the Presbyterians had no way of knowing that. She was fully conscious of her power there, and exercised it gently but regularly. The Presbyterians understood the power of habit, which had been at least half her reason for choosing Old First over others in the city.

Katherine did not choose to serve on either the nursery committee or the floral committee, nor did she attend the semiannual Young Person's Pancake Breakfast, or the Presbyterian Women's Wednesday circle, or the Presbyterian Women's Sunday circle, for the Presbyterian women who worked on Wednesdays or had otherwise fallen out with the Wednesday crowd could no longer be trusted to sit through a meeting without resorting to spiritual violence.

This year the denomination had formed a Presbyterian Lay Committee to investigate the national decline in membership, and Katherine had not joined that either. Old First had not been so alert nor prone to stocktaking since 1855, when an unnamed trustee had proposed installing a pipe organ "for the attraction of young people and strangers." The trustee had been successfully obstructed until 1886, so Katherine felt no urgency as far as the Lay Committee was concerned. The church had then enjoyed a substantial period of relevance and authority well into the twentieth century, with the congregation swelling to a height of 1800 in the twenties. Hardly a breath of doctrinal controversy had endangered it since Harry Emerson Fosdick entered into the modernist debate with a Sunday sermon entitled "Shall the Fundamentalists Win?" in 1922. After delivering it he was warmly praised and encouraged to resign, and thereafter threw himself into the welcoming arms of the Baptists uptown.

It was not as if the elders uniformly disagreed with the modernist position. In fact there were plenty of sympathetic members within the ranks, but the sermon drew an answer later that summer from Reverend Macartney in Philadelphia, in the form of "Shall Unbelief Win?: A Reply to Dr. Fosdick," which moreover was printed and circulated for "15 cents the copy" throughout both cities and within *For the Faith* magazine. Macartney had additionally threatened him with a series of papers "in defense of the cardinal doctrines of the Christian religion," which hardly anyone wanted. William Jennings

Bryan got wind of the dispute and began making rattling noises about a formal resolution of confirmation of doctrine, at which point the trustees began to ask themselves, Had not Dr. Fosdick, though estimable in many respects, been after all ordained a Baptist, and might therefore be inherently susceptible to the sin of personal charisma? And while it could not be denied that Dr. Fosdick certainly knew how to pack them in, had not the marbling in the central aisle cracked under the weight of the additional rented pews, as sure a sign of hubris and rupture as anyone could ask for?

So Fosdick had been gratefully returned to the Baptists, now burnished with the medal of honorable conflict, and replaced by a Dane called Moldenhawer, who dedicated a new chapel in 1938 and preached mildness until his death a decade later. Privately most of the Old Firsters considered themselves well out of a pretty near miss, since Dr. Fosdick later went on to appear on the cover of *TIME* magazine and publish vulgar, helpful little pamphlets with titles like *The Power to See It Through* and *The Secret of Victorious Living*, which were later republished in the *Reader's Digest*. Now the pastorship was sensibly shared between two men, like the old Roman consuls, in order that the one might keep a check on the ambition of the other. They were both named John. One was called Macnab and the other Mellin, and each had very little to say on the subject of victorious living. If either of them might have been at times spiritually inclined toward progressivism, both knew better than to confuse preaching with pamphlet making, and together they set a comfortable walking pace for Old First's portion of the body of Christ to follow.

Old First was ideally suited to Katherine's tastes in many respects. Neither of its pastors preached using that casual, everyday tone that had come to infect so many other pulpits in the country, and if one of the Johns was sometimes liable to digress on the nature of cooperative education, at least he never pointed out individual members of the congregation—"And this means *You*, friend!"—which Katherine would not have believed any clergyman, regardless of creed, capable of doing until she had seen it with her own eyes at a Christian Brethren service downtown during her first year in Manhattan. Nor did either of the Johns try to show off his seminary German by quoting Ebeling or Bonhoeffer. The length of service never ran under fifty-five minutes nor over seventy. Some churches' ideas about punctuality began and ended with the start of services, letting themselves get carried away during the Prayers of the People or extending the processional, but Presbyterians had just as strict a dislike of untimeliness at the end of things as they did at the beginning. Here the Spirit might be permitted to brim, but it never overflowed.

Katherine had intended to shed the dim Baptism of her troublesome youth upon her removal to New York, but it had taken some time to decide where next to fix herself. She spent her first year in the city on an irregular pilgrimage, running in a mostly clockwise spiral whose center began two blocks west from the Biedermeier. She had decided against an early inclination toward Episcopalianism, considering it too precipitous a social advancement to attempt in a single move. She kept in mind the old prompt that a Methodist was a Baptist who had learned to read; a Presbyterian a Methodist who had gone to college; and an Episcopalian a Presbyterian who had joined the Social Register. There would be hardly any point in attending church at all if she spent the whole service in a panic about the suitability of her shoes and her handshake, or worrying how to properly address a bishop if she was introduced to one. Besides which, it seemed to her that there was something cringing, possibly even un-American, about the idea of a bishop, so it had been the Presbyterians after all. There was a comfortingly square and in-the-road presence about the Presbyterians. They had a good hospital system a little further uptown and were well represented among senators and presidents. One might be born, shepherded along the passage of an orderly, useful life, and die, all within the same comfortable envelope of Presbyterianism.

The building itself was an unfortunate mishmash of architectural elements, as the original architect had attempted to pattern the building in Gothic Revival after the St. Saviour Church in Bath as well as the entrance to Magdalen Tower in Oxford. To this rather alarming jumble had been added a secondary complex in Prairie School style in the 1930s, as well as a fence along the southern border, half-cast-iron and half-wood. The sanctuary was ringed by a series of stained glass windows, some Tiffany and some Charles Lamb, and all of them garish in the extreme. Katherine was seated today underneath the St. Bartholomew's Day massacre window, which featured a smiling Huguenot in pink tights, whose head was wreathed about in masses of purple and orange grapes.

There were a number of good reasons for attending services semi-regularly, although not so often as to run the risk of being drafted onto committees. It was the likeliest way to begin a well-organized week. Sundays without church were apt to slide into untidiness, in Katherine's experience. One always slept in too late to make any use of the morning, yet somehow without ever producing the feeling of being really well rested. This turned the afternoon into a panic as one attempted to make up for lost time, trying to squeeze together too many errands that had little or nothing to do with one another. This would be followed by a worn-out, empty sort of evening, surrounded by a lot of boxes and things that now needed to be put away, feeling quite unequal to the task of even going to bed, and wondering why she hadn't made plans to go out with someone, as she realized she hadn't spoken to a soul aside from a sales clerk, nor seen a friendly face all day. Church was a remarkably useful place to organize her thoughts, not to mention an opportunity to be quiet and yet still remain part of a crowd. If she had no close friends among the congregation, still she could count on being welcomed by name, and hearing her hair or her shoes warmly remarked upon. In church she could speak in unison without having to initiate conversation, privately judge the sermon, be stirred during the voluntary, weep a little in public without fear, reflect without the morbidity of her bedroom, wear something slightly uncomfortable and yet becoming, and set herself apart from her largely nonchurchgoing friends, all the while feeling that she was pushing the dark and unpleasant disheveled figure of Monday a little further back into the wings. There was also something about meeting occasionally with the same group to contemplate some particular aspect of a vast and alien consciousness that appealed to her. In spite of (or perhaps because of) this, Katherine remained suspicious of everyone's motives for attending church except her own, and made sure to keep away at least one Sunday a month.

Besides this, Katherine had a dim yet definite understanding that between unattached women and church existed a powerful, slightly frowsy magnetization—unless one moved conscientiously in another direction, a future of committee work with other semiconscripted unattached women with no recognized leader among them became inevitable. If women in church were a dime a dozen, *young* women (which in church meant anyone under forty) were at least somewhat rarer and therefore presumably more valuable. Katherine thought it important to capitalize on value while one still had it, although how exactly she was capitalizing on anything by occasionally skipping church she couldn't rightly have said. Possibly there was a connection between this slight religious skittishness and her impulse for hotel rather than apartment living, a desire to establish social connections rather than social ties, to be known enough to be greeted but not asked favors of, to be not without social recourse but neither to accumulate commitments. So Biedermeier girls who wanted to establish themselves as friendly "go-alongers" signaled friendliness by making themselves available during the same hours as the hotel and propping open a bedroom door in accordance with others, while those who wanted to signal independence kept slightly eccentric schedules, always preferring to plant small but easily readable indicators rather than state an open preference that might get in the way of someone else's independence.

This line of thinking had led Katherine directly to a question she had been mentally putting off for some time, and she puzzled through it during the better part of both the invocation and the assurance of pardon: *Why* had Carol never treated her to lunch? Or if not lunch, then tea or some other little thing? Carol was not eager to collect favors and debts like Kitty, and in almost all things concerning others was rigorously fair, so that Katherine had scarcely realized just how unbalanced the scales between them had become. She herself had, from time to time and without thinking much about it, offered to treat Carol because it was easy for her to do so, or she was feeling particularly flush and wanted to transmit her happy state to another. There had been no great expense—matinees, sandwiches, cups of coffee, bus fare, once a cocktail—and they had been spread out over a year, maybe two, always offered spontaneously and at intervals sufficiently distant that no pattern would be noticed for some time. She had done this without, she thought, anticipating any immediate return of the same but trusting generally that Carol kept track of little social debts much as she, Katherine, did, making a note of it in her diary along with other incidentals before, without either urgency or dawdling, looking for later opportunities to discharge them. She resented the loss of those previously untroubled feelings about Carol more than she minded the cost of a movie ticket. Even more troubling was the spectral possibility of herself as an exacting, ruthless sort of person who scrupulously held everyone to account. In this light her usual habit of noting social costs alongside the affairs of the day ("Tuesday, lunch Anna [$2, hers], south elevator stuck at third floor, reply M, remember ironing, meeting 12th street 6, read Gardiner in PM") looked shabby, even dismal. Was there something unusual in this? What did other people, besides Carol and Katherine, do in such cases? In what manner had Carol been raised, if she did not share Katherine's habit, and had most other people been raised like Carol or like herself? Of course the characteristic feature of *other people* was that they could not have been raised by the same people who had raised you, so it should not have been so surprising to learn that her social anxieties, whichever details she believed essential in the written account of any given day, were not universally shared. Despite having come no little distance herself from her family home, Katherine found it difficult to think of people's habitual routines as anything that was possible to choose or invent for one's own purposes. She almost always attributed daily habits to inheritance rather than to deliberation.

There was the secondary question of whether Carol was herself aware of this lopsidedness, or whether (as Katherine had herself been until the present moment) she was unconscious of it, the answer to which must surely be teased out before Katherine could tackle the third question—namely, what was to be done about it. But she found it a decidedly unpleasant prospect, pawing over every recent interaction in the hope of discovering some small detail, either in Carol's expression or look or turn of phrase, that would suffuse a moment which had until today seemed unremarkably friendly with an unpleasant, subterranean layer of new significance. It felt like replacing the friendly light of a good candle with a flash of cold lightning. If Carol *was* conscious of it, was it because she was worse off than she had been willing to admit? In that case perhaps Katherine had, without ever meaning to, made things even harder for her. It was difficult to imagine how a person might politely refuse an offer to treat, Katherine realized. Or perhaps it was because Carol liked Katherine well enough as a part of the machinery that kept the Biedermeier operating, but didn't want to encourage an outright friendship between them, in which case Katherine had failed to notice not just one but a series of graceful hints in her rush to establish her generosity. In this version of things she was guilty not just of being intrusive but also tasteless, trying to use money to buy what only conversation and mutual inclination could purchase. That Carol might be a chiseler Katherine felt safe in dismissing. Carol neither dropped hints nor picked them up. Either she was unaware of what she was doing, or she had private reasons for keeping herself at a distance.

What did it mean, then, that Carol accepted treats in such a placid, dispassionate way, seemingly unconcerned with whether she might be able to reciprocate in future? And what could she, Katherine, do about it? She could ask Carol outright, but she didn't like to. You might ask a man friend, "Why don't you take me out to eat?" (only if he had already taken you out to dinner, and you were sure that he knew how to take a joke from a girl in the right spirit), but it felt somehow impolitic to ask it of a fellow woman. It was a confining sort of question, much too much like "Are you free Thursday?" for Katherine to consider asking it with a clear conscience. She could stop treating Carol until or unless she noticed and offered to treat *her*, but that felt cheap, even deceitful, and what if Carol never noticed the change? She seemingly hadn't noticed the pattern to begin with, so it was hard to take as an article of faith that she'd notice any variation in such an incidental practice.

Or Katherine could carry on as she had been doing, every so often paying for Carol's inclusion in some event or other, only this time with the uneasy awareness that she was doing so out of obligation, with no expectation of return. Katherine did not consider herself an essentially timid person but if backed into a corner preferred to stay there rather than behave badly, according to her own reckoning of bad behavior, which included even the appearance of stinginess, grudge nursing, itemization, and unsportsmanlike behavior. Perhaps in that case she ought to stop keeping a written record of small favors between friends. It might prove unsportsmanlike after all. One kept count of the score during a game publicly, for everyone to see, not privately in a diary.

It was only when one of the Johns declared, "The Lord bless to us the reading of His Holy Word," that Katherine realized her own mind had been wandering (and after congratulating herself on her steadiness and focus, too). She had scarcely enough time to leap to her feet and join the rest of the congregation in the answering hymn, "Let all mortal flesh keep silence," and that jumping-jack maneuver still preoccupied her thoughts afterward in the coffee hall.

"There really isn't enough time between the readings and the hymns," Altheah agreed. "And I do think you're right about Shakespeare, because those filler words always stand out a great deal more than any of the *thee*s or *wherefore*s—at least to me they do—but at the same time one doesn't like the idea of walking back from the lectern and just standing either, not while everyone else is still sitting down. It feels too close to loitering. Is it very ridiculous to worry about this sort of thing? You've got to tell me if I'm boring you terribly."

"Not at all," Katherine said. "I think I know just what you mean. That is, you know that of course it isn't the most important moment of the service, but it is the moment you've got to worry about as you go from being *part* of the service back into being a congregant again, which almost no one else has to do except the readers. You don't want to look like you're in a hurry, or as if you were trying to prompt everyone else to stand on your say-so, which standing by yourself might very well do. It *is* difficult. And of course it's important. It's not the *most* important thing, of course, but it still matters. You're shaping the direction of the concerted attention of about five hundred people. That's something, after all."

"That's precisely it," Altheah said, with real warmth. She was the best type of lay reader, Katherine thought, because she was eager to avoid the appearance of self-importance that so often came with the office, without ever forgetting that it was her duty, in the manner she moved and spoke, to contribute to the general graciousness and solemnity of worship.

Katherine briefly considered saying something to that effect, but decided against it on the grounds that sympathy was already flaring up between them to a dangerous degree, and she risked inviting excessive interest. There was a distinct art to good after-church talk. Instead she murmured something tactful and nodded vaguely, and then after trading a few less keenly felt remarks about the weather, which was fine and seasonable, and the sermon, which had to do with whether Paul's taking-up of Eutychus in Acts should properly be considered a resurrection from the dead, in the manner of Lazarus and Tabitha and the daughter of Jairus, or whether it should be considered instead a *revival* and therefore merely a simple healing miracle, like that of the beggar at the Gate Beautiful, Altheah drifted away.

Katherine had sometimes wondered why attending church seemed to prepare one so inadequately for encountering one's fellows only a short while afterward. The best and highest goal that after-church talk could aim for was not to damage the feeling that church had wrought in someone else. Possibly it was too jarring and immediate a change to ever be really free from awkwardness, to go from singing the Doxology in four parts, shoulder to shoulder with the body of Christ, to being crowded into a stifling reception hall, drinking coffee from an urn in mismatched china and trying to talk softly about small things to half a dozen different people at once. But perhaps they felt it jarring, too.

Of course there was another excellent reason for not wanting to come to church so often one began to be expected there, and it was ridiculous not to have considered the Alcoholics Anonymous meeting that met every Friday evening in the Old First basement and which, except for the first three months after her arrival there, Katherine had faithfully attended for nearly all of her ten years in New York City.

If Katherine was not ashamed to call herself a woman alcoholic, still she was not proud of it, nor did she consider it an accomplishment worth bringing up in ordinary conversation. It would have, in fact, made ordinary conversation impossible with the Sunday congregation, and not because they were too unyielding either. It was an admission that by its very existence cut off the possibility of further discussion. One's companion could not say anything in response that was not either intrusive or censorious, and thus feel correspondingly censored, and besides which might now feel additional pressure to disclose something personal, even disgraceful in exchange, to even out the imbalanced sense of exposure. It may have been no longer unacceptable to acknowledge the alcoholic, but even these days it did not do to invoke him in the present. One might admit to having an alcoholic in one's family tree, or somewhere in the hinterlands of one's more distant acquaintances, or even say, "Such-and-so goes to AA," if his drinking career had been particularly remarkable, and expect to hear in response "That's the boy!" or "Good for him." But it was never a socially correct answer to everyday questions like "What will you have?" or "Join me for a drink," which was not even a question and could not politely be demurred.

And Presbyterians, Katherine had learned, just as often drank sherry after church as they did coffee. They also used real wine for Communion, a revelation that had shocked her almost as much as the fact that they celebrated Communion every month. After that first jarring experience Katherine made sure to avoid church every fourth Sunday, rather than risk a scene. Katherine had grown up in a teetotal church, which considered Communion a very special occasion indeed, celebrating it no more than four times a year, and always with little thimbles of grape juice so tart that the inside of one's cheeks tingled unbearably after. And of course she had almost never been drunk on Sundays, Westerville not only having been a dry city for nearly one hundred years but additionally serving as headquarters to the Anti-Saloon League after it was driven out of Washington, DC. The town still kept Prohibition, as did a number of other Ohio river towns, in as cheerful, placid, and determined a fashion in 1955 as they had in 1929.

———··———

It had been on the ninth of September, 1955, that Katherine Heap had been driven from Westerville to Chillicothe by her mother, where she boarded a bus for Cincinnati, departing from it on the Ohio State Limited, which arrived in New York City at 9:30 the next morning. She might have departed from Dayton on the same line, but which-ever train she chose, it still meant she had to begin her journey east by first traveling west for several hours. She wore a tightly woven gray woolen suit she reserved for long-distance travel, and stout shoes. People who did not walk often ought to wear thick shoes with heavy soles for a long journey, she had once read, but those who intended to make a business of walking should be as lightly shod as possible, in order to let the ankles toughen. She did intend to make a business of walking once she had settled in New York, but stout shoes were all she had in the meanwhile, and it seemed backward to buy a new pair before leaving home until she had worn out this one. In her pocketbook were a pair of Crescendoe gloves, an appointment book, her father's watch, an envelope of traveler's checks, and a letter of introduction to the Peabody accounting firm, from a cousin who had worked there two years ago as a junior bookkeeper.

"When you're settled," her mother said, "you might write and let us know what you need. We can send it by freight. I don't like to think about what can happen to good furniture in a boxcar, but there's no point in sending it before you've found something that's fixed."

"All right," Katherine said.

"I hope you'll take care of Mr. Heap's watch," her mother said. She had kept the old-fashioned habit of referring to her husband as Mr. Heap even to her children. Katherine was distinctly aware of an inner wrench; she was not likely to hear anything so homespun for quite some time. Mr. and Mrs. Heap displayed their considerable affection for one another through various ambassadorial devices. Whenever one was absent, the other spoke for them in the most respectful and ceremonial of terms. "It's worth the keeping of."

"I will," Katherine said. She did not like making promises to her mother; she was only too aware that her record on that score was dismal. It would have been much better to treat the watch casually, and just as casually display it in excellent condition years from now, without drawing attention to it.

"I'll wait until you're on the train to leave," her mother said, "but I'll do my waiting inside the lounge, where I can look out the window, and say goodbye to you here. This is for the steward, and this is for the porter. You ought to tip them both. Good luck to you." She quickly pressed Katherine's hand and then withdrew back inside the station.

Katherine was then twenty-two years old and three months sober. Ohio being the original headquarters of Alcoholics Anonymous, the first group in Akron having started meeting together in 1935, meant that even a small village like Westerville supported several meetings a week, one at the hospital, one at the Methodist church, one at the Kiwanis club, and one held in a member's private home twice a month that was just for women alcoholics. Katherine's drinking career had not been especially long, lasting only a little over four years, but its progression had been swift and the final drop abrupt; she was then the youngest member of the Westerville fellowship by several decades.

The Heaps were an old family, at least by Midwestern reckoning, having established a branch in Westerville by the time of its incorporation in 1858. But even the very oldest families rarely outlive three oaks. Certainly neither of Katherine's parents ever seemed conscious of having to steward anything like a family character outside of what was generally owed to children by right of birth. Like most parents of their era, they hoped for the dispersal, rather than the consolidation, of their legacy, mentally settling their offspring in every far-flung corner of the country. The Westerville Heaps were by and large a dry family. Even a careful examination of their lineage, traced as far back as it was possible to go, would have produced no more than two or three suspected drunkards, none of them after the nineteenth century, and the last of whom, a bachelor uncle graciously donated to the railroad in the 1880s, had turned into a remarkably steady citizen upon his removal to Arizona, where he was in later years elected twice to local government. Those Heaps who remained in Westerville practiced a mild form of religion, some worshipping at the Church of the United Brethren in Christ and others with the Methodists. In neither case was their attendance regular, and both sides were eccentrically born high-minded Victorian atheists, of the sort who tirelessly cataloged the whole world from top to bottom during that most frenetic and middle-class of centuries, who became botanists, geologists, and ornithologists, and delighted in any scientific pursuit that required one to go about with a logbook and a miniature hammer. The family had more regularly produced at first orchardists, who cultivated excellent apple trees of golden Pippins (which they valued all the more highly for having once drawn the ire of the visiting Johnny Appleseed, who as a Swedenborgian objected to grafting on the grounds that it hurt the trees, which the Heaps at once dismissed as religious quackery and enjoyed as notice from a celebrity), and later schoolteachers, principals, and headmasters, and especially prided itself on the education of its women.

Katherine's own mother had been granted a degree in sociology from a ladies' seminary in 1928, and as she was herself the eldest of six (of which all but one survived infancy), the family had long cherished a dream of sending Katherine back East for college. She had exhibited a modest talent for languages as a girl and was considered by her parents and her own teachers a largely tractable child, reasonably studious, prone to no more than the gentlest of wanderlust. Her daydreams tended to run shallow, and if her attention was not always easily held, it was at least easily recalled, and she had in fact been on track to receive admission both at Elmira College in New York and at the Pennsylvania College for Women after graduating high school, when suddenly and without any serious prior indication of trouble, Katherine began to exhibit signs of near-total collapse and, almost without knowing how, having seen so little of it in her young life, to drink.

She "began to drink"—a phrase that communicates nearly nothing except an automatic progression of cues, that calls up the meaningless image of some indistinct and general figure, never an individual, pounding the bar in rumpled shirtsleeves, heedless of the speeding train bearing down on him from just off-screen. Katherine's drinking more than baffled her mild and even-tempered parents; it overturned them. There had been no new stressors added to her life, no social loss or rupture that might have added undetectable forms of pressure eventually leading to a breakdown; the scales of her days remained as evenly balanced as they always had been. She had not acquired any recent dangerous acquaintance, was not a hard liver, demonstrated no marked or new interest in men, music, and dissipation, demanded no new terms out of life, and made no statement of independence or rebellion that they might have either tolerated or forbid.

From one day to the next and in all other respects Katherine's life looked very much as it always had, except she drank. In a family of near teetotalers, in a dry city, in a semidry state, as a young woman of seventeen, whose sex and background and class none of which should have predisposed her to such a thing, seemingly happy with her lot in life, and with both limited funds and opportunities to procure liquor, she swiftly progressed from friendly drinks at a small party to dizzying, incomprehensible bouts of near annihilation, which she herself neither understood nor could scarcely be said to enjoy, except for that very first night when, deep in her cups, she thought madly to herself, *This then is life—and they have kept it from me—they knew this was life and they kept it from me.*

———··———

"Are you leaving, Katherine?" Altheah had rematerialized by her side after some interval. "Can't I persuade you to stay a little longer? Only what you were saying about the order of service was *so* helpful, and the Overtures Committee is meeting in the Alexander Chapel this afternoon."

How nice it was, to be wanted to stay! But it would not do at all.

"Possibly another time," Katherine said guardedly. "I'm afraid I'm wanted at home."

Later discussion with her AA sponsor, Arthur, determined that this counted as a promise made, regardless of the "possibly" hedge, and that Katherine was in fact honor bound to keep it at the first opportunity.

"You can always say no when people ask you something," he reminded her, "but if you *don't* say no, you've got to live up to it. You make an awful lot of promises, even by alcoholic standards, Katherine."

"I know it," Katherine said. "I can't help liking Altheah, and wanting her to like me; I just wish she liked me without wanting to see any more of me."

"You do realize, of course," Arthur said, "that everyone on the Overtures Committee is responsible for presenting requests to the General Assembly, too?"

"How often does the General Assembly meet?" Katherine asked, horrified.

"Only once a year," Arthur said. He was a cradle Presbyterian himself, although situated much further uptown at the Brick Church on Park and Ninety-First Streets. "Of course, it's being held this year in West Virginia."

Katherine groaned.

"Yes, it's very difficult to attend church and avoid church life at the same time," Arthur said. "I wonder when you'll stop trying to do both." Not for the first time, Katherine thought that Presbyterians must belong to a particularly unfeeling limb of the body of Christ.

Chapter Four

INCOMPREHENSIBLE
DEMORALIZATION

After graduating high school Katherine worked several afternoons a week in an accounting office in Westerville's little downtown district, typing copies of letters that the accountant had already dictated to his secretary and addressing envelopes, and at that time there was still a streetcar running between her home on the north side of the river, the accountant's office, and the nearby city of Columbus, which had never harbored the Anti-Saloon League and marked 1933 as the end of Prohibition, as did the rest of the country. There was still at this time, her parents believed, every reason to hope for the best possible outcome, and Katherine had no cause to doubt them except for the inner certainty that the next time would look very much like the last had. She might go as long as ten days between sprees.

For Katherine there did not seem to exist that happy state in which many alcoholics and near alcoholics drift along for years, sometimes for an entire lifetime—that of habituation, where each crisis, however desperate, may afterward be succeeded and even diminished in power by a lengthy period of maintenance. For Katherine the crisis was immediate, chronic, and merciless. No double life was possible for her, whereby a steady surface might have for years concealed the growing dependence underneath. Between the stages of germination and harvest there was almost no interval of maturation; the compulsion to drink flourished, even when a drink was neither welcome nor able to satisfy. It grew altogether more like a mushroom than a weed, requiring no tending, no sunlight, no particular food or environment to thrive, swelling rapidly to pale maturity, seemingly capable of reproducing itself spontaneously. Within weeks of forming the habit, she began to find the sight and smell of liquor entirely repulsive, and viewed the likelihood of her next drink with genuine fear and abhorrence. Shaky but eager to collect herself after her first bout, her inner sense of fitness and any awareness of an ability to meet and face the moment of crisis folded swiftly and completely after the second.

Shortly after turning eighteen she one day regained consciousness inside a hospital, at first cocooned in a delicious warmth that brought with it a sense of being wonderfully blunted all over, then gradually becoming aware of an insensate dullness in her right foot. It had been badly broken. There was of course no memory of having broken it, nor indeed of having been brought to the hospital. Katherine could find no mental gap between the awareness of noon, health, and work and the onset of disorientation, immobilization, and the sight of a lot of people running to and from her bedside in white smocks, having awoken to one state without ever consciously departing from the other. Stranger even than that unaccountable spell of lost time, no one else could tell her how she had broken it, either; whatever accidental collision, deliberate self-injury, or involuntary lapse of control that caused it had apparently taken place out of all possible human sight. She had not even been found where she fell. She learned that, incredibly, she had the night before walked home, dragging her dead foot behind her in the dark, then been found sick on the porch.

After two weeks in traction Katherine was discharged from the hospital and sent home with a pair of crutches. In another eight weeks she was able to walk without them. But she did not return to the accountant's office downtown, and there was no talk of her getting another job.

While she was still laid up in the hospital, the doctor directing Katherine's treatment had invited her parents into his office to discuss her prospects, having noticed her condition on admittance, asking if she had ever made trouble for them before. The Heaps denied this, which he had of course expected, but were so consistent in this assertion that he by degrees began to give way.

"Never a highly strung child?" he asked. "Never fitful, not prone to moods either especially high or low, nothing like that elsewhere in the family?"

Not highly strung, never given to throwing or having fits, moods invariably composed.

"Your daughter is perhaps hopeless of her future? Disappointed in love, recently parted from a strong attachment—perhaps a childhood companion—a loss in the family, the forfeiture of a scholarship?" No, none of those. Future had seemed agreeably, if not spectacularly, bright. No recent loss of friends, no emotional rupture. No marked change in daily routine. Only a sudden cratering of the ground beneath her and an abrupt pitching forward, then straight down.

The doctor of course believed this to be a face-saving lie. Either they did know the cause perfectly well but were too embarrassed to own it to him, or they were ignorant of the cause, being too trusting or too oblivious to have caught it in time. But as she had only damaged herself, rather than run someone over with a car, he did not push further. He advised them to keep their own liquor locked up. When they admitted they kept none in the house, he suggested they keep a stricter eye on her.

"What she likely needs is not a change of pace," he said, "but a solid, dependable routine," after which he politely dismissed them from his office, believing that in doing so he was sparing them further embarrassment from needing to tell lies again.

And of course he had been disgusted by the conversation itself. He regretted having had to introduce the subject of Katherine's drinking even indirectly in the first place. For a young person (he could not quite think of her as a young lady), who by all other indicators appeared to have been normally brought up—but it was nothing like the sort of exculpatory trouble one associated with normal youthful esprit—this was worse than unhealthy. Once, as a boy, the doctor had seen his dog running through the kitchen proudly carrying its own waste in its mouth, the sight of which had affected him intensely; he did not consciously think of it now, but experienced a similar determination to avert his attention until the scene had passed.

Mr. and Mrs. Heap, we have already said, were both possessed of mild and agreeable temperaments, which equipped them very badly indeed to handle the present moment. Their minds were not dull, yet they lacked the type of imagination that might have allowed them to help their daughter. That she was suffering was obvious. That she was conscious of having made her parents and her sisters suffer equally so—that she sincerely did not wish to drink again, and had not in fact wished to drink the last time she got drunk either—all that was obvious to them, too. That there was no apparent origin for it, no family precedent to be found in their own generation, or even in their parents', which might have led them to anticipate such a habit, almost throttled their ability to decide upon any one course of action in favor of another.

The other children were substantially younger than Katherine. (The sibling who had not survived infancy had been born shortly after her, leading to a subsequent gap of several years before the arrival of the next.) And so they were innocent of any suspicion that something more than a broken foot was wrong with her, and their parents took the doctor's suggestion of a dependable routine as a promise of a cure. She was brought home and kept there. Just as all talk of another job had vanished, so too did any of Elmira and Pennsylvania; college and the East were entirely evacuated as subjects of conversation, for fear of possibly creating a shock. If anyone made naive inquiry, Katherine was staying at home to help with the other children, which was no more than a slightly old-fashioned thing for a girl of her age to do. That her own mother had gone to college was credible, but it did not generate an automatic expectation; there was no need for the maneuver to be repeated in every generation. If Katherine recovered only to find life had been made impossible for her—the Heaps were at least as concerned for their daughter's welfare as they were for what might be said about her, and it is not against their credit that they considered both questions with equal weight when planning for her future.

During the first part of her convalescence there was no talk about liquor; the Heaps did not mention it for fear of mortifying her and Katherine because she did not want to press her luck. All parties hoped to forget what had already passed. There had been a stumble, even the loss of some real good, but no painful reminder from *them* would inflame it. All parties resolved to turn the stumble to account, and looked ahead to a future that, if not so bright nor expansive as had been previously hoped, was now all the steadier and surer for its diminution. And of course, unable to walk for very far unaided, and without the slender financial reserves afforded by her job downtown, Katherine could not have gotten anything to drink, had she wanted to (and she did not want to). But then, a week later, when that sweet little idea arose—what did the combined force of all those concentrated hopes, all that joint resolution amount to? With every reason not to drink, with hardly any conceivable way of getting anything *to* drink, Katherine exhibited previously unknown and subterranean reserves of cunning and resourcefulness.

She got it; she got spectacularly, radiantly drunk; she was happier than any creature now living; she was entirely healed; she was more well than she had ever been; she had a hundred glittering futures ahead of her; she was the beloved eldest daughter who enclosed the fondest hopes of her doting, handsome parents; she could traverse the entire length of the porch railing without stopping; she could climb a tree; she fell; again she broke the right foot; again she tried to walk inside; again her white face was sick; again the hospital bed; this time with no cocoon of warmth, no delicious blunted feeling to temper the nauseating heat of the shattered joint. The foot was broken; the foot was doubly broken, being but so recently mended; the bones of her foot were as good to her as soup.

Katherine was very, very sorry then, as sorry as she had ever been. Her parents were sorry too. They became, if anything, even more courteous and soft-spoken to one another than before, each acutely conscious of the tender contrition of the other. The doctor was very angry with them, and again advised a strict home routine and stricter surveillance. It was then that Mrs. Heap, in her heart's ache, hit upon an explanation and a plan: their mistake had been in keeping Katherine at home *without also keeping liquor there*. When the insane urge had struck her daughter, she had been without recourse, almost forced out of the house in search of relief—*without even her mother to help her*, Mrs. Heap thought with no little guilt.

Next time (there was now no pretense that there would not be a next time) would be different. A small reserve of strong liquor, kept somewhere in the house under strict observation—locked—with Mrs. Heap holding the only key—not for the purpose of inducing drunkenness, which both Mr. and Mrs. Heap would have shuddered at, but solely to relieve agony *in extremis*—in only the most urgent of cases—with the bedroom door safely locked and the window safely fastened shut, to prevent a third fall—would allow Katherine to again be brought home, and kept there.

She had been a child, and then she had been a drunk, without ever passing through any intermediate stage that might have substantially distinguished one from the other. Now she accumulated very little society outside the home, and did in fact help with the children, usually during the first half of the day. The mysterious glamor of her afternoon withdrawal to a closed room upstairs made her no less popular with them—for extreme agony proved to be a daily visitor with her, and if she could not depart from a state of everyday consciousness quickly enough, she grew frantic, even desperate. Mrs. Heap could not have guessed, when she brought her daughter home from the hospital a second time, either how frequently a case could be considered urgent, or how cheaply relief might be purchased to everyone's satisfaction.

Nor could either Mr. or Mrs. Heap begin to understand how such mellow and humane parenting could have produced such rebellion— and yet it was rebellion without direction or end, for she made no plans to leave them. Equally mystifying, Katherine, who had never been melancholic as a child, who gently enjoyed the company of other children, who tolerated the instinctive hero worship of her much younger sisters (and being very young herself at the death of their second child, did not take it especially hard), who had suffered no mistreatment at school, no serious injustice or interference from strangers, no trespass on her rights by the world, yet now seemed to bear life a grudge better suited to one who had been orphaned by war and privation. But Katherine was only wretched, and made others wretched, when alcohol was too long withheld from her. She revived like a flower on being watered, and became for several hours glassy and sociable, wonderful with the children and charming to her mother, who carried always on her person the very key to Katherine's health and happiness. Katherine and her mother had worked out a slight signal between them, by which Katherine would indicate whenever she found the shallowness of her inebriation intolerable, and Mrs. Heap would vanish to make arrangements no stronger than were absolutely necessary to defer catastrophe. So Katherine's life from eighteen on grew itself more and more tranquilly childlike, founded on obedience to her mother and attachment to a bottle. With real affection on both sides and the best of intentions on Mrs. Heap's, things became often unbearable between them; things continued.

"Today's no good," one of Mrs. Heap's children was heard one afternoon to remark to her fellows on the landing. They had trooped halfway up the stairs, eager for an omen, elected the next-eldest from amongst themselves to peep through the keyhole in Katherine's door. "It's an upstairs day. Let's go back down."

The next day the ringleader had been radiantly comforted on Katherine's contrite return: "And did you miss me terribly, darling? I missed you. Today you shall have whatever you like, even unto half my kingdom, by way of consolation."

The other children grew a little older, knowing only that Katherine was sometimes lovely and sometimes ill, and when she was ill she could not bear loud noises, and positively must be left alone upstairs. Since she was not their parent, they developed no desire to learn about something that could only be unpleasant. Like most children they had a native allegiance to health, and preferred concealment of anything potentially disfiguring or unwholesome. Children may be curious about many things, but very rarely the troubles of grown-up persons, unless those troubles directly threaten their own peace of mind. This is perfectly natural and healthy; children already have more than sufficient demands on their still-limited abilities. In latter cases, the children invariably grow old before their time; any little man or woman who jumps at sudden noises has been prematurely aged by overeager interest in the private concerns of others. The other Heap children kept their youth until such time as they could exchange it for a suitable adulthood, and did not further investigate the plausibility of their happiness. Three more years passed.

The tenacity of youth is remarkable. Despite Katherine's ongoing participation in her own confinement, despite her many attempts to disown the inheritance of strength and resilience that always accompanies adolescence in at least some degree, health persisted within her—mangled, shrunken, and impaired as it was, nevertheless she did not entirely succeed in subduing it. The effect of that remaining wholesome impulse in her resulted in an occasional desire to be out of doors—a third time, incredibly, she fell, and on the same bankrupt foot. This time she did not attempt to return home, instead dragging herself into a neighbor's barn, where she was found several hours later and once more taken to the hospital. On the second day of her admission the signs of delirium tremens were unmistakable. She was removed to a dependent ward for drying out, and the Heaps began to be talked about. Westerville was not an especially small town, with nearly five thousand residents, and it was not so very unusual for a young woman to break a bone or stay at home that Katherine's predicament excited much comment, but finally the limits of guaranteed privacy had been breached, and speculation set in.

Katherine, who had become accustomed to the submerged and glittering existence of a sea diver, now had the sense of being abruptly hauled out of a grotto, where both sound and light had been softened by a couch of deep water, and onto the blazing noonday deck of a shadowless ship. Here was a sudden, hideous close to what now seemed such a sweet and gentling employment. She thirsted, and there was no water; she perspired, and there was no relief; she alternated between frenzy and exhaustion, and there was no rest; she burned, and there was no coolness. She dared not close her eyes, which invariably set the room spinning around her, and she hated to open them, for there were often little occult figures on the foot of her bed, bobbing their heads together and gabbling softly. Time did not pass for Katherine in those few days. She found herself suspended within a petrified and unceasing moment, which continually poured over the edges of her perception without ever draining away, until at some incoherent threshold she was once again shunted back from hateful eternity and into time. To return to her former way of living was impossible, she now knew. It had come to a pitiful, degrading, and definitive end in that barn, and any relapse would mean forfeiting the hope of ever seeing a welcome look on a familiar face for the rest of her life.

And Katherine, who was desperate not to drink, also knew that this desperation could provide her no protection whatsoever, that nothing her family might have to say on the subject, however kindly meant, could possibly be any good to her. The danger she felt that was forever bearing down on her was of a type entirely unknown to them. It was as if she were uniquely subject to a sort of earthquake that produced sensations which no other human person ever felt or saw.

So on the fourteenth day of her confinement Katherine yielded readily to the visitors from Akron, two well-dressed and complacent-looking women who had been ushered in and seated at either side of the foot of her hospital bed.

The first meeting of Alcoholics Anonymous had begun nearby in Akron nearly twenty years earlier, and the ward Katherine found herself in had long been frequented by members arriving in groups of two or three to speak with the drying-out cases. Some of the drying-out cases threw them right back out again, and in such instances they departed more or less cheerfully.

Women drinkers were by no means a novelty among their ranks, and she had been speaking with her visitors for practically half an hour before it dawned on Katherine that they might be like her. She had been entirely at a loss for the reason for their visit. In her still-muddled state she had believed them to be acquaintances of her mother's, and it had taken all of her wasted resources to make conversation.

"Now for myself," the stouter of the two was saying, "I somehow managed to avoid falls like yours, although I could hardly say how. But my God, how I *stole*!"

"Oh—did you?" Katherine said uncertainly.

"From the housekeeping budget, from my sister, from the collection plate at church. . . . I've never worked, you see, so I couldn't steal from the office, although I'm sure I would have if I'd ever gotten half the chance."

"I opened the girls' piggy bank on several occasions," added the other readily. "Needs must when the devil drives."

"And invariably," the first woman went on, "every time I thought I was on the verge of conquering the thing, sure as shooting that was the start of the next slip. The more I didn't want to drink, the likelier it was bound to happen. As I'm sure was the case with you, dear," she said, nodding to Katherine in so cheerful a fashion as to border on the inhumane. "I'm sure you had no intention of ending up here again, did you?"

Katherine could not speak.

"I haven't shocked you, have I?" said the stout woman. "I don't say any of this at your expense, dear. I only mean that shame is no help to anyone in your position, or in ours. But you drink, don't you?"

Katherine nodded.

"And you don't exactly know why, isn't that so?"

"Yes," Katherine said. It seemed impossible to answer this merry directness with anything else.

"It was just like that with me," the woman said triumphantly. "It was just the very same way with me, and every time I fell—not down the stairs, but within, you know—I was as shocked and horrified as if I'd just been bounced off the roof. Worse still, it didn't matter how horrified I was, or how much I wanted not to do it again; it was like the law of cause and effect had gotten uncoupled when it came to me, somehow. But don't let's worry about it just now. If you want help, you've only got to say so. It'll work for you like it's worked for us, sure as fish is fish."

"The really good news is," the other one said, leaning closer to Katherine as she did so, "is we're all a great deal more like each other than we think. Your days of being unique are numbered." She smiled, as if that were supposed to be good news, and Katherine smiled back, not having the energy to resist further.

The women went on talking for at least another hour, about something Katherine could neither grasp nor retain, and by the end of their visit she had agreed to be released into their care.

Chapter Five

THE LAST OF OHIO

During the months of Katherine's convalescence in Akron, Mrs. Heap came to believe that she would be unable to endure even the briefest of reunions. Again there was no quarrel, no recrimination. She said only to Mr. Heap, after the second week of their daughter's removal, how pleasant the family atmosphere was: "And it would be a shame for everyone if we were to spoil it, because I don't think we can call these last few years a success, really." To which Mr. Heap certainly agreed.

It was not that Katherine had been *un*helpful, but that perhaps they had less need of it than they had when the other children were younger. And it was undeniably true that without Katherine, the mood in the house had been beautifully rinsed. Most of all, although she did not say so to her husband, Mrs. Heap thought that if she saw Katherine's face at their front door again she would want to scream.

Despite this discomfiting new aversion, she still took an active interest in Katherine's recovery, writing faithfully twice a week and encouraging her attendance at meetings. She also made arrangements for Katherine to go East after her time in Akron, having written to a cousin on her mother's side of the family who had established himself in New York City after the war, saying it was Katherine's wish to see something of the country now that the other children were growing up, relating her experience at an Ohio accounting firm, and inquiring whether he might consider writing a letter of recommendation on her behalf—realizing a letter of recommendation was of course itself no guarantee of employment—and assuring him that anything he might do in the way of helping to get Katherine situated would be very welcome, and that her parents would happily contribute some money toward her settlement, if he knew of someplace decent for her to stay. He did know, he would write, and he would be happy to help; as it happened the Peabody firm was almost always looking for reliable girls, and if money was no object knew of a very good hotel. If money were some object he knew of several others, very nearly as good, and after that there were always advertisements to be found in local newspapers.

So Katherine was dispatched, first from the hospital in Akron to the home of a local member of Alcoholics Anonymous during her first few shaky months of sobriety, whom she only ever knew as Dierdre A., then to her parents' doorstep, where she found arrangements already made for her, a trunk already packed, and a very cheerful chorus of "goodbye and good luck" from everyone she had ever known before while being driven very steadily by her mother to the station in Chillicothe, her father and the children staying behind and waving from the porch. From there, as we already know, she caught the bus bound for Cincinnati before making the Ohio State Limited, which arrived in Manhattan five days a week, a few minutes after 9:30 a.m. By three in the afternoon her trunks were unpacked in a bare room on the Biedermeier's third floor facing east. It had been as sudden and as sweeping a change as any she had experienced, and she had a distinct feeling of having been delivered, in both a postal and the traditional sense.

By the following Wednesday she had started work as an assistant accounting clerk at Peabody on West Forty-Third Street. There she made fifty-five dollars a week, an amount that at first terrified her, a single paycheck being more money than she had ever handled at once before. It was enough money to think of squandering it. She dreaded the return of the impulse to waste above all things, remembering what a spendthrift she had been with time. There was a perverse appeal in the knowledge that today would be obliterated in the same way yesterday had been (and she had only ever experienced the wasting of time as an inevitability; it had never come to her as a question, to be decided either for or against, or a matter of will that could be accepted or resisted).

Her fellow Ohio AA members had been cheerful almost to the point of irritation on that front. This was a frequent occurrence in the early days of her sobriety—finding that everyone else shared an intimate knowledge of her own fears without, somehow, feeling any longer the weight of them. "Of course you'll want to waste it," Deirdre said, after Katherine had called her to confess her anxiety the night before her first payday. "I can't think of a more sensible impulse. I see a bed, I think of sleep; I see money, and I think of how to get rid of it as quickly as possible. Fifty-five dollars is too steep a responsibility for a good alcoholic. So is fifty-five cents. But you still have to learn how to live in the world with money and other people in it, and you might as well start now." Dierdre had written her own letter introducing Katherine to several members of AA living in the city, as well as a list of meetings she was to attend regularly. This included the Friday night gathering in the basement of Old First

Church, which was where she took her first paycheck still in its envelope, jittery and miserable, and revealed what felt to her like a sign of inexplicable depravity: that somehow, getting the money that was owed to her for two weeks' worth of work, in exactly the manner she had been promised she was going to get it and precisely on time, felt like an unfair burden, even an insult, and she resented being made responsible for it, because among other things, it meant she would have to open a bank account.

"Which I know is a perfectly ordinary thing for a person to do," she said, "only I don't know how I'm supposed to choose which bank to start an account with, or what I'm supposed to say once I get there, and I didn't want to ask anyone at work how to do it—it seemed like such a backward question, and it made me feel especially conscious of the fact that almost before I became a person I was a drunk first, and worse than that a drunk who hardly even went anywhere or did anything, a drunk almost without a past—and once I *do* open it I'm going to have to go to the bank for the rest of my life, and there's a part of me which really, truly, sensibly would rather die—only I came here tonight instead, so I guess I'm not quite ready to die just yet." That there was general laughter at this last part she remarkably did not resent, possibly because there was nowhere else she would ever have said anything like it. In meetings she was almost never ashamed of having been a drunk, because it made her useful to others, but everywhere else she felt the weight of it keenly. Another fellow even offered to accompany her the next morning to the branch of her choosing, and somehow or other she had managed to accomplish the task with very little trouble.

That this was regularly the case with the little offices of independent living gave Katherine no little trouble. So often she experienced a sudden, not-very-pleasant revelation about some minor task associated with daily acts of administration: that it was the simplest thing imaginable, that there was nothing in the world that should have prevented her from having done it years ago, that her lapse into alcoholism was as inexcusable as it had been incomprehensible, and that everything she had wasted, her own time and the even more valuable time and energy of her family, her potential, her most receptive and educable years of life, the chance to form lasting friendships with people her own age, had been doubly wasted in her case, without even a colorful history to show for it. A few years only—but what years they had been, and how much had she forfeited in dissipating them! Even after her sober years in New York began to outnumber the years she had spent drinking, the self-consciousness of having burned through a critical period did not leave her, and she maintained a profound dread of failing to "do her share." When Katherine was not at work, she went to AA meetings; lucky there were more of them in New York than anywhere else, even Ohio. When there were no meetings, she helped out around the Office for General Service, scheduling members for twelfth-step calls, taking hospital referrals, proofing the monthly bulletin, responding to letters of general inquiry, and answering the phone. When the Office for General Service was closed, she made herself useful around the Biedermeier—so useful that before the end of a year she was able to quit the accountants and move her things downstairs to take up the full-time position of first-floor director, which came with the additional benefit of being paid only fifty dollars a week. Katherine's first arrival to the city had been in the autumn, and her first-floor removal in the height of summer, so for several years she continued to underestimate Stephen, having never seen him in action on Moving Day. Mrs. Mossler had apologized for not being able to afford any more, but Katherine had announced the cut with great relief to her Friday night fellows, seeing it as twenty dollars less to worry about every month. It had lifted a real load off her mind.

Katherine left enough of each paycheck in the bank to keep her account open, and used it for clothes and other incidentals. Her rent, already significantly reduced to begin with since becoming an employee of the hotel, she had persuaded Mrs. Mossler simply to withhold from her salary.

"If only they made more girls like you" was all she had said after Katherine made the request. "You're very easy to make happy. You just want more responsibilities, so long as those responsibilities don't extend to money." In this detail, as in so many others, Mrs. Mossler proved satisfyingly understanding and incurious.

Katherine's other expenses were few: she had received scrupulous dental care as a child and had no problems with her teeth. She set her own hair, only getting it cut every three months. She seldom went to the movies, contributed a quarter a week when they passed the hat for business expenses during meetings, and got most of her books at either the Biedermeier's or the public library. The rest she sent home in her monthly letter.

While Katherine had still been convalescing in Ohio, Deirdre and another woman had taken her through the twelve steps. She had no objection to talk of God, especially when it was kept respectfully vague, found the principle of "usefulness to others" an invaluable fortification against the idleness of shame, and when the time came was only all too ready to make amends to her parents. Always conscious of having wronged them seriously, she now felt newly able to see her way toward an honest attempt to repair what she had broken. She did not believe she presumed too much on their affection for her, and had been adequately prepared by Dierdre and Margaret for the very real possibility of a rebuff. She felt, she believed, truly ready to own her prodigality, her selfishness, her perversity, and would not be overwhelmed by any just recrimination that might follow. But she was less well prepared for the serenity of their reception as she enumerated her wrongs to them, along with her intention to make up for them. Where she was repentant, they had been gracious; where she felt grief, they were sanguine. Without dismissing the truth of these admissions, and without ever shading into coolness, they diplomatically accepted her apologies without committing themselves to anything like a calendar of amendment. And Katherine, feeling herself to be very much in their debt, did not wish to press a conversation that they seemed to think unnecessary, if not exactly unwelcome, so it was not until quite some time had passed that she realized nothing at all had been restored between them, that they did not want to repair the ties that had once connected them, that expressing her regret had been not only presumptuous but additionally painful—had been in fact a continuation of the wrongs she had committed against them, not an alleviation. They were amiably fixed against reconciliation, and Katherine could find no purchase on the smooth surface of their politeness. Her mother answered her letters faithfully at the end of every month, acknowledging receipt and offering general updates about the family, but asked no questions and offered no response more personal than "I am glad to hear you are still attending your meetings, and hope they continue to help you."

Mrs. Heap did not understand how sincere parental compassion could have led to such an unnatural and disordered relationship, could not have explained even to her own husband why the idea of seeing their daughter again, even after the years of her sobriety exceeded the term of her drunkenness, would have felt like a violation against decency. They had meant well. Their joint decision to oversee Katherine's drinking had harmed her, perhaps as much as she had harmed them, and Katherine herself was earnestly penitent, had been steady and consistent in reform, made no inopportune demands for renewed closeness, continued to repay what she had cost them, and furthermore had been genuinely ill, as the Akron doctors had taken pains to inform the Heaps; all this Mrs. Heap could freely admit. But she did not suggest that she visit home again, and if the door to the bedroom that had once been Katherine's was ever unexpectedly closed at the end of the hall, Mrs. Heap felt a hysterical urge to run down the stairs and out of the house.

She did not encourage Katherine to write to her siblings, and Katherine did not dare to do so without a clear invitation, feeling that to do so would mean provoking disloyalty, even corruption. She was not invited to visit home again, and did not ask; her parents did not suggest she quit New York City and she did not imagine it. She remembered, from what little instruction she had received from the Methodists of her youth, the doctrine of imperatives, which taught, "In essential things, unity; in doubtful things, freedom; in all things, charity," but she could not bring herself to follow it. When Katherine doubted, she froze in place until some external force released her. She did not look for signs, since she did not trust her own interpretation of them; either something else would lift the spell of uncertainty and immobility, or it would not. In this way she plotted the boundaries of her own understanding as a series of freedoms, bound on all sides by stillness. There had been times when she thought briefly of applying to college, of leaving the city behind and tramping to Yellowstone— but she worried about somehow violating the terms of her semiofficial banishment, of incidentally spreading additional pain and shame in the exercise of too broad an independence.

"Then go and be useful to someone who *wants* you to be useful to them," Deirdre had said after allowing Katherine a few minutes for tears. "And unless your parents explicitly tell you not to do it, keep sending money. That's just about the only amends that nobody ever turns down, because it's never intrusive. And cheer up—you're young yet, and you haven't even killed anybody."

Privately Katherine thought Deirdre had failed to understand the uniqueness of her situation, that since Katherine's drinking had been so cloistered and domestic she had relatively few people to try to make amends with, which made any failure loom disproportionately large. Deirdre in fact understood this perfectly well, and said as much: "If you'd had a longer list of people you'd hurt, you'd think *that* was worse, because it provided further evidence that you're a truly bad person who'd alienated practically everyone she met. There is no unique situation for any of us. There must be at least fifty other girls in this country with practically the exact same history you're so sure sets you apart. You just haven't met any of them yet. But you will, so stay on the lookout."

Whether there were in fact fifty other women with Katherine's particular history, who drank almost exclusively indoors and under quiet parental supervision, she did not know. If there were, none of them ever came to her meetings. But nonetheless she did keep a lookout for them, and in the meantime managed to lead many a shaky newcomer through the first few steps herself; in so doing she discovered the real pleasure that came from being of use to other people. This was nothing like the polite fiction about staying at home to help her mother with the rest of the children after high school. Even when she had managed to be of actual help then—and she *had* been fond of the children, whatever else—it had been incidental and without design, toward no greater end than the pleasant passing of a few dry hours. If anything, these brief moments of alignment with the official story made the underlying lie seem all the more powerful.

If making fifty dollars a week had felt like too great a responsibility for her, somehow listening to someone else haltingly relate the most shameful and intimate episodes of their lives and saying, "Yes, I've felt that, too," was perfectly natural, and her powers entirely equal to it. Elsewhere she might mistrust, even avoid, disclosures of privacy, but in these cases she felt as admirably suited to it as an expert craftsman feels with a sculptor's chisel in hand. She did not mistake this usefulness for genius—she understood perfectly well that any other member of the fellowship could have served just as effectively in her place—but she no longer sought out evidence of her fatal uniqueness. To feel useful, after having done so little, to feel no *more* or *less* useful than anyone else after having so much to be ashamed of, brought with it a satisfaction no less persistent for being quiet.

And if sometimes she still felt an uneasy lurch at the sudden conjecture of what her mother thought of her, or a flash of profound loathing at the unsolicited memory of something particularly degrading, she followed the advice she had been given by the good-humored old Irishwoman whose name was, incredibly, Colleen, and who had made herself Katherine's first sponsor in the New York fellowship.

"That sort of shame is above our pay grade, and has to be kicked upstairs," she had said, meaning there was nothing to do but pray about it. Prayer, she had given Katherine to understand, was better utilized as a system of disposal for useless things like excessive guilt, self-pity, morbid dwelling on the past, impatience, and officiousness rather than as a department of inquiry. Besides which, she had said, if feeling ashamed over being drunk could have gotten anybody sober, there wouldn't be a single alcoholic left in the country. So Katherine prayed that she might be relieved of shame, and spent a moment or two wondering whether the prayer had worked before she gave up worrying about it. She could never discover to her own satisfaction whether this chain of events was a genuine spiritual practice or mere sleight of hand, but something about declaring herself unqualified to cope with shame, rather than merely averse to the experience, worked in dispersing it.

It was not lost on Katherine that she had in some ways simply exchanged the framework of her parents' house for the Biedermeier's slightly larger one, and that any seeming difference between her old life and the new was cosmetic, not structural. Here she was not *contained* but essential, perched on the edge of a hundred other small independences, moving among them only as she was needed or wanted, bound only by the laws of ordinary politeness. She found life in New York often amusing, her duties in the hotel light and satisfactory, and her work in AA meaningful. If she was also convinced that life could not hold out any very exciting possibilities for her, she might very well be excused in thinking she had already used up her fair share of them.

The Biedermeier had many comfortable qualities, and some of its residents certainly considered it their home, but no hotel, however intimate, could ever be mistaken for a house. It would never have been possible for Katherine to hide in her room here, or to be locked and confined within it. Her room made up the entirety of her residence there; there was only one door. Like an atom, it could not be any further partitioned into any constituent parts that might be cut off from one another or set somehow at odds. It possessed the admirable quality of indivisibility, which often bolstered Katherine's spirits on particularly dull or dispiriting afternoons. There was nothing that could be called subterranean in her room, no chamber that could be shut up and hidden from itself or its owner. Subversion, repression, and compartmentalization were structurally impossible. She was nonetheless conscious that her work and residence at the Biedermeier constituted a material step downward for her socially; her grandmothers and great-grandmothers had been mistresses of staffed households and occasionally members of trained profession, who would certainly have understood a "first-floor director," whatever that might mean in theory, to in practice refer to someone junior to a housekeeper.

But practically everyone in her grandmothers' generation had been either a mistress or a servant, most of them servants. Why compare herself to the dead ranks of the old world, especially now that she had so decisively quit it? If the compass of her life was less grand than theirs, nevertheless it was more securely her own, and she was not ultimately responsible for anyone except herself. (*Did* this contradict the first principle of usefulness to others? Surely not—surely a person could only be useful insofar as they had not been counted on in advance.) *They* might have shuddered at the prospect of having to enter a shared hallway before reaching the bathroom; *she* might have cringed on being helped out of a tub by a maid.

Yet if the whole world had seemed made up of mistresses and servants to Katherine's grandmothers' generation, theirs had never been the only world on record. Not everyone at the Biedermeier considered their residence there an indicator of decline. Pauline Carter, of the second floor, moved into the hotel only a few years after Katherine, but might have come from an entirely different planet altogether.

She had grown up in Yorkville, where she had been raised chiefly by her paternal grandparents, Judith and Clarence Carter. They were committed anarchists of the old school of the "propaganda of the deed," and both as firm as two sinews. They had never married, although they lied about this to the census man every decade and occasionally wore cheap rings until they broke or fell off. It still deeply distressed them that several of their children had fallen into matrimony, even thirty years after the lapse. Family life, two wars, television, and the entirety of the twentieth century had failed to make any real impression on them. They dated the fall of man to 1848, to the Springtime of the Nations, that year when more than fifty European nations had, without any formal coordination, begun to throw off their governments—and within a year almost all had either been beaten into counterrevolutionary repression or given up and gone back to sleep after acquiring a new head of parliament or being granted a nominally independent second newspaper. As far as Judith and Clarence were concerned, the world had deteriorated in both strength and spirit with each subsequent year, and by rights should have gone up in flames at least twenty times over. Their own children proved, at least in comparison with the rest of the world, only mildly disappointing; some of them married, but at least none ever became useful. Both of Pauline's parents had left New York shortly after her birth, her mother joining up with a constellation of hitchhikers with vague ambitions of traveling to Black Mountain College, her father joining the Mohegan Colony upstate. Judith and Clarence considered the baby something between an apology and a tribute, and set to work trying to redeem something out of her.

The two had known Johann Most from his days working at an explosives plant in New Jersey (in fact it had been through Most that they were first introduced), gathering information for the pamphlet he would later publish as *Military Science for Revolutionaries*. Most hoped to make up for the woeful gap in bomb-manufacturing knowledge between German and Austrian anarchists, whose explosives failed often and with embarrassing regularity, and Russian nihilists, who counted a number of skilled technicians in their ranks and whose explosives were reliable. He had almost no faith that Americans could be persuaded to blow up anything important, and scarcely bothered to try; the greatest violence he had experienced in-country was when Emma Goldman once horsewhipped him across the face after he ignored her during a lecture. This impressed him, but he considered it a singular act, rather than an indicator that the national spirit was worth rousing further. Both Judith and Clarence remained passionately attached to Most, since it was from him they first learned how to mix dynamite, and regularly took him into their home between prison sentences until a few months before his death in 1906. That Most's own grandson served as an air force gunner during the Second World War and later a radio announcer for the Boston Celtics seemed to them the most hideous mutilation of his legacy imaginable, and they often tried to cheer one another up by saying that if only they had known, they would have strangled him in his crib in honor of his grandfather's legacy.

They had named Pauline in honor of typesetter and failed assassin Pauli Pallàs, whose execution inspired a friend and comrade to bomb the Liceu opera house in Barcelona in 1893, possibly as a reminder that failure could always be turned to revolutionary account. Failure was of primary interest to Pauline's grandparents, who had watched the world decay from a place full of anarchists to socialists to trade unionists and finally to federal employees. The family's origins were a jumbled assortment of German Jewish, Swedish, Irish, and some Slavic strains, most of whom had found their way to Yorkville by way of Dutchland, or Little Germany, as the East Village was often referred to in the mid-nineteenth century by its neighbors. Most of these ancestors continued to slowly drift uptown for the next half century, picking up the pace after the *General Slocum* disaster of 1904, when more than a thousand Germans, mostly women and children, drowned during a church outing in the East River. The community's survivors subsequently removed up to Yorkville almost at once. Pauline's grandparents took no chances with her; she was taught to swim first as an infant in the sink, then a little later in the washtub, and when she was four was dragged down every summer to the WPA pool by her grandfather, who tied a rope around her waist and held on to the other end, walking alongside the water's edge and keeping pace with her while she thrashed around. They often impressed upon her not only the importance of mourning the benighted state of a world that had been so rapidly drained of its revolutionary fire, but also a sense of personal responsibility to compensate for the inadequacy of her parents' generation.

They used the Godwin family tree by way of illustrating this inherited tendency toward moral degradation, and inculcated in Pauline an early horror of the life of the only surviving child of Mary Wollstonecraft Shelley and Percy Bysshe Shelley, Sir Percy Florence Shelley. *Sir*—what a descent in two short generations! Mary Wollstonecraft and William Godwin, dissenters and free lovers, a radical and an atheist, gave way to Mary Shelley, a novelist and reformist, who gave way to the Third Baronet of Castle Goring, a member of the Royal Thames Yacht Club, the High Sheriff of Sussex, who was called a "gentleman" by *Vanity Fair* and hosted private theatricals in his home. Privacy! Privacy! Always the hateful retreat into privacy, which was the enemy of thought and progress. That this couple, who had once hoped to live to see the yoke of marriage dismantled, might have their legacy wiped away by a single worthless grandson, who lived to amuse himself and his friends on his own personal stage, on his own personal yacht—"He ought to have been strangled in his crib," Judith would say, nearly shaking with indignation.

"It's a wonder I survived my own infancy," Pauline said to Judith once. "I must have been as strong as Hercules, living with you two snakes." To this crack Judith, who had been a terribly affectionate parent, laughed with undismayed pleasure.

For Pauline, the Biedermeier was a necessary, if temporary, compromise with the world after the many sacrifices her grandparents had made to raise her. As far as she was concerned, it was located about halfway between the Ritz-Carlton and the fleshpots of Babylon. Where Katherine was delicate, Pauline was frank; where Katherine was morbid, Pauline was healthy. "Living between the two of you is terribly restful. It makes me feel so balanced by comparison," Lucianne often said.

Chapter Six

A GINGER ALE DINNER

All was not well in Lucianne's room on the third floor. She had been sent the day before to cover the National Horse Show at Madison Square Garden for the *New York Herald-Tribune*'s society section. This was not in itself exceptional, except for the fact that there were now considerably fewer newspapers carrying a women's page than there had been when she first came to Manhattan in 1956. Lucianne had spent the last several years ignoring every newspaper strike (of which there had been several, the latest of which was presently in its seventeenth week) and heroically resisting editorial pressure to cover anything *substantive*, a dark and odious little word some of her colleagues began bandying about after a number of papers either eliminated the women's page altogether or, worse, tried to turn it into the mirror image of the city page, cramming it with depressing features about the conditions in state-run orphanages, or violence in the home, or prisons. This was all done at the expense of the gay, the elegant, the socially significant, and the beautiful, and Lucianne felt it was her moral duty to repel it as much as possible. "A man ought to be writing that," was her frequent answer to any editor hoping to trick her into writing about new treatments for syphilis, or conditions for workers in the garment district. "That's a job for a man, and you're not going to get me to take it away from him. I'm here to write about the things they can't, not try to ape what they do, and badly." For Lucianne, anything that could not be done with graceful, immediate success was not worth doing. She knew nothing about syphilis or garment workers, and she did not want to learn; she knew about horses, Anglo-Japanese ceramics and lacquerware, day boating, and nouvelle cuisine, and she wanted to be useful in ways that only she could be. Neither did she prefer to cover divorces, affairs, or engagements. These she considered the necessary but hardly attractive essentials that made the beautiful life possible, and did not care to discuss them any more than she cared to discuss foundation garments.

The show itself had been crowded and exhilarating, with sufficient surprise in the final race to lend color to a column. Lucianne had even bumped into an old friend of hers, Sidney Avery, and gone afterward with him to dinner at a crowded little Hungarian place way up on 111th Street. It was the sort of place where seemingly every dish fell into one of two categories—either a modest two bites of something very hot and scented with cinnamon sealed up in pastry, or a steaming platter of soup as wide as a man's head. They both loved it, and had steadfastly kept it a secret from every other newspaperman of their acquaintance for years. The trouble had begun after the arrival of a silver basket full of hot little silver dollars of fresh bread but before the *palacsinta*, when Lucianne realized two things with a sudden flash of horror: first that she was very much in love with Sidney, and second that he was not going to order any cocktails.

Lucianne was no more than a garden-variety social drinker, but not to have a single drink with dinner meant no lingering, no loose ends, no going to a movie or dancing afterward, no long drifting walks home by way of the park. It meant either that Sidney had somewhere else to be afterward or, worse, that he was not having as good a time being with her as he had guessed he might when he first asked her to dinner, and was now regretting having made the invitation.

Why did this kind of feeling always conjure up a desire to bargain with the universe? All day long she had caught herself on the precipice of offering a mental exchange: "If I do *this*, he will feel *thus*; if only he felt *that*, I would always gladly do *this*." She had a tendency to forget between romances the extent to which falling in love made her magically minded. She wanted to contrive great events, to re-create a particular evening over again in her head until she was able to cultivate the exactly correct attitude, appearance, and demeanor that would guarantee success. Last night had not gone badly, she was sure of that much, and Sidney had been attentive, even affectionate, but by no means definitive. He had never tried to be sure of her, and never came close to declaring himself. And at dinner—he had ordered ginger ale for the both of them.

This she had not expected. It rattled her to such an extent that she had almost begun to cry in front of the waiter. It was only thanks to her own quickness of mind that she had kept her tears from spilling at all. First she looked very carefully around the room, widening her eyes as she did so, then blinked sharply several times in succession before commenting on the liveliness of the crowd and asking him about the Lipizzaner in the third exhibition.

Ginger ale! And not to have seen it coming before he ordered it, that was the greater humiliation. There was of course no question of enjoying herself now. Whatever she might have considered a successful evening together five minutes ago was quite dead. She could dimly see, as if at the end of a long corridor, her own front door, and herself slipping behind it at the end of a gratifying dinner, well supplied with excellent conversation, and Sidney none the wiser; Sidney turning away from her door and thinking what an easy, engaging companion she had made, Sidney grateful for her uncommonly good spirits, Sidney conscious only of having been one of two young people who sincerely liked one another having passed a mutually agreeable evening together, Sidney braced and happy, Sidney already forgetting the pleasure of her company, so seamlessly congenial that it slid out of mental keeping once she herself was out of sight.

To make it to that door in two or three hours without Sidney ever suspecting her of disappointment, of having cherished any particular hope that he had failed to meet, to look plausibly content and not as if she were straining to appear gay, *this* would be a success now.

But ginger ale! Wasn't that worse than "Just water, thanks," in some crucial, submerged way? It wasn't as if Sidney were a teetotaler. Hadn't he ordered cocktails for both of them often enough when he had taken her out before? Of course ginger ale was worse than water. A man might just order water because he was distracted when the waiter stopped by, or didn't yet know quite what he wanted but didn't care to admit it, or because he simply didn't feel much like having a drink just then, or for any other of a half dozen reasons Lucianne couldn't quite develop. But he would only ask for ginger ale—*two* ginger ales—in order to depress an unwelcome expectation he feared his date might harbor.

And he had not ordered ginger ale only for himself. He had ordered it for both of them. That was unequivocal. He had feared that Lucianne might have been angling for him. Worse than that, he thought her so willfully obtuse, so self-deceived, that she would not have recognized any discouragement less subtle than two glasses of ginger ale. He might as well have ordered her a child's birthday cake, and a little hat with streamers on it. What a miserable gap between hope and pity that moment had revealed!

"I suppose it might have been worse—he could have ordered me a glass of milk," she wrote later in a letter to her sister Giuliana. The name Giuliana was an affectation; the Carusos had been settled in this country since the days of New Netherland. At that time they were known as the Cayruses and had been banished from the Piedmont region, along with twenty other Waldensian families, by the Duke of Savoy. From there they had slowly drifted northward until reaching Holland, from where they fled Europe altogether, eventually making their home in Nieuw-Amstel on the Delaware River. They had been Protestants before the Reformation and Americans before 1776; if the *Mayflower* had beaten *De Vergulde Otter* by a decade or two, it had not been by very much, which made the family's vestigial Italian extraction a slight mark of distinction, like a Chippendale cabinet or a chariot clock. It was not until the nineteenth century that the family had begun to style itself Caruso; they did not discourage the mistaken belief that there must have been some distant connection to the singer, whom they occasionally made reference to as a poor but brilliant relation. Lucianne wrote to Giuliana, who was her junior by sixteen months, at least twice a week. The two had not been especially close as children but, whatever qualities either may have thought her sister lacked to sustain an in-person friendship growing up, had as adults found in each other a remarkable affinity for correspondence, and letters traveled thick and often between them. No small amount of Lucianne's wonderful composure was due to her letters to her sister. In them she found she was genuinely able to convert disaster into anecdote, and in doing so came to derive real amusement and pleasure from things that would otherwise have distressed her. With Giuliana she could be wry, resigned, impatient with her own absurdity:

If I'm really honest with myself, which of course I would rather not be, Sidney hasn't really flirted with me in months, not really. He's often sincere and almost always affectionate, but he doesn't flirt. I have accepted the ginger ale with quiet good humor, let me tell you—he won't have to make me take my medicine more than once. And I know how dull this sort of thing is to anyone outside of it, that it makes me a dull and selfish correspondent, because all I want to discuss are the ups and downs of each day based on how often or how warmly I hear from him, which cannot possibly interest you as much as it interests me. So I promise you won't have to make me take my medicine from you more than once, either.

But that letter to Giuliana was as yet unwritten, and Lucianne was still in the depths of her wretchedness. She must have begun to bore him! When could that have started, and how in the world could she have missed it? But he had been glad to see her there; he had been busy with work, yes, but despite being busy he had clearly been glad to see her, had introduced her to a colleague of his, and if she had mentioned feeling hungry (had she?) it had surely only been in passing, not as a hint. Lucianne took real pride in not dropping hints, although of course she did it, just as almost everyone does at least once in a while. Certainly if she had mentioned it—and she was not at all sure that she had—it had been merely in passing, and there had still been a comfortable amount of time before Sidney ever mentioned dinner. And she was sure that he had brought up the question of dinner without prompting. If he had not wanted to take her to dinner, surely he would not have asked her? Or if he had wanted to signal nothing but friendship, surely he could have brought his colleague along with them. That he had taken her to dinner alone surely meant something.

Whatever he might have meant last night, today she would not trouble him. If he had meant to put her off, looking for an excuse to talk to him could only irritate him, and if he had not meant to put her off, if last night had not been definitive (but of course it had been definitive) she must give him a chance to miss her, to think of her, to want to speak to her again, this time in the manner of his own choosing, and at his own timing. It may or may not have been definitive, last night, but certainly he had not repulsed her, and that was something. She had not been entirely pushed away. This left her with a sacred charge to safeguard, to carefully inspect for signs of tender growth, and a reason to remain silent she could be really proud of, so that when Sidney ever felt—but of course she had been repulsed. It was only politeness that had led Sidney to ask her to dinner in the first place. He had felt forced even into the ginger ale.

She could only ever feel herself fly or drag along the ground, depending on how persuasively she was able to recast the events of the night before in either a hopeful or a depressing light, and herself as either a figure of divine favor or a worthless encumbrance. But if Sidney had liked her, had really liked her, nothing in the world could have stopped him from ordering a drink that promised something. A cocktail did not necessarily mean something between a man and a woman, it might just be social, but it at least left room for the possibility of something. Whereas a ginger ale began and ended with itself. It changed nothing, transformed nothing, elongated nothing. And she, Lucianne, must be nothing in return. From this point on she would hold herself entirely back. She would be noncommittal where she wanted to be open, she would sit still where she wanted to rush, she would never say more than she meant to, she would never say anything coarse or cheap that might ruin the image he had of her—

She was not *crucial* to Sidney, that was all. He enjoyed her company enough to talk to her when they met unexpectedly, and even well enough to sometimes take her to dinner (although never too late and nowhere they might run the risk of dancing), but he was not thrilled by her, she could not thrill him, or make him nervous or shy of her in any of the ways that she would like to. She was not crucial. Oh—he did not love her, and there was nothing to transform her out of ugliness! He did not love her, and she was well and truly ugly!

Not only that, but to have mistaken their connection so badly, and so completely, that was worse still. She thought that because she could accurately guess some of his thoughts about horses and people that she knew his heart, and that knowing his heart was the same as winning it. What a failure of that social shrewdness, of which she had always been so proud, and so unjustly proud at that—she had seen only what she had wanted to see, and only from the most flattering of angles. Well, last night had put a stop to any of *those* illusions, at least. That was something to be grateful for, if nothing else. She would never suffer illusions again. He had been near her all evening, had shared dinner with her, had walked down the street with her and never once been troubled by their proximity, had never once felt an impulse to put his arm around her, had never felt the twisting of a great need. Sidney had passed a pleasant-enough evening with a nice-enough girl, and nothing remarkable had happened—how could that have ever felt to her like a success? What on earth did it matter whether he thought her disappointed, indifferent, sane or insane, dead or alive? He had been so careless about nearness, hardly seeming to notice if they touched when he pulled out her chair or steered her through a crowded entrance, neither minding nor preferring to be any closer to her than ordinary graciousness required. But Sidney was so magnetic, always flush with masculine health and success; there must always be women striving for admittance with him, and conspiring to extend an incidental brush as long as possible, and he must have become purposely ignorant of the language of touch in order to maintain a sense of privacy as a result. It was hateful of them, to have so obstructed what would otherwise have been the broad and smiling highway to his heart.

Friendship was such a lovely thing. Why couldn't she feel for Sidney the same friendship she felt for her other men friends? These she adored with a real ease, and without suffering. Her affection for them was capacious, expansive, and yet portable, easily stowed away when called for and stored against later use. If she could adore Sidney without suffering, she might call him up today, never mind that scarcely any time had passed since she last saw him, and ask what he was doing later. She might even tease him for not taking her dancing last night, knowing that any mock accusation would carry with it absolutely no potential for harm, no weight to injure him, that he might tease her in turn for being demanding, overbearing, ruinously self-centered. She could look at him, and he could return a steady gaze. There would be no limits on what they could look at, or what their eyes might take pleasure in. They could talk so freely, and so playfully, and she could be perfectly happy with him. And she *would* be perfectly happy, Lucianne knew, on the strength of that single free and open conversation, even if it lasted only for an hour, and never again occurred between them. It would be somehow like shaking hands with him, and it would mean candidness, equality, fraternity—but this made Sidney sound like the French Revolution.

Again with the "if, if, if"—"if only" this happened, she would be forever grateful, or never want anything again, or always feel happy, or try to offer God some sacrifice in exchange, as if love had ever been kick-started by an artificial mechanism snapping into action, had ever been conjured into being with the mere activation and focus of the will. Now she was straying into really dangerous territory. She must not try to insert herself into his life, or try to behave in whatever manner she guessed he might find the most lovable. She would not call him, she would not arrange to pass by his offices when he was most likely to be leaving for lunch, she would not try to prod him into action, would not force a conversation by artificial means—

"I do think I must have been made all the things that I am so that I might change him," she wrote later to Giuliana. "I was made ardent, and all those other things, in order to draw him out, to trouble his remarkable calm, only he doesn't know it and it would spoil everything if I tried to mangle the lovely silence between us with announcing it. He's either got to see it for himself—that's *his* job, not mine—or at the very least get hit by a taxi so I can forget about him, or nurse him back to health, or something."

Whatever Sidney felt for her, it was not incompatible with being often separated. They had parted last night with no definite plans to see one another again. If he had felt anything like what she did, he would have found this unbearable. And yet he had borne it. He would have been eager to plan their next meeting, he would have found it necessary, but the night had come to an end, and Sidney had walked away from her door, and still they had made no plans to see each other again. He could cheerfully contemplate the next week without Lucianne in it. Between herself and Sidney there was *no plan*.

Lucianne had never thrown herself at a man, but neither had she avoided the men she hoped would become her lovers. Not unless she had something very pressing to occupy her elsewhere, or was for some reason unfit to be seen; she liked to be available to the men she liked, and who liked her. But she would not see Sidney today, and she would likely not see him tomorrow, either. That would make two days, and practically two nights apart, and then it would grow longer every day—forever. The whole afternoon would pass by, and he would find in it no reason to think of her, or call. He would not make an exception in his habits for her. She could do nothing to move him; he might as well have been a piece of granite, or on the moon, or someone already dead and buried for three hundred years. "Why aren't you here?" was with her the only question love ever asked; on either side, whichever the answer, love was always silent. How was it that he could produce in her such frantic need, and yet experience no corresponding urgency in himself? How could such an imbalance of force exist? It should be impossible; it should violate one of the laws of physics.

Let the fever break today; let it break now. Let the fever lift. She wanted Sidney; Sidney did not want her; it had not come off; that was all.

If, after all that, it turned out that he *had* felt the exact same way about her, what would have followed? The relief of mutual avowal, yes, and the delight of coming together, but afterward, and always sooner than she expected it, the strangling of additional possibilities, the foreclosure of other evenings with other exciting new prospects and the capacity to incorporate new admirers, new lovers into the web of her life. And if Sidney could already make her dislike her own society to this degree, could already spoil the solitude in which she ordinarily took such pleasure, what other pleasures might he kill in her, perhaps without ever wishing to do it?

Sidney then must be a danger to her, must be avoided as a potential threat to her own life; suddenly the balance of Lucianne's afternoon shifted and she wished for nothing more than Katherine and Pauline's company, which as a rule she generally did not seek out. But today Katherine and Pauline would be perfect, Katherine because she always seemed to produce a powerfully neutralizing effect on one's desires—Lucianne always felt wonderfully boosted in equanimity after a few hours with Katherine, feeling as though whatever the rest of the day might bring with it, whether winning the lottery or being killed in a freak tornado, she would be equal to it—and Pauline because she was so unusually good-looking, in a way that complemented and even heightened Lucianne's own beauty, without ever stepping on her toes about it. Men who were drawn in by Pauline's striking warrior's face, rescued at the very last moment from mannishness by an occasional touch of delicacy around the eyes and mouth, found unconscious relief in the melting softness of Lucianne's, just as one who has stared too long at the Alps finds relief from snow blindness by turning his gaze to the meadow at his feet. And she had heard the two of them in the hall discussing some meeting or other of Pauline's that Katherine was supposed to accompany her to; there was no reason why she could not join them, even if it was some ridiculous assortment of longshoremen and old bearded Bolsheviks reminiscing fondly about minor royalty they had very nearly assassinated and streetcars they had once derailed.

The letter to Giuliana could wait. Lucianne shook all thoughts of Sidney from herself as she got out of bed, focusing instead on choosing a shirt to change into and how best to invite herself along once she found them. This could not be difficult; Pauline was always desperate for potential converts to the cause of old longshoremen, and the prospect of bagging Lucianne, who could scarcely tolerate reform, let alone revolution, would be too tempting to pass up.

If Pauline was still wearing brown, as she had been this morning, then Lucianne had better wear something blue, to heighten the charm of the differences between them. Luckily it would not matter what Katherine was wearing.

Chapter Seven

DRESSING TO MATCH

Blessedly, Pauline had not changed her outfit for the afternoon, so Lucianne had been right to choose something blue after all. She had been right about Katherine too, who was wearing a pullover Chelsea shift dress in black trim with an indistinct waistline that did absolutely nothing for her over a snap-in red chemisette. Choosing the wrong thing to wear was almost a talent of Katherine's. If ever there was an opportunity to dress for the occasion, to set someone at ease or to indicate professionalism, capability, and poise, Katherine could be reliably counted on to miss it. Lucianne, who was easily fluent in the language of clothes, found the idea that a person would move to New York City and keep dressing like a person who never expected to be looked at completely baffling. It seemed to her antisocial, and very nearly rude, especially since on any given day in the city it was possible that as many as half a million people might look at you, and that degree of exposure ought to have counted for something. As a rule Lucianne did not expect beauty from others in order to find pleasure in looking at them. She considered herself more than broad-minded in her appreciation of unusual looks in a woman, and did not care in the least about color analysis or summers and winters or dressing to one's "type," the sort of thing that involved calling some women pears who ought never to wear turquoise, or other women ovals who should never own a dress with an empire waist. Anything resembling a magazine-quiz-style approach to dress violated her deepest principles, and seemed to Lucianne like an attempt to replace taste and thought with a system. In almost all things Lucianne hated systems. It was through clothes that Lucianne could speak without speaking, could contribute to the loveliness of a particular scene by way of heightening or contrasting or lending depth to it, could mold herself to an occasion and fit perfectly into it, or remake an occasion to reflect her own image if it called for improvement. She could put an employer at ease, radiate discretion, put other women higher on their game, reassure or distract a man, create an atmosphere of romance or grace or sophistication or even homeyness if the situation called for it. And fashion was honest; there was no mistaking the effect your clothes had on others, not as long as you were halfway decent at reading other people. If you had chosen rightly, people liked to look at you, and your instincts would be rewarded with a sea of considerate attention. Of course in a big city like New York no one was going to stop you on the street and tell you how good you looked, not unless you were a real knockout or looked like the wrong sort. A woman who did not take pride in looking her best, whatever that best may be, was unpleasantly alien to her, and she could no more understand Katherine's relationship to fashion than she could have understood it if Katherine went around cutting in line at the bank or taking seats away from little old ladies on the subway.

Pauline's meeting was far enough downtown that the journey felt charmingly novel rather than disagreeable. A shorter trip would have inconvenienced Lucianne more. Since none of them had any money they took the subway. Pauline had no money as a matter of principle, Lucianne out of extravagance, and Katherine because having money made her uncomfortable. She was perfectly at ease with her duties around the Biedermeier and her responsibilities toward the other girls, but whenever she was handed a personal responsibility, be it ever so slight, she found a way to dispose of it as quickly as possible.

Katherine took the seat opposite Lucianne and Pauline, directly underneath an advertisement asking, "The Girl Who Knows What New York City Is All About: WHO WILL BE THE NEXT 'MISS SUBWAYS' ? ? ?" Beneath this was a row of snapshots of five dark-haired girls, four of them pretty, all fresh and friendly looking. They were psychology students, they hoped for a career as an airline stewardess, they had been born in Poland and the Bronx, they were secretaries, they were taking singing lessons. The rest of the copy ran: "See Our LOVELIEST Subway Riders. . . . See the girls on WABC-TV CHANNEL 7 . . . or on this very train! Vote for Miss Subways by Postcard—Winner ANNOUNCED September 16th." The voting by postcard was new; when Lucianne had submitted her name and class photo back in 1959 the contest was still being judged by John Robert Powers, the well-known modeling agent. She felt rather sorry for this crop of girls having to submit to a popular vote. Being Miss Subways was surely democratic enough already. To win by consensus, rather than being selected by an expert, seemed more like luck than victory. Lucianne had been a John Robert Powers girl; he had personally selected her in the spring of that same year. It had been wonderful; all the fun of winning a beauty contest without having to do any charity work or wear a bathing suit onstage. You got an ugly-looking bracelet with a subway token on it and half a million people saw a picture of you looking wholesome, approachable, and enterprising but not too ambitious, which had made it useful for getting both dates and a job.

"Tell us about the new girls," Lucianne said to Katherine, hoping to keep the conversation general for as long as possible. If there were a break, Pauline might try to explain the nature of the political meeting they were going to, and Lucianne thought being warned in advance could only make things worse. It didn't matter if they were meeting to protest the war or to restage the Scopes Trial or to plot the assassination of Robert Moses. All she wanted was to get away from the phone for a few hours.

"There's not much to tell yet," Katherine said. "There's only two of them. There was supposed to have been a third, but she stopped replying to Mrs. Mossler's messages. The last one ended up in the dead letter office—I like to think she found a better offer or got married or something, but of course she could just as easily have been hit by a bus. Gia you must have seen, or at least her luggage. I can't remember the last time I saw that many boxes at the Biedermeier; Stephen must be as rich as Croesus by now."

"I haven't seen her yet," Lucianne said, "only her equipage. But *what* an equipage! I counted Bonwit Teller and De Pinna among them, and those were only the ones with writing on them. Thanks for giving me the stylish one, I ought to say. Unless the other one is grander?"

Katherine turned serious. "I hope you'll be nice to Ruth."

"Oh, so it's like *that*," Lucianne said.

"I'll be nice to Ruth," Pauline offered in mild tones. "Not just to make up for Lucianne, either. I hear she's out of work." Pauline felt a natural kinship with anyone who was unemployed, which the unemployed did not always sufficiently appreciate. "Where did you put her?"

"On your floor," Katherine said. "At the end of the hall, next to Josephine. I thought maybe Ruth would appreciate an older, sympathetic type, but one who wasn't too motherly either." Josephine was, after Mrs. Mossler and J.D., the eldest among them, although she had only come to the Biedermeier in '61, after her apartment had been knocked down to make room for the expressway. She had been a newspaperwoman, had lived in the same three-room apartment since getting divorced in 1937, had gone around with Alexander Woollcott and some of the peripheral chairs of the Algonquin set, and claimed once to have seen Noel Coward playing the piano at the Stork Club "not with his hands, but with his characteristic part, and quite well too," at three in the morning. Now she lived on Social Security, wrote the occasional sketch for *Harper's* or even the *New Yorker*, and would almost always draw a caricature for anyone who asked, which went a lot further with the girls now than the Noel Coward story. Lucianne kept hers pasted to the mirror hanging on the back of the door; it was flattering without appearing to be trying to flatter, which she appreciated as a mark of real talent.

"Does that mean she's hopeless like Kitty? Or just a little lost?" Lucianne asked.

"Kitty," Pauline said, "is not hopeless. Kitty just isn't built for independence. She needs people, which happens to be true of everybody."

Lucianne considered it dangerous territory anytime Pauline took the opportunity to discuss People-with-a-capital-P, especially when Lucianne wanted to discuss people as individuals, usually in the interest of examining their shortcomings. Pauline had an unshakable faith in the rightness of whatever it was the People did, and that faith often seemed the strongest whenever a person was behaving particularly badly, Lucianne had noticed. But Pauline was remarkably sanguine about bad behavior, at least about the kind that Lucianne considered the least pardonable—conspicuous self-pity, fishing for reassurance, lack of poise, an inability to pay one's own way—and only grew more tolerant and understanding the further somebody trespassed on her goodwill. Sometimes this worked out in Lucianne's favor, although on those occasions she thought only that Pauline was being unusually reasonable. The rest of the time it struck her as a supreme waste that Pauline's best qualities, her greatest reserves of patience and even affection, were specially lavished on those least suited to appreciate it, while someone like Katherine, whose temperament made her uncommonly well suited for Pauline, was with her only a friend of afterthought. Not that Pauline disliked Katherine; in fact they got on very well together. But there was within Katherine no resistance that Pauline might galvanize herself with. It was also true that Pauline liked to disagree, even to quarrel, with anyone she felt at all close with, while Katherine made a point of avoiding argument. Part of this must have been because it was her job to solve disputes among residents, and did not want to work off the clock by arguing in her limited free time, but no one could get close to Pauline's heart without providing serious opposition, and no one could get close to Katherine's without demonstrating a preference for harmony, and so their friendship remained an easy one, without ever touching or troubling either of them very deeply.

Lucianne preferred stronger attachments. She did not require profoundness or great intimacy from all her friends, but whether they saw one another often or infrequently, she liked to feel that when they spent time together it was not due to convenience or mere proximity, but a careful and deliberate act of will. She had a special horror of being instrumentalized, and mistrusted anyone who, like Kitty, cast their dependence widely and indiscriminately onto other people, while on the other hand anyone who was willing to help Kitty, even if it happened only once and purely out of a sense of obligation, at once became Kitty's friend, whether they had intended to or not.

"Nobody's built for independence," Lucianne said. "That's why being independent is an accomplishment that's worth being proud of—which also happens to be true of everybody."

"Ruth does remind me of Kitty, in some ways," Katherine said, "although I've only met her twice now, and it really isn't fair to try to assess her character yet. She is trying very hard to make a go of living here, I think; she's training as a hairdresser right now and I've offered to let her practice on me later tonight—"

"You didn't," said Lucianne. "Katherine, you didn't. You can't let someone who reminds you of Kitty even in the least little bit anywhere near a pair of scissors. That's taking even your martyr complex too far."

"She's not going to *cut* it," Katherine said defensively. "It's just a shampoo and set. And I don't think letting some poor girl wash my hair comes anywhere near martyrdom. She seems to want to fit in, and I'd like to help her get the chance, which is something I'd have thought you of all people would appreciate."

"All right," Lucianne said, "you win! I'll retract all my pointed edges, and only show my softest parts if I'm ever trapped in an elevator with your mouse. And thank you, by the way, for giving me the city mouse for a floormate, and not the country one." She laughed a little to make sure Katherine realized she was not spoiling for a fight, that she had only meant to tease her to the point of fun. She really liked Katherine, even though Katherine failed to live up to almost everything that Lucianne considered important—which was not to say that she liked Katherine *for* those failures, either. Lucianne's vanity did not extend so far that she wanted to surround herself with satellites to reflect her own glory. She liked it when other girls looked well, spoke well, and made a good impression, so long as she herself made a good impression too.

Katherine also smiled, and there was no trace of a sulk in the corners of that smile. She was a sport.

"I do wish you'd told me about Ruth earlier, Katherine," Pauline said warmly, but without any real recrimination. She either had not noticed, or did not care about, the quarrel Lucianne and Katherine had just narrowly avoided. "I'd have asked her to come along with us. You know how important it is for us to reach young people, and how closed off so many young people still are to anything further left than the DAR, and anybody who's out of work has not only the time for meetings but a chance to really ask themselves what society is *for*—"

"I'm here," Lucianne interrupted, only half joking, "and I'm young, relatively speaking, and as it happens my family is even a little bit older than the DAR. Doesn't that count for anything?"

"Oh, you Rockefeller Republican types don't count," Pauline said. "You're here in body, but not in spirit, and I don't intend to waste my breath trying to win you over. I'm not religious. I don't hope to convert my enemies, just defeat them."

"She's here as a prisoner of war, then," Katherine said. "Is it like a scavenger hunt? Do you get points for bringing along society girls or yacht club boys with you?"

"A prisoner of war, nothing," Pauline said. "Lucianne is the fifth column's fifth column. My greatest ambition for her is that we can arrive at a nonviolent agreement in exchange for some free sandwiches."

"I'm not a Rockefeller Republican type," Lucianne said, more offended by the thought of being a type of any sort than by the particulars. "For starters, I don't vote Republican. I don't vote at all." This was only partly true. Lucianne did vote on occasion, once back at home and at least twice since moving to New York, but just as often she forgot until after an election had passed. She rather enjoyed the way the news scandalized people of almost any political persuasion in her class. It was a wonderful way to rile up a detached date, too. There was something about a man who, not five minutes earlier, had been as indifferent to her as to a baked potato, suddenly taking her arm and talking warmly to her of *duty* that felt tremendously stirring. It lent heroic proportions to what might have otherwise remained an entirely flat evening.

"That's why she's such a useful enemy," Pauline said, grinning. "She's not an idealogue, she's just conventional. All I've got to do is change the conventions and then she'll be on my side anyways. I wish you could convince all your sorority sisters and their husbands to follow in your footsteps, Lucianne."

"It's not that I especially object to left-wing ideas," Lucianne agreed, "it's just that I object to having to change anything. If I get a cookie with raisins in it, I don't ask the baker to make me a new one because I don't happen to like raisins. I just pick out the raisins and eat around it."

"This is why I never waste time arguing with Lucianne—I just wait for her to bring up the subject of food, and then I feed her," Pauline said to Katherine. "But come on, this is our stop." And she stood to go.

A man in a light suit who was holding the doors open for their exit said something tasteless in a polite and friendly voice as they walked out of the car past him and onto the platform. Since Katherine and Pauline seemed not to hear him, Lucianne decided she would decline to comprehend whatever it was he had said too, instead flashing him a bright smile that acknowledged only the friendliness of his tone, but not the words themselves.

From the station Pauline led them through a rabbit warren of side streets where all the storefronts extended onto the sidewalk, so they had to dodge racks of men's shirts and folding tables with heavy-looking cloth handbags, cheap paperbacks, and table lamps just to keep up. Sometimes one of them had to drop briefly down into the street and hop back up onto the curb again wherever there wasn't room for three to walk abreast. They went down a flight of concrete stairs, passed through a steaming basement underneath a cafeteria, then up two more flights of stairs into a packed room that could have been holding a church supper or a subscription dance, except that both of those would have drawn a more homogeneous crowd.

To Pauline's credit, and somewhat to Lucianne's surprise, there were a great many young men present. Lucianne admired anyone, man or woman, who had a lot of men friends; she considered it both an indicator of talent and a willingness to work hard. Katherine was less impressed, if only because she had grown very used to men in large groups through her years in AA. Aside from a monthly gathering just for women held privately in a West Side apartment, most of her regular meetings ran male, the only difference being that the meetings uptown drew veterans of slightly older wars than meetings below the Park, where the veterans tended toward a more recent vintage, with wives and young children. Men were scarcer on the ground at church on Sundays, of course—between college age and their fifties most New York men became evasive on the question of worship—but were still no remarkable sight in church basements on weeknights. The night before, Katherine had in fact been the only woman, and the youngest by at least two decades, at the Friday night business meeting, which had as usual run late after at first looking like it was going to conclude on time or even early. The coffee cups had been washed and spaced out to dry, the books and folding chairs piled away, the treasurer's report and the minutes from the last meeting approved, and Stanley R. had been on the verge of making a motion to close up for the night, when Fred H. uncharacteristically raised his hand to raise a point of new business.

"I don't know if anyone else has noticed this," he said slowly, "but I've noticed that lately when we ask about anniversaries at the start of the meeting, a lot of the people who raise their hands, especially some of the newer people, will say something like 'I'll have six months next week' or 'I'll have two years on the seventeenth,' and everybody will still clap the same way they do for someone who's celebrating a real anniversary. I don't know where folks are getting this idea from. It seems to me like it's spreading, and I think it's risky. We're not a time-travel society. If you're going to celebrate six months' sober next week, then you ought to come back next week and tell us when it's really happened, instead of announcing it in advance and taking premature credit. And where does it end? I'll have eight years sober, in five more years. I think we ought to do something about it. That's just what I think."

Suddenly every other hand in the room was up.

"I think we make too much out of anniversaries to begin with," Walter T. said. "There are times when the last Friday of every month feels like a children's birthday party. We don't need awards, or cake, or tokens or things like that. Sobriety is a serious business, and the blessings of recovery are rewards themselves. We ought to be thinking about the next day ahead, not celebrating what happened last year."

"I mostly agree with Walter," Katherine said, "I don't think much of the birthdays. But I do think we ought to keep the announcements and the chips for the newcomers, for anyone who's feeling shaky and still counting days. I think that's important." Nobody was prepared to defend the new practice as such that night, although Douglas D. thought there was no harm in applauding milestones now and again, and that it wasn't as though they were handing out Mother's Day corsages. A number of other members took the opportunity to raise additional complaints about how newcomers spoke in meetings, and it took some time to get back to Fred's original point.

Then Arthur C., the eldest fellow by at least ten years, asked how they proposed to stop newcomers from saying whatever it was they damn well pleased. "I don't mind saying that if the first time I managed to cobble together a few months' sobriety, after the shaky wreck I'd been, if one of you had interrupted me the first time I tried to celebrate a milestone and told me to shut up and come back in a week, I'd have walked out," which set most of the hands going again. ("If that was all it took for you to walk out, Arthur, then maybe you were just looking for an excuse to get going!" "We could always refund people's applause in the event of a relapse!")

Many of the others agreed with Fred. Stanley worried about cultivating an "aristocracy of old-timers," which emphasized quantity of time over quality, and suggested doing away with lengths of time altogether, so that everyone celebrating in the same week did so on equal terms, which confused almost everyone else and required several rounds of further explanation before it was shouted down. A few of them denied the existence of the trend altogether. Arthur wanted to know how exactly they proposed to stop people from announcing their anniversaries in advance, to which Walter suggested taking a group conscience; Arthur countered that the group conscience had no business trying to preempt what somebody *might* be about to say, to which Katherine proposed adding to the anniversary announcement, "Is there anyone here celebrating an anniversary this month *on a date no later than today?*" which nobody else but her liked, and also required several rounds of explanation before being similarly shouted down. At this point Fred, who had not spoken since he first brought up the issue, suggested tabling the remaining discussion for the next business meeting, since it was already almost 8:00 p.m. and he had promised his wife he would be home in time for *The Sammy Davis Jr. Show*. This was also shouted down in favor of an immediate vote on Katherine's proposed change to the script, which still nobody liked, but nonetheless carried the day with nine votes in favor and five against, until Gerald E. argued that the vote had not been properly proposed according to Robert's Rules of Order and the results were dismissed.

Fred now made another motion, this time to close the meeting, but he was again outvoted, since everyone else had been cheerfully animated by the altercation and wanted to stick around to further tear one another to pieces on additional points of order. Fred then loudly stacked his own chair in the corner and left muttering darkly about the perversion of God-given instincts; half an hour later Katherine rather wished she had thought to leave with him, especially when the final vote in favor of raising the issue to the General Service Office had to be postponed to the next business meeting anyway, when it was discovered that the meeting's elected General Service representative, Mickey P., was away in Indiana visiting his mother. Mickey's final report came after his return in October, when he informed the group that the General Service Office had decided the question was ultimately a matter of group conscience; the vote was tabled amid a general uproar.

The men at Pauline's meeting were of a decidedly different sort to the Friday-night crowd at Old First, of course. It was a joint venture, put up by Students for a Democratic Society and an unrecognized offshoot of the Workers Defense League, in the interest of coordinating draft resistance efforts and infiltrating the AFL-CIO. While fewer than half of the AA men wore suits to meetings, only one did here, a slightly pop-eyed young man in a morning coat who couldn't have been much older than twenty. When he turned around to look at them, Katherine saw he had a chain of daisies threaded through his collar instead of a tie, and prodded Lucianne lightly in the ribs.

"These are the stakes!" Lucianne stage-whispered. "To make a world in which all God's children can live—or to go into the dark. We must either love each other—or we must die!"

Pauline gave her a puzzled look.

"The stakes are too high for you to stay at home," Lucianne quoted. "*Vote for President Johnson on November Third.* Oh, Pauline, I refuse to believe that even you don't know that one."

"What she means—what she wants to know, and I do too," Katherine said, slightly tilting her head in the boy's direction, "is who's your friend wearing the daisies?"

Then Pauline grinned too. "Oh, *that*," she said. "I thought Lucianne was losing it or something. His name's Harvey. I don't know him well or anything. But it's sort of a left-wing tradition that the youngest of the youngbloods dresses as formally as he can afford to, while everybody else sticks to turtlenecks and honest rags. But come on, we've got to find seats before he comes over to try to corner me into introducing you."

"I hope you weren't thinking of keeping us apart," Lucianne said in mock-offended tones, although she permitted Pauline to hustle her down the aisle and into a half-full row. "Imagine keeping something like that to yourself."

"I mean it," Pauline said. "He's a relentless little urchin. No phone number is safe with him." Harvey, meanwhile, had settled himself next to a group of older men wearing frizzled beards (Lucianne was surprised by how pleased she was to see there were still bearded revolutionaries; it was a little like seeing the Grand Canyon for the first time and realizing it lived up to all your expectations from photographs), shooting looks at them only every five minutes or so.

"It's hard to imagine him doing very much damage," Katherine said.

"Though he be but little, he is fierce," Pauline said. The woman sitting in front of them turned around to raise an eyebrow, and Pauline gave her a half nod by way of apology.

"But nothing's started yet," Katherine whispered.

"That's only half-true," Pauline whispered back. "We start the meeting like Quakers, in silence, until someone is moved to act as clerk." This was a recent tradition that had so far proved very effective, since the sort of person who was usually moved to speak first rarely wanted to act as clerk, who did nothing but read the agenda and facilitate discussion. The silence lasted for several minutes, and made for a pleasantly restful beginning.

A heavy-looking man who seemed to be in his middle fifties had been moved to act as clerk; he had deep-set sideburns and wore a cape the color of tinfoil, but he discharged his duties with surprising grace, always calling on those who seemed hesitant to speak and making the most enthusiastic wait their turn. During the impromptu poetry performance that arose after the first half hour of earnest discussion, he also acted as timekeeper. This was not, Katherine and Lucianne came to realize, because there was anything like a limit on how long anyone might choose to read poetry for, but seemed to reassure the performers, who always wanted to know how much time had passed, and to announce how many more poems they were going to read after each one ended. This was useful because otherwise it might have been impossible to know where one poem ended and the next began.

"I'll read two more poems. Sorry, what time is it? Yes, I'll read two more poems."

"How much time have we got left?" A heartless shrug. "How much time has it been?"

"I've got a few more poems here. . . . I'll read three. . . . I'll read four more poems. Is that all right?" Another poem. "I'll read three more poems now." Another poem. "I'll read two more poems now." Another poem. "This will be the last poem I'm going to read, then."

It helped that Lucianne did not care for poetry, made few distinctions between good or bad verses, and had no expectations of being pleased by anything about the meeting, so to her own surprise and amusement she realized she had frequently enjoyed herself, even in the prolonged silences when no one as yet felt moved to speak or when the poets of the moment fumbled through their notebooks, unsure which one to read next. An older woman with dyed red hair talked about *Griswold v. Connecticut* and dismantling the Comstock laws for ten straight minutes without ever setting down her peacock-print carpetbag. Next an Eastern European girl with the face of a cherub, who walked with a blackthorn-wood cane and was dressed all over in black (the effect was pleasingly and incongruously matronly, rather than dramatic), led a discussion on curb and sidewalk zoning regulations as they had affected street actions against the war. Then a weedy young man brought out a concertina and played a song called "The Hammers Kept Red Time," which nobody else seemed to know but which had a pleasantly boisterous chorus that Lucianne and Katherine both found themselves humming for days afterward.

He seemed ready to launch into the song for a second time, when he apparently thought better of it and said, "Let's eat," into the microphone. The room came to an immediate and joyful consensus, and the meeting was over. This seemed to have taken some degree of pressure off the young man, because he sat back down and resumed playing the concertina, while everyone else helped themselves to cut fruit and coffee and little Cuban sandwiches. First he played "I Dreamed I Saw Joe Hill Last Night," then "The Draft Dodger

Rag," then "Hallelujah, I'm a Bum," and then once more "The Hammers Kept Red Time." The room seemed evenly split between people who preferred songs about one big union standing in for all workers and people who preferred songs about not working at all. Lucianne disliked any song with a moral, but the little sandwiches were surprisingly good and the bouncing-saddle-like rhythm of the concertina faded easily enough into the background that she could comfortably ignore it most of the time.

As they nibbled, Pauline pointedly did not ask what either Katherine or Lucianne had thought of the meeting. She considered the question of enjoyment to be entirely beside the point and, if anything, treated their presence there as a matter of course and the least they could do, as if they had finally returned some overdue library books, but Lucianne couldn't stop herself from saying in light amazement, "Do you know, I *really* enjoyed myself," more than once. She could scarcely have said *what* it was she enjoyed beside the sandwiches—certainly not phenomenology or the history lesson in Comstock laws; she had not found the presentations politically persuasive, but all the same she liked the crowded little room, the unlikely jumbled confusion of the audience, and the sudden shifts between quiet and uproar. She found it winsome; she found it harmless; she could not imagine anything like power being present here.

Lucianne was on the verge of allowing Harvey with the daisy necktie to make her acquaintance when Pauline materialized at her left elbow with a man of middling height, who looked to be in his early thirties, in tow. Like almost all the other men present under fifty, he wore a dark turtleneck under a cheap coat with overlong cuffs. There was something cheerful about the manner in which he was badly dressed that distinguished it slightly from everyone else's bad clothes. It was not that he looked as if he did not care how he looked, Lucianne thought, but that he was determined to enjoy whatever he had on, even if it could not be made attractive.

"Tobias, these are some of the girls I live with I was telling you about," Pauline said. "This is Katherine, who could possibly be useful to us after a few years of half rations and reprogramming, and this is Lucianne, who will undoubtedly be among the first killed, but whose body might be broken down and recycled for nutrient extraction. Trust her with nothing. Lucianne, Katherine, this is Tobias Sterne, one of the nearly literate Linotype pushers at *Freie Arbeiter Stimme*—that's the *Free Voice of Labor* to you."

Tobias earnestly reached out his hand to both of them in turn. "Very pleased to meet you. Listen, you girls should know I'm not ambitious like Pauline here. As long as I can convince just one of you to stop contributing to society, I'll be happy." Katherine colored a little, but took his hand.

Lucianne did the same, then said, "I expected to see more young people here. Where's that wave of politically conscious youth in flower you're supposed to be leading? You're just about the youngest man I've seen here, apart from that stammering boy, and you can't be under thirty."

"Thirty-two," Tobias admitted cheerfully. "And you should have been here ten years ago. There wasn't a full head of hair in the room. Now we've got half a dozen fellows under forty-five who come almost every week. I call that very encouraging. And Pauline, of course," he said, nodding politely in her direction. "But you've got to remember your Red Scare was pretty effective. The government has spent the last two decades cutting off every revolutionary movement at the ankles. And of course, we've also got to compete with the Junior League."

There was no point in liking Tobias, who was dangerously easy to talk to, Lucianne decided. But he had a napkin-wrapped bundle of sandwiches in his coat pocket that was the same size as the bundle in her own handbag, and what would be the point in getting fond of somebody who couldn't afford to take her out to dinner? Besides which, she had enjoyed herself, but not to such a degree that she was interested in changing the trajectory of her own life; one had to draw a line against pleasure somewhere. It wasn't that Lucianne couldn't enjoy the simple things in life—she liked a sunset, a picnic, and a walk in the park as much as anybody—but the simple things were robbed of some of their appeal when they were the only things you could afford. And nothing lost its charm quite so quickly as a not-so-young man who was full of potential. You could hang almost everything on potential, at least in the beginning (and Lucianne had done so on more than one occasion, with more than one man), but it never held. Potential never seemed to be able to bear up under its own weight. It certainly couldn't bear up anything or anybody else. In fact, the more potential a nice and not-so-young man had, the more you were liable to hate him at the end of things. And Lucianne did not want to hate Tobias, so she only smiled at his joke instead of returning it, and let Katherine slip into her place in the conversation.

The real problem, as Lucianne saw it, was that unless you had given up the question of marriage entirely (and she was not at all sure that it was wise to do so; it seemed to her that giving up the possibility of marriage was a wildly idealistic thing that she herself could not afford to do), any man that you liked had to be seen through the light of a potential future employer as well as someone you might like to see socially. This put an awful lot of pressure on the men she liked, even if they didn't know it. Something she might have liked very much in a date wouldn't have been at all suitable in an employer, and so the charming and funny ones were made to seem professionally unreliable, and the reliable-looking ones seemed like conversational washouts. This *was* a problem, and Lucianne had no idea how anyone solved it. To her mind, the best attitude, if one couldn't arrive at a solution, was to hold everything and everybody very lightly, and to behave a little more carelessly with every year that passed after twenty-five.

After a few minutes, Tobias turned to Pauline and asked, "Have I completely lost my mind, or is that Bruno talking to Sam Dolgoff over there?"

"Bruno?" Pauline said. "I don't know. Where's Sam? I can't see him."

Tobias directed her attention across the tables to where the strangest little old man was carrying on a highly animated conversation with a tall, spare Italian man with a primly trimmed mustache. The old man was wreathed in both wrinkles and smiles, with worn and cheerful slits for eyes. His middle was almost perfectly spherical, contained only by a pair of old suspenders, and he had a thick curtain of gunmetal-gray hair that fell over his eyes, such that every few minutes he threw his head back to dislodge it in a swift, surprisingly graceful movement. The Italian stood almost perfectly still in a manner that suggested a mounting fury, and Pauline went white. "It's *Max*."

"Who's Max?" Katherine asked. "Who's Bruno?" Pauline was already halfway to the door, and Tobias put a polite hand about an inch behind Lucianne's and Katherine's shoulders as he hustled them after her.

"It's both," Pauline said as they ran down the stairs, placing a hand over her hat to keep it from sliding off. "He's always changing his name because he's on the run from the government. He's my other boss."

"The Italian anarchists don't know Pauline works at *Freie Arbeiter Stimme*," Tobias explained, "and the Jewish anarchists don't know Pauline works at *L'Adunata Dei Refrattari*."

"I didn't know that either," said Katherine. "What's *L'Adune*—what's the second one mean?"

"I don't make a habit of telling people about it," Pauline said, disappearing beneath the next turn in the stairwell.

"It's supposed to mean 'Call of the Refractaires,' but I'm not really sure what a Refractaire is supposed to be," Tobias said.

"Unmanageable," Lucianne added unexpectedly. "When you're breaking in a pony or a horse, if it's particularly unmanageable, it's being refractory. So you might as well call it 'Stupid, Stubborn, and Loud.'"

"I'll ignore that counterrevolutionary comment, because I know you're hopelessly indoctrinated and more to be pitied than censured for now. But I only know because I caught Pauline coming out of the *Refrattari* offices last year," Tobias said. "She looked like how I've always imagined Montresor looked when he laid the last brick over Fortunato. I've covered for her because as a general rule, I think it builds character to lie to your boss." By now they had emerged safely back onto the street, between a launderette and a covered fruit stall, and the conversation was able to resume at a more conventional pace.

"It wouldn't ordinarily be a problem, having a second job," Pauline said, "only Max—Bruno—and Herman—that's our boss at *Freie Arbeiter*—had a terrible falling out over Mark Mratchny's coverage of the Spanish Civil War in '39 and if either of them knew I was working for the other, I'd be fired for sure. I never dreamed they'd both be at the same meeting. They can't have seen each other, or we'd have heard about it, so I think it's safe to say Max can't have seen me, but what a close shave." She did not seem to be joking about the Spanish Civil War. Pauline was like that sometimes—she could take almost any problem in the present day with real ease and unconcern, but twenty-five-year-old grudges carried over from another country, in the time of their parents' generation, while she did not share them, she took in dead seriousness. For a revolutionary she had a surprising respect for her elders. At least it surprised Lucianne, who hardly gave a second thought to her parents, their world, or their values; her allegiance lay with convention, not with tradition, and convention always orbits the young.

"What you need," Tobias said, "is a couple of free drinks, and so do I. Some of the boys from work were talking about going to Gerde's up in the Village with a few college girls they met out pamphleting, and in my experience college girls like buying a round or two for the virtuous working class. What do you say we meet them and make sure they get their money's worth?"

No one else wanted to go home yet; no one had any money of their own to spend, and so Tobias's motion passed without objection. They turned to walk uptown, Lucianne being careful to stay on Katherine's left so she did not end up walking next to him. There was nothing like trying to avoid one likable man for forgetting another. Silently she blessed Tobias for making conversation that was just charming enough that she had to work to resist joining in, and scarcely thought of Sidney more than once an hour the whole night.

The next Lucianne heard of Sidney was from a reporter friend, who excitedly informed her that he had signed up with the coast guard in a respectable form of draft evasion. Lucianne was disgusted. There had been something appealing, even admirable about Tobias's frank determination to get out of military service, but Sidney avoiding it by halves seemed pitiful by comparison. "Ginger ale," Lucianne wrote to Giuliana, "again."

Chapter Eight

A HAIRCUT FOR KATHERINE

oth Gia and Ruth were moved in completely by the following afternoon. This particular Moving Day having brought in fewer arrivals than any year previous, the final count of Stephen's particular intimates for the year were: Katherine and Kitty on the first floor (Stephen liked Kitty for precisely the same reasons Katherine struggled to like her, but Kitty made Stephen feel heroic where Katherine could only be made to feel besieged), Josephine and Pauline on the second, Lucianne and Gia on the third. On the fourth floor were Posey Becker-Wolfe, a legal secretary, Helen Gibran, who worked at a piano storage warehouse, and Dolly and Nicola.

Stephen had dedicated the entire morning of Moving Day to Gia, an exclusivity that had been previously unheard and undreamed of by the other girls. Yet Katherine had been mistaken in thinking that Gia must have had more tip money at her disposal than her competitors; she paid the usual amount. Stephen had in fact, and for the very first time, made an exception for her.

That Gia was very beautiful must have played some part in his decision. Stephen was not especially susceptible to beauty, but he sometimes could be moved by it, and Gia was so lovely to look at that the work of stacking and unloading boxes into her room seemed like luck, even to the point of attracting additional luck to himself through this act of tribute. It was a pleasure to feel himself busy near her, to frame her cool and restful attitude with his own activity; that restfulness in turn framed his attitudes, such that several times throughout the course of that morning Stephen felt his own looks must have been enhanced by her presence. It was a curious blend of gratefulness and conceit that Gia produced in him, and he rather enjoyed the contrast between them. But there was more to it than that—Gia's beauty was so immediate and so pronounced that it had straightaway furnished a channel of easy understanding between them. Stephen received it as a piece of uncomplicated and impersonal good fortune, and Gia received his obvious pleasure as a relief. She was beautiful, and he was glad that she was beautiful, and he was not going to pretend not to notice or hold it against her. From the start they both felt entirely free with one another, while at the same time they felt a shared accord.

The things that belonged to Gia were also beautiful. She had come over in a cab from the train station, with a second car filled entirely with trunks and cases following just behind. Her mother, Stephen learned, had also done a great deal of Gia's wardrobe shopping over the phone in advance, and arranged for everything to be delivered directly to the lobby, so that all her various bags and furnishings washed up there together as if in a tide pool. Everything that ought to have been new was new, and everything that ought to have been old was old. The old things had been neatly maintained, and the new things were in good taste.

But in New York even a second-rate institution like the Biedermeier was not a stranger to beautiful women with good taste. They could be found on every block in every borough of the city, even in poor and unfashionable neighborhoods. What Stephen had found most compelling about Gia Kassab was her disarming honesty and singleness of purpose. She had taken off her gloves to shake his hand with real enthusiasm, and riding up in the elevator she had said something extraordinary when he asked what brought her to the city:

"I'm in New York to get married, only the man I'm going to marry doesn't know it yet. His name is Douglas Burgess, and he's an editor at Viking Press, and he used to go with my mother before she married my father, but of course that was a long time ago now. She doesn't know it yet either." Then she lit a cigarette and stepped out of the elevator.

Stephen was only speechless for a moment. In three steps he had caught up with her, and as soon as he could get a good look at her face he started to laugh. It was an innocent and friendly laugh, and there was no mockery in it, only astonishment. She laughed too.

"That's a hell of a plan," Stephen said, unlocking the door to her room and handing her the key. "Have you always been precocious, or was it a question of waiting for inspiration to strike?"

"Always," she said. "But I never had anything to hang it all on before now."

"Give me one too, will you?" Stephen said, and she handed him both a cigarette case and lighter. He waved off the lighter and produced his own, lit the cigarette, and sat down on the chair in front of her desk, in the farthest corner of the room from the door. "Thanks. Why now? I mean, if he used to date your mother, you can't have just met him or anything. What changed?"

"No," agreed Gia easily. "I've known him practically my whole life. But his wife died last month, and it took me a few weeks to quit my job and find a place to stay here."

Stephen whistled appreciatively. "You're in the wrong line of work," he said. "They could use you in the army."

"I wouldn't work half so hard for the army as I've worked for this," Gia said.

"How old are you?" Stephen asked her, leaning forward and reaching out his hand for another cigarette, which she offered him silently. "What have you been doing with yourself until now? Why him? And what does your mother think?"

"I'm twenty-one," Gia said, which was probably true, or at least close to the truth. "I was a dancer. My people are from Detroit. I've been dancing at the Chicago Opera Ballet for the last two years. I'm supposed to dance now that I'm here—at least that's what I told my mother—but I'll give it up as soon as we're married. I might give it up sooner. I don't know how Douglas will be able to see me on a dancer's schedule, and I think I should get an office job with an editor or somebody, which would make it easier to run into him. My mother thinks I'm a good dancer and a slightly dull girl, and I'm not saying a word to her about this until after I'm married."

Stephen started to laugh again. "Mrs. Mossler told us you were supposed to be very religious. I was expecting a painfully thin girl carrying a rosary and wearing a mantilla."

"I'm as American as anybody," Gia said, in a sudden flash of temper. "My people have been in the Midwest for eighty years, and we were just as Christian as the Pilgrims. And there's nothing wrong with wanting to get married. Everybody ought to get married."

"I am sorry," Stephen said, a little puzzled by how he had managed to offend her but eager to smooth things over. "I sounded like an idiot. I didn't mean anything by it. I'm not a Christian myself, as it happens, so sometimes I get—the wrong idea about things."

"Oh," Gia said, and she brightened again right away. If she was sensitive to even the suggestion of irregularity in herself, she did not seem to mind it in Stephen in the least. Now she grew candid and friendly again, and she lit her second cigarette in an attitude of perfect calm. Stephen, who was a chain-smoker, had already finished his, but was perfectly happy to sit a while longer with this curious, gorgeous girl before going downstairs for the rest of her things. "And I did go to church every week in Chicago, and I hope to do so here, too."

"All the while," Stephen told Lucianne later that afternoon, when he looked in on her room in between jobs, "looking like butter wouldn't melt in her mouth, and as if she were talking about making a date with a nice boy her own age she'd met at the Cornell Club, instead of her mother's ex-lover! I think she's a menace. Let's both be very much in love with her." Then he was off again in a shot.

As he delivered much the same speech to the rest of his intimates on other floors, the astonishing story of Gia's peculiar and glorious arrival spread rapidly throughout the hotel. It was true, as Gia had said, that plenty of girls came to New York, and to the Biedermeier even, hoping to get married. Usually, however, the hope was a general one—or, if the girl had a particular target in mind, she kept it to herself until after the ring rested on her finger and the date was set. Lucianne had a complicated relationship to the question of marriage herself. She liked being conventional, but what she liked best was being the most conventional, by way of contrast, among less conventional people. She liked going out with men, she liked falling in love, and she liked being in love; marriage was the point of all these little activities, and marriage would put a stop to them forever. She wanted to be asked, and she wanted to seriously consider the proposal—and at that point her ideas dissolved into a curious little mental blank spot, because she could never bring herself to follow them to their ultimate conclusion. Lucianne recognized something of herself in Gia's declaration—it was perfectly ordinary and entirely perverse.

One of the college girls Tobias's friends brought along to Gerde's the night before had been a psychology student. No one in their party had been able to resist improvising their dreams to her, and by the third round of drinks she had begun offering grand pronouncements about the significance of each:

"Sister, you wouldn't believe me if I told you, but I'm dead serious: In my dreams everything runs riot, nothing is ordered or under control, and time itself operates under new and baffling conditions I can't seem to understand no matter how hard I try. My whole family is so ashamed of me. Their dreams are perfectly productive, last exactly as long as a single night, and they always get sent away with a nice little prize, like the corn they're growing or the book they're working on, once it's finished. What I want to know is, what sort of fertilizer works on corn that grows backward?"

After a moment of carefully studied thought, the reply came: "It's your family that's backward, not you. Try sleeping on your stomach."

"Doc, you've got to help me. Every night it's the same: It's Carnival, and I'm trapped in some miniature European city, rushing through a cobblestone maze, and I'm being chased by a series of menacing figures. They're real shadowy—all covered in costumes and masks and bells and things. And I'm running and running, but I can't get away from them, and I can't see their faces. Finally I run indoors through a side door and join a party that's just sitting down to play bridge. West opens with one heart. What's trumps?"

Answer: "They're playing pinochle." Then, with that abrupt

change from hilarity to seriousness that so often accompanied a third round, she said: "Of course, the idea that the dream is built out of the dregs of the day is itself a compromise with rationalism, because it suggests that nothing in the sleeping mind can exist without coming from some initial sensation in the waking mind, like all a dream can do is rearrange mental furniture."

"But that *is* all dreams do," one of the other college girls— Lucianne could not remember their names—had said in reply. "That's why everyone else's dreams are so tiresome, and no one else ever wants to hear about them. That's why everyone's been inventing dreams for you to analyze, instead of telling you real ones, because the real ones aren't half so interesting."

"All dreams are interesting," the psychology student said imposingly, "and that's why almost everyone is afraid to talk about them, and pretends to find them boring."

"What bothers me about dreams," Katherine said then, "is how you can never find the point where—maybe I ought to say *when*—things break down." She had ordered Shirley Temples all evening, although still she had kept up with the group's pace and was currently drinking her third. "I never become late in a dream; I always *find* myself rushing because I've become late without realizing it, and I can't find out how it started."

"You could call that curious," Pauline said, "if you wanted to stretch a point, but I don't really see how you could call that interesting."

"Every night you step outside of time," the psychology student said, "and find yourself already subject to various conditions, where nothing ever comes first, where time is stopped and all times are the same but somehow you are still late, and you want me to believe that isn't interesting? I banish such speech from the table," and here she made a lavish sweep with her empty hand, "and I sentence you all to another drink!" The edict met with universal approval.

For some reason Lucianne could not quite formulate, Gia reminded her very much of that college girl, whom she never saw again (although she had, in fact, been cheerfully stuck with the bill after all, and had just as cheerfully discharged it, which made her enormously popular with Pauline and Tobias's friends). Possibly it had to do with a sense of encountering something singular—something ordinary, something perverse.

———••———

Ruth Morton Carpenter had brought very little with her, and what she did have she carried herself. She was very taken with the green wing chair, the rock-maple bureau, the two lamps, one sitting on the writing desk, one standing on the floor, and the narrow bed. Katherine came by to see how she was getting along only to find her already entirely installed in her room. Ruth wanted nothing, needed nothing, only a repetition of the promise that she would be allowed to practice on Katherine's hair after her return from Pauline's meeting.

"I'm not exactly sure when that might be," Katherine had warned her. "We may go out for dinner or drinks after. I don't want to put you out if you're tired from your trip or anything."

"That's all right," Ruth had said. "You won't bother me."

"We might not get back until late," Katherine said.

"That's all right. I don't mind" had again been Ruth's reply.

In this strange compliance she was at least unlike Kitty, who was herself forever apologizing and as a result always happy to traffic in apologies as a kind of stock-in-trade. But Ruth had more of an air of renunciation than remorse, and skillfully blocked the possibility of apology from either direction.

Josephine, whose room was just next door, had not taken to Ruth after all, Katherine was disappointed to discover. Apparently Ruth was not willing to be sketched, not even briefly, not even in fun; she seemed discomfited even by the possibility that someone wanted to look at her long enough to draw a likeness, or thought that she would want to look at herself. She was not even bad-looking, although Josephine's caricatures were never mean-spirited, or even photo-accurate, just a few quick lines to outline something immediate and reminiscent of the girl's personality. She had nice gray eyes, reasonably attractive clothes, and her hairstyle was becoming, but she absolutely refused Josephine's sketching, and went cold and silent at further attempts at conversation. Josephine was in turn bewildered by Ruth's unexpected stubbornness in refusing her and, as her pride had been hurt, gave her an exaggeratedly wide berth from then on, as if to say: "Who *knows* what might set her off next—better let her have her own way in everything, just in case," even though no one else ever saw Ruth putting her foot down over anything.

Pauline, several doors down, took a kind but general interest in Ruth, but Ruth did not care for general interest or, seemingly, for anyone who shared the floor with her. She was, however, interested in Katherine, in Stephen, and in the girls on every floor but the second—apparently according to the order in which she had met everyone.

Katherine had come up to the second floor with Pauline when they returned home from Gerde's to look in on Ruth and try to get out of the promise she'd made to her. Truthfully, Katherine had regretted making that promise ever since telling Lucianne about it on the subway that afternoon. It was late, well after midnight, and Katherine tried to put things off until the morning, at first saying politely but insincerely that she was sure Ruth wouldn't want to go to all that trouble at this hour—but Ruth did, very much, and wasn't in the least bit tired, and had everything already arranged in the bathroom at the end of the hall.

"Well, I am tired," Pauline said blithely as she abandoned Katherine, making for her own front door, "so if you've got a hair dryer hidden in there somewhere, heaven help you if you turn it on, because I'll smash it first chance I get."

Things went every bit as badly as Lucianne had predicted they would. Ruth spent almost the entire time apologizing, first for taking up so much of Katherine's time, then for the mess she expected she was going to make of her hair, then for the temperature of the water, then for the smell of the setting lotion and the sharpness of the clamps on the rollers, until even Katherine's patience was tested. Then Ruth apologized for Katherine's badly concealed temper, which made Katherine feel even crosser, but guilty too. So when Ruth reread the instructions on the setting lotion and saw the style called for hair "no longer than chin length," and bangs too, and burst into tears, it was Katherine who suggested that they might as well cut her hair while they were at it.

"After all, it would be a shame to waste all this time and effort," she said, trying to sound game, which was no small effort while she was still bent backward over the sink.

"Oh, but I couldn't," Ruth cried, "I just couldn't, not after I've already made such a mess of a wash and set, I couldn't *possibly*."

"What do you think you'd rather do, then?" Katherine said in the brightest tone she could muster. "See if we can make something out of the style, even at this length? Or wash it out and call it a night?"

This only made Ruth cry harder. It seemed that there was no suggestion she found bearable, and it was only after serious persuasion on Katherine's part, still half-crouched as she was, that Ruth so much dared to go and fetch the scissors. Afterward Ruth insisted that Katherine leave her to clean up, that it was the very least she could do, although Katherine had been reluctant to leave her alone, feeling somehow responsible for the total breakdown a simple shampoo had brought about.

Lucianne stopped dead in her tracks when she walked past Katherine's room the next morning. "Oh, Della," she quoted in amazement, "you won't believe this, but I sold my pocket watch to get the money to buy you those combs—"

Tears came into her eyes, and she was shaking with laughter as Katherine darted up and grabbed her by the wrist, pulling her inside and closing the door after her. "Listen to me," Katherine hissed, and told her everything that had transpired in the second-floor bathroom the night before.

"And with every cut," Katherine told her, trying very carefully not to laugh, "she apologized again, as if she were cutting out my heart. I almost thought she was, by the end. I felt like Rapunzel— every snip of the scissors was accompanied by a single tear."

Lucianne, who felt no such compunction, continued to laugh uproariously. "Oh, Katherine, you can't say I didn't warn you—how on earth did a chin-length bob turn into *that?*" For on Katherine's head was a coif the likes of which Lucianne had never seen. She was positive, for that matter, that no one had ever seen its like before. Approached from the left, she looked as if she had started to grow horns. Approached from the right, she looked almost human; faced directly on, she looked as if she had narrowly escaped a mechanical accident.

"*It was the bangs*," Katherine insisted, before giving up the fight herself and beginning to laugh and cry in turn. "Oh, I don't know how it happened. I was upside down the whole time, and couldn't see a thing besides Ruth's face—and she looked so stricken already, I could scarcely tell the difference until she'd made me half-bald. Don't you dare say a word. Ruth was on the edge to begin with; I don't think I can be held responsible for how she'll act if she thinks anyone else has noticed."

This set Lucianne off again. "*One dollar and eighty-seven cents. That was all. And sixty cents of it was in pennies!*"

Later that day Katherine, with a silk scarf of Lucianne's wrapped attractively around her head, had stopped by Ruth's room to inquire how the trial at the hairdressing school had gone.

"Oh, by the time I made it in, they said they'd already hired someone else, and were full up," Ruth said. "Can you believe it?"

Katherine could. "Some girls have all the luck," she said, and was proud of how evenly she managed to say it.

Chapter Nine

A FAIR DAY'S WAGE FOR
A FAIR DAY'S WORK

By the end of Moving Day, Stephen had made more money in a single workday than he had made during the entire month of April. For all that the residents bewailed, usually to his face, how cash conscious he became during this season, Stephen felt that he more than earned his commission and that no other mover could be had in the city at so reasonable a price. "Muzzle not the ox who treadeth out the corn, dear hearts" was his only response to such complaints. "Remember, the laborer is worthy of his hire." On May first he moved pianos, bureaus, dressers, antique trunks and potted palms, hatstands and coatracks and glass vanities rattling with a dozen delicate brush bottles, tracing and retracing the same hundred steps to and from the elevator on each subsequent floor, arranging and rearranging furniture in every possible configuration, and answering to a hundred bosses instead of one:

"Mind the dirt falling out of the pot, Stephen—careful, you'll track it all over the rug."

"I don't think it looks quite right in that corner after all. We'd better put it back to where it was in the first place."

"That's not my chair. I don't know whose chair that is, but that isn't my chair. This one's *rattan* backed. Whose room were you in last? You'd better go back and see if she's got mine. You'll know right away; if there's anything in her room that's suspiciously taste-ful, it's bound to be mine."

And the residents who never purchased his services were even worse. The ones who stayed put on Moving Day he considered more or less to be stealing from him. The ones who moved without his assistance, who prided themselves on becoming independent of him, often liked to celebrate their newfound self-sufficiency by borrowing his tools:

"Stephen, you're not using your second trolley cart just now, are you? Can I borrow it? I'll use the service elevator so as not to dis-turb you, if I can just get the service-elevator key from you while I'm at it—"

"Stephen, are there any of these washtubs left downstairs? Only they're just the right size for my linens and bedding, and I've already filled all my suitcases."

"Stephen, do you happen to remember which knot is best for a rope pulley?"

At this last question Stephen had come to a dead halt and in-spected the stairwells on the first three floors for any jerry-rigged pulley systems, finding and untying two of them while strongly sus-pecting several others had been hastily dismantled before he had a chance to discover them. News of Stephen's whereabouts nearly al-ways outpaced Stephen himself, despite his best efforts.

Sudden wealth has a habit of breeding dissatisfaction. It was like this with Stephen, who had worked at the Biedermeier four years now, and spent every May brooding equally over his grievances and treasure hoard. Twice he had attempted to use his Moving Day income to ask Mrs. Mossler for a raise, who was inclined rather to the opposite view—namely, that Stephen's annual springtime bonus more than made up for any possible shortcomings (which she would not admit) in his regular salary.

"What *do* we pay you, Stephen?" she asked after he had pled his case for a third time. Abstraction was not something Mrs. Mossler had to affect in order to get out of discussing a possible raise; she came by it honestly, but Stephen resented it all the same.

"Dollar an hour. Which happens to be a quarter under minimum wage, you know. Pauline told me. She says it's all right to leverage the power of the state to fix prices as long as it's in the favor of the workers."

"A dollar and a quarter an hour? I'm sure that can't be right." Mrs. Mossler's ideas of fairness were anchored securely somewhere around the year 1927. Sometimes this had a surprisingly progressive effect on her—she had mostly missed the first Red Scare due to her youth and entirely ignored the second—while at other times, like the present conversation, it meant a stubborn refusal to acknowledge that the present was in any way distinct from the past.

"It's true, Mrs. Mossler. State legislature voted to bring the wage forward from a dollar-fifteen just last October. I could write to the assembly and ask for a copy of the ruling, if you don't believe me."

"Of course not, Stephen; don't put yourself out," Mrs. Mossler said automatically; she resisted any increase in spending as a matter of course, but nevertheless still disliked the idea of putting Stephen to more trouble than was absolutely necessary.

"We could unionize, you know."

"Who could unionize, Stephen?"

"Myself and the other operators." This was a maddening complacency. Stephen sounded rather like he was threatening to go on strike with his own grandmother. Neither Stephen nor Mrs. Mossler ever mentioned, during what was seemingly becoming an annual exercise, that he could easily get another job, one that paid a man's wage. (This was because both Stephen and Mrs. Mossler were polite by nature as well as by training.)

Stephen did not want to get another job for several reasons: First, although he had not attended any classes in the last two semesters, he was still technically enrolled at Cooper Union and found it important to still think of himself as a student "in between things" rather than a former student, and second, he did not like to work. The truth about the world, Stephen believed, was that almost no one likes to work (and he was not alone among Biedermeier residents in this belief) and that real happiness lay in finding the sort of people whose patterns of work avoidance most closely matched one's own and hanging on to them for dear life. At the Biedermeier Stephen hardly ever worked, not even on Moving Day. Wasn't just about everybody living in the hotel his friend? Wouldn't he be sitting down at those very vanities and writing tables, admiring the potted palms when he was invited round for sandwiches, playing those pianos on a slow and empty afternoon? He was never expected to stand at attention or keep his eyes forward in the elevator; whenever someone got on board, it was bound to be a friend of his, and it was understood that Stephen would talk to his friends just like anyone. On busy days Stephen might travel five miles just running back and forth throughout the hotel—taking Pauline up to the eleventh floor—carrying a message from Mrs. Mossler to Katherine—running out to the drugstore for more bobby pins for Kitty who couldn't leave the phone—but this was not work, this was no more than occasionally undertaking an errand for a busy friend. Besides which, Stephen liked being around women, and women usually liked it when Stephen was around. There were some men who liked being the only man among a group of women; such men were of too variable a type to be classified as either wholly good or wholly bad. Some of them were selfish in a delightful way, and some of them were selfish in a tiresome way. Others spent time with women in order to not think about themselves at all. Stephen did not belong to any of those types. He simply liked being around women as much as they liked being around him, and the relationship between this marked preference and his own sex seemed to him purely incidental.

In any other hotel he would probably be forced to wear a hat with a cheap elastic strap that snapped under the chin. In any other job, he would have to set himself a little apart, would have to stand and speak and even think differently during working hours, would have to become Stephen-at-work every morning before he could be released back into his own Stephen-ness at the end of the day—unthinkable! And no amount of money could make up for it. But he still wanted the money, if he could get it.

"The other operators . . . ? Oh, you mean Kitty and Carol. But the hotel doesn't pay them half what it pays you, Stephen. It couldn't possibly. They don't work anywhere near your hours, and besides they never have to carry luggage or anything."

"That don't enter into it, Mrs. Mossler. It's the principle of the thing. We do the same job, so we have the same interests. And we could still unionize, you know," Stephen said seriously. He had been perhaps a little less than half in earnest during the entire conversation, but it did seem to him that Mrs. Mossler ought to give it at least as much attention as she did to replacing the flypaper in the utility room.

"Oh, could you?" Mrs. Mossler said in an earnest yet distracted tone. "Only I'd really rather you didn't, Stephen. It would be such a headache, and I already have more to deal with than I can really manage. Patricia and Carol have been using my pinking shears to cut out paper dolls, and paper is the one thing that dulls the edge of pinking shears, and I can't even afford breakfast anymore." In this she referred to a hotel matter as if it were a personal problem, which she did so often that Stephen no longer found it alarming. "Here's a quarter, if you're short this week," and she actually pressed the coin into his hand before wandering off, leaving Stephen feeling equal parts exasperated and affectionate.

He decided to look in on Pauline, who could always be counted on to provide an antidote whenever he felt himself growing too sympathetic toward Mrs. Mossler: "You must never think of anyone who employs you as a human being, Stephen. It's absolutely fatal." But he went to see her by way of Mrs. Mossler's office on the ground floor first. He could not in good conscience keep the quarter.

Stephen appreciated Pauline perhaps more than anyone else in the building. Her politics were unusual inasmuch as she knew exactly what they were; most of the residents had no more than approximate commitments and vague allegiances. In this Stephen was part of the general rule, rather than the exception. He did not like to work, it is true, but he considered that a personal matter, and a question of individual skill in getting out of it while drawing as little attention as possible, rather than an interest which might serve to unite him with others. What Stephen wanted more than anything was to be able to pretend he was not working while he was at work; cultivating a sense of fellow solidarity with other workers was at direct odds with his heart's desire, so he cheerfully ignored them. (Possibly it was for this reason, among others, that Mrs. Mossler had not taken his threat of an elevator operators' union seriously.) Besides, strikes were something he associated with his parents' generation, like drape-cut suits and Peter Pan collars and the WPA.

Pauline would have liked to see a greater display of fellow feeling from him, Stephen knew, but was heartened by his openly avowed workshyness, and counted him among her victories. She did not mind vagueness as much as she minded coziness, which she considered her great enemy under the Biedermeier's roof. (Outside the Biedermeier she considered her greatest enemies to be, in no particular order, the police, Westchester County, the *New York Times*, Parks Commissioner Newbold Morris, *Liberation* editor Roy Finch, Jimmy Breslin, and a Kips Bay truant officer named Courtenay Odell.) This was not to say Pauline disliked comfort, or even personal luxuries; no one who had seen Pauline's wardrobe could accuse her of scorning pleasure. But she considered coziness a dangerous step on the road to loving privacy, of making a novelty, even an indulgence, out of eating dinner alone. Solitude was not, for Pauline, an end in itself; she often suspected Katherine, whose fondness for the cozy was well known, of having no greater ambition than having a place to toast cheese by herself, and worse, for congratulating herself on choosing snugness and seclusion over marriage in the suburbs, as the better and more radical option. So many Biedermeier girls who congratulated themselves on not fleeing to the suburbs after a year or two that they shut their minds up and forgot the world entirely, taking their intermission from life and cultivating only their own little plots of dreamy solitude. And what was the point in living all together, if only to continue to live so decidedly apart? "To have gotten away from their family homes is the right start," Pauline once told Stephen, "only so many of them seem to think that's the end of it. And you've got to be careful about it, because anyone who worries that you're going to take their privacy from them is likelier than ever to start shutting their doors to you."

After Pauline, Stephen liked Dolly and Nicola best. Dolly was enormously cheerful and Nicola was conspicuously well adjusted.

Dolly's last name was O'Connor and Nicola's was Andelin; Dolly worked in a bar and Nicola worked in the back room at Loehmann's. They were also lesbians. They were not lovers, or if they ever had been, Stephen thought it must have been over between them some time ago. Both Dolly and Nicola had been at work for several years on separate novels loosely based on their contemporaries at the Biedermeier, only Dolly called her hotel the Hyperion and kept a scrupulously faithful account of everything she saw and heard, and Nicola called hers Fontainebleau and more or less invented things as she pleased.

Dolly and Nicola were reasonably well understood by everyone in the hotel according to her abilities. Lucianne suspected all women who lived in women's hotels of being washouts until proven otherwise, herself excepted, and considered lesbianism merely an ordinary stable vice that was apt to develop along with boredom, jealousy, overeating, and neuroticism as a result of prolonged confinement. A good woman, to Lucianne's mind, was both valuable and rare, like in the thirty-ninth Proverb or the little girl from the Longfellow rhyme who, when she was good, she was very, very good but when she was bad she was horrid. Girls were cheap and men were valuable, and that was all there was to it. She believed that what she called "that sort of thing" was only appealing to a small pool of rich girls and a slightly larger pool of very poor ones, along with a handful of likely congenital cases. It was like trying to make a living as a poet or something: possibly all right for a girl with a lot of money, who didn't especially care about other people. But what were two girls with no money supposed to do for each other? Not to each other— that much seemed self-evident and straightforward—but *for*. Where would they get their dinners? Who was going to pay for it? And who in the world was going to sell it to them? No, middle-class girls could scarcely afford to be very interested in that way of life, at least for very long. Possibly this was why she approved of, and even admired, Pauline's improbable handsomeness, which nevertheless successfully encompassed beauty, while on the other hand she considered Dolly, who had no beauty at all, merely unwomanly. That there were women of this type, whose mannishness did them no credit, did not trouble her deeply, but she did wonder from time to time: Where was the future in Pauline's looks? Women were supposed to age into handsomeness, not out of it; how could such an eternally boyish face enter maturity? But that was Pauline's problem.

On another end of the scale, Mrs. Mossler understood the limits of her own ignorance, and never tried to learn more than she had to (whether about Dolly and Nicola or anything else) for her own good. She had still been at school herself during the final days of the unconcealed and unselfconscious passionate friendship, when smashing and spooning prevailed on the grounds of every ladies' seminary, conservatory, and academy from Maine to Michigan. Mrs. Mossler—still Emmie then—had grown up in warm proximity to a crowd of flesh, only to emerge blinking into a mighty cold world, where suddenly everyone was expected to keep her distance from friend and stranger alike, and the innocent, ubiquitous touch of her youth was newly awkward, cumbersome, and shameful. She did not understand what had brought this change about, and she did not like it. She liked Dolly and Nicola very much, and was only dimly aware of the gulf that she knew she must be very careful to skirt whenever she saw or spoke to them. They in their own turn understood her friendly terror, and considered it an act of joyful chivalry to escort her past their borders, unedified and unharmed.

At the very end of the fourth-floor corridor was J.D. Boatwright, whom Stephen adored, a feminist of the very oldest school and a former Lucy Stoner who was seventy years old if she was a day. The Lucy Stone League, a group of mostly journalists who wanted to keep writing under their maiden names, had come into being under Ruth Hale in 1921. It was one of a seeming thousand little penny-ante women's groups that had sprung up between the wars, the kinds of groups that recorded with portentous delight "the first woman from Massachusetts to complete a bachelor of science degree" or "the first-ever lady over thirty to stop for lunch by herself on the Bronx River Parkway"—what Pauline called "the archival traffic in female detritus" and what nobody else in the building thought to call anything. No one ever knew what her initials stood for, although Lucianne liked to claim that either James Dean or John D. Rockefeller had been named after her. She had been a minister's daughter, a real blue blood from the old days of Henry James's New York, and had been working on a biography of George Sand for as long as anybody could remember and which no one expected she would finish.

Sadie, Patricia, and Carol all lived in a big suite on the eleventh floor, and of course it was possible that Ruth, now on the second floor, might amount to something, although privately Stephen considered it unlikely they would ever become particular friends. Kitty's sort of helplessness could be poignant and even charming, while Ruth's sort of helplessness, which he suspected concealed an underlying indifference for life, put Stephen slightly on his guard. And of course he had seen what she had done to Katherine's hair.

———··———

The horse show article had barely paid to keep Lucianne in stamps for the next two months, and her stenotype training-by-correspondence was going exactly nowhere. Lucianne liked to think of herself as a self-starter, which is why she often felt better having four "gigs" going at the same time than she ever did with traditional employment. But she was not a self-starter, and although she invariably felt better when she first took on two freelance writing projects, a babysitting job across town, and a new correspondence course that promised to retrain her for one of the most rapidly expanding and highly remunerative industries of the decade, within a few weeks it was always the same; something had unexpectedly come up that meant she could not find the mere thirty minutes a day the correspondence course required, the kid got croup or some other communicable disease requiring quarantine or his mother's sister moved into the apartment to look after him for free, and the freelance articles took three weeks to get started, an afternoon to sit down and properly write, and another three weeks to get paid. Worse still, her union severance from her last telephone operator job was running out. Lucianne had done nothing to help organize the union, and occasionally complained about it when she was invited out to dinner if she thought the men treating her would appreciate a little anti-union sentiment, but she very much appreciated the severance just the same. She had tried not to think about it, she had tried quietly panicking, and she had tried violently daydreaming about being suddenly rescued from her predicament by receiving an unexpected inheritance or marrying a very rich and very ill man who had only weeks to live and wanted to cause a little feminine happiness before he died, thereby impressing Jimmy Breslin so much that he either wrote a "JFK's Grave-Digger"–style column about her simple, plucky, heartwarming attitude toward being a working girl in the modern era or demanded she be given the job of society editor at the *Herald-Tribune*, possibly both.

Finally, and no sooner than she absolutely had to, Lucianne faced it: She needed a job, a real one, and that right soon. It would be faster, she thought, to try to get an *old* job back, rather than look for a brand-new one from people who did not know her—or, failing that, to try to extend an occasional freelance relationship with the *Herald-Tribune* or the *Journal American* or *McCall's*. But all three of her editors thought that things between them ought to stay the way that they had been. Would she like to come in next week and go to lunch? They would be happy to talk about future columns, but although they highly valued her unique contributions, they were looking for something different, quite different, from their full-time staff members, although what that something different was, none of them were willing to say.

Things eventually got so serious that Lucianne got dressed up one Friday afternoon and "dropped by" the offices that had employed her last, before her stint at the telephone company, under the guise of visiting an old colleague and friend (really just an old colleague) and taking her out to lunch, meanwhile discreetly investigating whether they might be willing to give her back her old job, which had been proofreading copy for a restaurant menu–supply concern. Lucianne had forgotten the colleague's number so, rather than hunt through the phone book, merely turned up at the offices at ten minutes to noon, pretending to have been in the area already for some trivial reason and "thought I'd come and look you up, Rosie, and see if you were free for a drink or some window-shopping on your lunch break." Rosie had been slightly mystified by Lucianne's sudden turnup but was nonetheless willing to be steered around some department store windows and to supply Lucianne with the latest odds. Lucianne had been unwilling at first to come right out and say that she was hoping to be rehired, but Rosie had failed to pick up any of her hints, and her lunch break (as well as Lucianne's patience) were both running short when Lucianne finally put the question to her.

"Oh," Rosie said, a little stupidly, "but I thought you were writing for newspapers and things now."

"Yes, I am," Lucianne said, "and I like it very much, only—it's not so much a job, what I do for them, as it is—an occasion. And what I'd like is a job, and since I used to do *this* job pretty well, I thought Mr. Gourley might be able to give it back to me."

"But are you sure you'd want it back?" Rosie asked. "Only I remember how excited you were when you left—"

"Yes, I remember how excited I was then, too," Lucianne said sharply. "I don't know how else to put it, Rosie, but things have changed for me since then, and not in an especially promising fashion. I'd wait tables, only every place I've asked expects you to have waited tables somewhere else first, and I can't very well turn call girl, because I share a line with eight other girls on my floor, so the johns would never be able to get ahold of me."

Rosie promised she would ask, and Lucianne bought her a drink, which she couldn't afford, by way of apology and thanks at once, before returning her back to the office, feeling a little tipsy and a little humiliated and ready to quarrel with anybody the first chance she got.

———··———

J.D. was quietly popular at the hotel, particularly among the residents of the fourth floor, who treated her as something between a pet and a college dean. Part of her popularity might have been explained by the curious mixture of reclusiveness and regularity that characterized her routine; part of it might have been explained by the glamor of her fashionable, continental ugliness. She never wore anything but black, and whatever she wore was always buttoned or fastened or closed right up to the very top of her throat. She had a long and elegant horse's face, a powerful gaze, dark eyes, and half-moon glasses. She also had a neat little mustache on the corners of her upper lip, which she evidently took sufficient notice of to ensure it always remained tidy and locked in place, but never to remove it, and wore Spanish Leather behind her ears, which reminded many of the residents fondly of their grandfathers. She was of middling height and excruciatingly correct posture; Dolly, who had been scribbling notes for an eventual novel hunched over in bed before she fell asleep, often wondered whether she sat like that at her desk, too, but never dared to ask. J.D. rarely left her room before three in the afternoon, and almost never left her door open to visitors; she went to the New York Public Library on Wednesdays and to the French Institute Alliance Française every other Friday for research.

"How much more do you suppose there is to learn about George Sand?" Dolly had once asked Lucianne, who could curse a little in French and was therefore the residential expert on Continental history, philosophy, and letters. "Wasn't she the one who lived with that fellow who was already married?" J.D. had just sailed through the dining room on her way back from the French Institute, pocketing two diagonally sliced liverwurst sandwiches and an apple before shutting herself up for the weekend to write.

"I know she lived with Chopin for a while," Lucianne said, considering a moment. "Most of my French has to do with the dirtier Toulouse Lautrec pictures and an old paperback of *Bonjour Tristesse*, though."

"I don't think she could have," Dolly said. Each was perhaps both equally as lost as the other in the moment. "I thought she was later than Chopin. And I thought she lived with that old critic, the one with three names and that big Victorian mustache."

"No, you're thinking of George Eliot," Lucianne said triumphantly.

"No, I mean the woman who wore men's clothing, and had all those affairs, and wrote novels, and called herself George," said Dolly.

"That's George Eliot," Lucianne said. "And I know you're always thinking about women in men's clothing."

"You're putting me on," Dolly said. "Katherine, don't you know the one I mean?"

Katherine looked up, startled. "I know there's Charles Dickens, and then there's Edgar Allan Poe in there somewhere, and a little later Virginia Woolf came along. But anything deeper than that beats me, kids. Blame the one-room schoolhouses of Ohio." Her heart raced a little faster as she joked. Katherine still froze up whenever the conversation veered too closely to college or things most people were supposed to have read or seen in adolescence, since she worried terribly about inadvertently betraying just how much she had missed, and raising speculation as to why she had missed it.

"What did I miss? You look like you're trying to solve a murder," Posey asked as she sat down to join them.

"None of us knows the difference between George Eliot and George Sand," Lucianne said. "I'm the closest, because I know they're not the same person, and one of them was French, but that's about all I've got."

"And one of them dressed like a man," Dolly added, "which is important even if Lucianne thinks it's disgusting, and lived with married men, possibly including Chopin, but we don't know which."

"I don't think it's disgusting, exactly," Lucianne said, without rancor. "I just think men happen to look better in men's clothes than women."

"You haven't seen me in a dress," Dolly said.

"I don't exactly count you as a woman, either," Lucianne said, "although maybe if you ever put a little effort into it—"

"I think that's actually a point in favor of my side of things," Dolly said. "And let's not argue about dresses."

"You're both right," Posey said.

"About Dolly being a woman?" Lucianne asked, for once a little behind on the conversation.

"About George Eliot and George Sand," Posey said. "They both wore men's clothes, and they both called themselves George, and they both lived with married men, and they were both women, more or less."

"That can't possibly be right," Dolly said.

"Dolly's right, for once," Lucianne said. "There can't have been two women novelists calling themselves George, living in both trousers and sin, at the same time."

"That's true enough," Posey said, "since there was also George Egerton. Also christened Mary, also lived with married men, also wrote novels—"

"How do you boo people in French?" Dolly asked Lucianne.

Lucianne made a guttural, inquisitive sort of noise, like an owl that had flown into a tree. Dolly decided against imitation and simply started throwing things.

None of them cared to ask J.D. anything about George Sand, rightly intuiting that to ask her about the project was to implicitly cast censure on its colossal prolongation. But she did not always work on George Sand. On most weekends she set her notes to one side and wrote letters to her grown children. She wrote to them faithfully, and they to her intermittently, although always in friendly and respectful tones. One, a daughter, lived in Chicago, where she had married a man who worked for Abbott Laboratories, and the other, a son, traveled for a pharmaceutical concern based in Cleveland. J.D. had married early, and unsuccessfully; her parents had been against the marriage from the start, and as she had never before gone against them in everything, they felt all the more outrage that she could behave so deceitfully, ungratefully, and selfishly over something which affected them at least every bit as much as it had affected her. Her father had been a very severe minister of the Calvinist variety, and her mother had been an equally severe member of the congregation. Neither did her eventual divorce do anything to reconcile her to them. They had always known she would come to regret the error, and did not consider it adequate compensation for the loss they had suffered. J.D. had not been well after either of the births, and her husband, who had been very seriously alarmed by the form her unwellness had taken in both instances, finally dropped the children off at his in-laws' doorstep before departing for parts unknown.

At first J.D. had not felt sufficiently recovered in either body or spirit to retake the children, and when at last she did make an appeal to her parents, some ten months later, the attempt was timid, even pitiful; she had reverted almost completely back to the cringing condition of her own childhood, and meekly accepted "No" as her answer. A little later she asked her father if she might write to the children, and after some consideration he consented, although he reserved the right to read and, if necessary, edit both her letters and theirs. So her son and daughter grew up in the same home as their mother, but without her; they played with her old toys, climbed the same trees, and learned to read from her old spelling books. She felt a ghostly sense of proximity, knowing that they were separated more by time than by distance, as if their childhood were a spiritual continuation of her own, and sometimes that sense even comforted her a little. She was a strong writer, and while for the first few years the children made for pretty indifferent correspondents, having no strong attachment to her, as they grew older came often to appreciate and even enjoy her letters, full as they were of interesting tidbits and observations about life in New York, which seemed to them very exciting, and eagerly curious about the things that interested them. When her son had been six and her daughter four, J.D.'s father had suffered a brain hemorrhage, which slowed his speech and his gait only a little, while remarkably softening his attitude toward discipline, and he became amazingly tolerant toward his grandchildren in ways neither his wife nor his daughter could ever have imagined. His wife followed suit, as she did in all things; if Lyman thought a thing was right, then it *was* right, and while her transformation came about as a result of the will, rather than a sudden change in temperament, it was nonetheless every bit as marked as his, if also slightly stiffer and a little less natural seeming. So J.D.'s children rather enjoyed being raised by the same people who had made childhood a terrifying place for their mother. Mostly she was glad of this, rather than envious, since she had thought of herself as an unfit mother—otherwise why would her children have been removed from her care? Surely a fit mother would have been able to keep them, so that their loss became proof in itself that she had deserved to lose them.

Today J.D. was writing to her daughter, christened Irma, but everyone but J.D. called her Rebecca. J.D. strove to keep her tone light and cheerful, since she feared that her last letter had strayed too closely to guilty reflection and self-recrimination, and that it had been because of this unwanted pressure that Irma had not replied for several weeks:

You should know that I am now the official caretaker of half-a-housecat, a rust-colored animal I have started calling Rufus because his coat is so orange it looks almost red in certain lights. I consider him half-a-housecat because he has dwelled for at least some length among civilized people, since he is neutered and does not seem to mind being stroked under the chin, although he doesn't wear a bell or a collar and I am fairly certain he has no fixed abode. He started appearing at my window every few nights last month—the first time it must have been almost midnight, and I was so engrossed in my notes (you may remember I was revising the chapter on Sand's medical studies with Dr. Deschartes at the time) I hardly noticed him until he started butting his head against the window and yowling as if I had locked him out. He must have climbed the fire escape, but what drew him all the way up to the fourth floor is beyond me. I opened the window, and he jumped right down onto my desk as if he had done so every day of his life. Since then he has become more or less my most regular visitor, and brings me news and gossip from the neighborhood, plus occasional evidence of his street fights (I believe he wins most of them) in exchange for a warm place to curl up and the occasional olive. Rufus adores olives, tomato slices, cheddar cheese, and ice cubes; perhaps unexpectedly, he does not like milk. He turned over a bowl of it only last week, and I was all afternoon trying to get the smell out of the rug. Milk is a very thick smell, with a tendency to linger; it's a very unwelcome guest in that way.

J.D. stopped after this. How much did a young wife, whose world was only beginning to open up, really want to hear about her strange old mother's relationship with a stray cat? Was this not just as tiresome, in its own way, as a letter that was overly pleading, overly emotional, that trespassed too much on her daughter's good nature? She knew her relationship-by-correspondence with both children was largely dependent on her ability to sound cheerful, unconcerned, and generally interested in their lives without prying. She must not bore them, and she must not intrude—but she was already forbidden from talking about the past, and there was so little in her present to talk about, so if they did not answer her questions and furnish her with details from their own lives, what else was left for her to say to them? She started over:

I have recently acquired a cat, in the informal way that cats usually join a household; I wonder if you and William ever think about getting a pet. All is well in George-land, and I still hope to have the manuscript ready for review in the fall. I had thought about taking a vacation once the Beast is off my desk and cluttering up someone else's. Are there any places you recommend?

But this was obviously fishing for an invitation. She started again.

There's a very determined red cat at my window. I think you would like him. I've named him William Rufus—Rufus for short— after the Norman king and son of the Conqueror, and not McKinley's Secretary of State, although the latter William Rufus did look more like a housecat than the former, if pictures are anything to go by. I hope you're enjoying the same nice spring weather in Chicago as we are here. Don't worry about writing back if you haven't got the time—Much love to you and your William, who looks nothing like a cat at all. Yours affectionately, J.D.

The other unexpected change Rufus had wrought in J.D.'s life was that now she left her door open for much of the time. This was ostensibly so he could come and go as he pleased, but had the happy knock-on effect of bringing more visitors to her room. In a later postscript to her daughter, J.D. added,

I would never have guessed that so many young people maintained an interest in the life of George Sand, but I have been very heart-

ened lately by how many of the girls here stop by with questions about her work. This evening alone has brought three inquirers to my door. I have also been asked to join an informal committee on the question of breakfast by some of the residents of the eleventh floor, so you can see I keep busy here.

Chapter Ten

UBI SUNT

Katherine had dutifully related to Mrs. Mossler each breakfast solution proposed by various residents during her rounds. Mrs. Mossler had listened carefully to each, and agreed readily on their various merits and shortcomings, but as none seemed notably stronger than any of the others, was unable to bring herself to choose one from among them. If she were ever cornered into answering directly, she would admit she was still "thinking it over," which *was* true inasmuch as she was in a state of chronic indecision and anxiety, but not at all true inasmuch as she never arrived at anything resembling a decision. It fretted her to no end to think of the residents going without breakfast; it was a crushing blow to her sense of providing a haven for working girls; it was degrading to the morale as well as to the pocketbook, and she eventually decided to stop thinking about it altogether. Amazingly enough, before the year was out she was once again half-convinced that there *was* still a daily breakfast service—because with Mrs. Mossler, to *wish* for something was the first step toward achieving it, so that she often considered things she merely hoped would come to pass in the future to be already as good as accomplished—and carefully avoided venturing onto the residential floors until after ten in the morning in order not to be confronted with evidence to the contrary.

The weekly rate remained the same, the longed-for urn of coffee never materialized in either the library or the cafeteria where dinner was still served ("For *now*," Lucianne was often heard to say darkly, "but you can be sure they're going to try to starve us out before winter"), and overall levels of hotel theft rose correspondingly as girls sought to compensate their losses by hoarding soap, matchbooks, trays, shower caps, hand towels, fountain pens, and stationery.

Carol composed an *ubi sunt* poem in the style of Baruch and tacked it over the door to the library:

> *Where are the breakfasts of yesteryear?*
> *When did Helen eat? And where did Thaïs dine?*
> *Where are the covered plates, the covered cups,*
> *The coddled egg, the coddled girls who ate them?*
> *Where is the coffee, which sweetened our breath?*
> *Where the shredded wheat, the cold limp toast?*
> *Those who hoarded up silverware and bowls, in which men trust,*
> *They have vanished, and returned to their hometowns,*
> *And no others have arisen in their place.*
> *Timor prandium conturbat me.*

Within a few days the note had been so thoroughly covered in responses as to be completely illegible. J.D. had been so overcome, both by the change in routine and the sudden jolt in memory that had accompanied the unexpected sight of Latin, that she immediately wrote out as much as she could remember (which was two and a half more or less accurate stanzas) of *De Brevitate Vitae* underneath it. Pauline had contributed a line about how "hearts starve as well as bodies" without either bread or roses. Someone else—Carol suspected, but could not go so far as to accuse, Patricia—had struck out *prandium* in red ink and written *IENTACULUM* over it, followed by *Video meliora, proboque, deteriora sequor.* The rest of the responses were in English and some very rude French (Lucianne again), as very few of the residents of the Biedermeier had experienced the benefits of a classical education.

"What I really hate about it," Lucianne said to Katherine that first cheerless morning, "is not so much that the breakfast was particularly good, and therefore worth missing, because of course it wasn't, but it means having to leave my room, and quite possibly the building, first thing in the morning, and to a person with even the slightest delicacy of feeling that can upset practically the whole day."

Lucianne had caught Katherine washing her private china stockpile in the shared hall bathroom only the week before, and had managed to secure for herself a standing invitation to drink coffee in Katherine's room each weekday morning as a result. Not for the first time did Katherine bemoan those keen and unsettling instincts for survival that would have more fittingly suited Lucianne—who had no business being on Katherine's floor at that hour in the first place—for life in the jungle than in Kips Bay. But still, it was better to have been found out by Lucianne rather than Kitty or Ruth or many of the others. All Lucianne wanted was the best that she could get for herself, which Katherine considered quite an easy position to do business with, herself.

Carol, Patricia, and Sadie began conducting nightly raids on the cafeteria, either at the tail end of dinner service if Esther, whose nature was forgiving and whose gaze was blessedly vague, was on kitchen duty, or after hours if Lela, whose gimlet eye missed nothing under the sun, who stood at least eight feet tall in stockinged feet, whose nature was grim, and whose boots (it was well known) were hobnailed with broken glass and human teeth, was working instead. On nights Esther worked they wore their winter coats to eat, even though the weather was splendid all May and the building was outfitted with a remarkably efficient steam-heating system. They would take a little bit of everything for the first course, then every couple of minutes one of them would jump up and exclaim:

"Will you look at that? I've forgotten a napkin," at which point one of the others would say,

"And what am I doing with two soup spoons and no fork?" to which the proper response was,

"I'd better get another coffee cup—this one's chipped. Or looks like it's about to chip any second, anyway," and then they went back to the buffet line, stuffing as much of whatever they could into their pockets till they bulged to absurd proportions. This little bit of theater was mostly for their own sakes, as Esther did not need it and Lela would never have countenanced it. But it boosted their morale to make a game out of it, like children who make believe at being prisoners of war, and made their borrowing feel playful rather than desperate.

Like Robin Hood and his Merry Men, the Quaker Girls stole according to a strict code. "We'll never steal the last of anything," Carol said seriously, when they were first working out how to make up for their lost breakfasts, "and never keep anything perishable in the room longer than overnight." (This rule was very quickly thereafter amended to "two hours," although the following winter Patricia had the bright idea of hanging a jug of cream on a piece of rope outside their bedroom window to keep cold overnight, which worked very well until she tried to get artistic and use a blue ribbon to tie it, which tore immediately in the first storm of the season, to predictable results.) Other rules included no more than one sausage per person per day and no starting fires in their room to reheat leftovers.

Lucianne considered this petty level of food theft beneath her, and aside from getting her coffee from Katherine in the morning, simply gave up breakfast altogether and angled for more invitations out to lunch on the days she went to the *Herald-Tribune* offices, while on other days she started telephoning some of her more successful men friends a few minutes past eleven, trying to sound smart and cheerful and like someone who would brighten up a tedious Wednesday afternoon if only they would ask her if she was free in an hour. She also began a brisk trade in slug tokens meant for tricking the subway fare box before the turnstile. She could buy thirty washers at the hardware store for twenty-two cents, or twenty play coins at Woolworth's for a dime, and it took all of ten minutes to punch holes in the middle or file down the edges slightly, then sell the slugs at a nickel apiece (which still undercut the New York Transit Authority's going rate by a dime), which made for a tidy profit, even if sales did slow down after the first month. She considered that, as a former Miss Subways herself, she was more than usually justified in riding for free. She justified selling the slugs inasmuch as she considered the other Biedermeier residents members of her court. She was not selling to the general public, but to a select and needy few.

"When housewives economize," Lucianne said by way of explanation, "they cut down on spending at the butcher. Well, I don't have the kind of money to afford to shop at the butcher. Since I can't cut down on discretionary spending, when I economize, I have to economize on following the law. I simply look at the legal behaviors I can no longer afford to keep up, and I cut them out."

Some of the older residents, such as Josephine and J.D., who had not left the building for work in years, had neither the resiliency of youth nor the quality of originality that might have made such a change feel slightly frightening but still something like an adventure, which might bring with it the possibility of being sharpened rather than like a sudden and terrifying pitch suddenly downward. J.D. had not quite been able to grasp the news all at once and required confirmation of the disappointment from three different girls before she was able to reliably retain anything like a memory of the loss of breakfast.

But Josephine had felt the pinch at once. She had lived so long at the margins of existence that she felt quite sure there was nowhere lower for her to drop *to* without exiting entirely the signposts of respectable life as she knew it. Aside from a brief and momentous run of plenty for a period of about six months in 1927, Josephine had scraped for as long as she could remember; it was the price she had gladly paid for independence. Her room was small, her lunches irregular, her clothes inadequate; she walked everywhere she went and patched her shoes; when the shoes could not bear another patch, she walked shorter distances, and less often. She affected a dislike first for the radio and later for television, and found it easier to decide that the theater had lost its appeal than to think of it as an expense she could no longer afford. She retreated socially rather than try to entertain her friends in shabbier style than in years past, while they in their turn assumed she must be too busy for her, and then thought of something else; gradually New York shrank to the size of her bedroom window, and now even that image was threatened. She dried her socks in feeble little strips over the radiator, where they looked like a miserable and cartoonish parody of bacon frying on the stove. (That might make for a good cartoon; she should write to Herbert and ask him what he thought of the idea.) Things had declined for her so slowly and so steadily it had seemed impossible to ever reach a point of crisis;

Josephine had been discouraged for so long that she had forgotten the possibility of despair.

She thought about going out—but where was there to go that did not cost money? She could take a walk; the fresh air and the activity would sharpen her appetite; she would see food at every corner and would not be able to buy any. There was the library. She could go sit among the books and the dirty old men and the sound of nobody talking—no, thank you. She could fish coins out of the fountains in Central Park—but people would see her doing it. She could try and go after dark—but she would be frightened, and she might lose her footing, and fall in, and then she would be wet and cold and frightened and alone and out of doors, and too ashamed to call for help, which would certainly be a worse position than feeling hungry but dry and mostly comfortable in her room, where no one could see her. The longer she stayed in her room and rested quietly and did not move, the longer it took to get really hungry, and the less she minded being hungry to begin with—but that meant giving up people. . . .

She could go to the Automat, and for a nickel she could get a cup of coffee with as many refills as she could stomach, and cream and sugar too. That was something. And she could sit there as long as she wanted, and nobody would tell her to move along, no waitress would come by to present her with a bill and an expectant look. . . .

But there would be people eating stewed chicken and buttered rice there, with biscuits the size of baseballs, and macaroni au gratin, still as hot as an oven, tucked into square ceramic dishes and bubbling like a church organ, and gleaming rows of sandwiches on soft white bread just behind the glass. There would be ham steaks with glazed pineapple and maraschino cherries. There would be plates with nothing but three thick red slices of beefsteak tomato, with just a bit of salt and pepper shaken over them at the last possible moment, and fresh pickles. There would be steamed green peas with mint, and little brown pots of Boston baked beans, and cream soups, and roast beef with good Sunday gravy on it, and there might be scallops, too, or lobster Newburg—and crisp salad, almost ice cold, where the dressing was carefully kept at room temperature in its very own jug, so that the cool lettuce and the warm oil did not meet before you ate it—and lamb with mint jelly, and curried lamb with sautéed apples, and raisin compote, and deviled kidneys, maybe. And it was spring, so there might even be asparagus, just a few spears of it, and scarcely cooked, with a thin little slice of lemon draped over them—and young turnips dressed in butter and vinegar. There would be cold melon, and peach halves, and jugs of buttermilk, and huckleberry pie, and green-apple pie, and lemon meringue, and cherry, and coconut cake with apricot sauce—and she could sit there and watch the whole city walk past her, press a little token into the back wall, and pull all these wonderful things to eat right out of the building.

But the Automats were closing, hadn't Katherine said? So it had closed; it was already gone; there were no more marvelous lunches and dinners hidden in the walls; it was like any other building in the city now; you could pull apart every door and wall and ceiling and never find anything to eat inside it, except for maybe rats. So she could not even go watch other people eat, because in other restaurants, you had to order something first if you wanted to sit down and look at the people eating inside. And things were no good for her, and things were only going to get worse. There was nothing in the world better than walking into a restaurant with money in your pocket. Just a little money—not very much—but a regular and steady supply of just enough money—that was the passport to freedom and ease, and it made waiters look at you with welcome in their eyes, and it made pleasant neighbors out of strangers, and she could not get any more of it. She had extracted all the money from the world that she had known how to get, and she did not know how to get more. Her income had been fixed for years, but the world was not fixed—every year every thing cost more and more; there seemed to be no limit to how rich the world could get around her, while she sat at her little table with her nickel's worth of coffee, and watched prosperity rolling in and around—but never in her direction.

Where had all her money gone? Surely she had made enough throughout the long course of her working life to retire in comfort, but there was no evidence of that work as far as she could see. Her mind rebelled at the prospect of its all being gone. There must have been something to show for those fifty years, it must have gone *somewhere*—she had lived in New York, in a rented apartment instead of a home, and later in a residential hotel instead of her own apartment, because it had meant less she had to take care of, meant she could be independent, meant that she could be closer to people, to crowds, to *New York*—but now the people did not do her any good, and New York was as far away as the moon. What good was independence in your old age, if you did not have the money to back it up? You needed money to live in New York, and she did not have any; therefore, she did not live in New York after all, and it was as simple as that.

Her meals had been spare and carefully measured out since 1939, which was the last year she had received alimony; there was nothing else that could absorb this blow, nowhere else she knew to cut back to compensate for the loss of breakfast, and she immediately telephoned her sister in a panic.

Josephine's sister was named Inez, had been remarried after an early divorce for fifteen years to a man who taught high school mathematics, and lived in Philadelphia under conditions of slightly less shabby gentility than Josephine. She disliked panic, discussing money, and being asked to discuss a problem she could not solve.

Josephine considered her terribly cold, but this did not stop her from calling every time she worried, which was often.

Inez had listened to her for all of five minutes before saying, quite naturally, as if it were the most ordinary thing in the world to propose to her, "Don't you think it's time you moved to a home someplace? It's ridiculous, a woman of your age living in a big college dorm, and if they're not going to even bother to feed you, I can't imagine why you'd stay there. After all, it's not like you go out, and New York is so expensive. I'm sure you could find someplace quite cheap in—oh, anywhere, New Jersey or Massachusetts or anywhere."

Josephine had for once been so startled that it had the curious effect of temporarily curing her panic. She felt immediately and profoundly calm. "Well, now, there's something to that," she said. "Although there is my work, of course."

"What work?" Inez said, not unkindly. "You draw a few pictures a year and mail them to the three magazine editors who still remember you from the old days. You can use the mailbox in a nursing home just as much as you can in a hotel. And you know you couldn't live with me and Roscoe," she said, even though Josephine had not asked, "because there simply isn't room, and besides his son David likes to stay with us when he's in town, which it's looking like his work is going to do more and more, and I couldn't come between a father and his son, just for a sister."

"That's certainly an idea," Josephine said. "I'll think about that. Possibly you're right."

"Well, I don't mind saying that I think you're taking this mighty well, Josephine," Inez said. "It's nice to hear you're willing to be practical for once. I don't mean to say that I think it's the best place in the world to be, of course," and Josephine noticed that Inez did not again use the word "home" for the rest of their conversation, "or that it won't be an adjustment, but my goodness, some of these places have tennis courts and bingo and are full of interesting people, and it's certainly better than starving to death in some cheap old hotel with a lot of coeds and hippies stepping over you."

They spoke for another few minutes before Josephine could get off the phone and properly think about what had just happened. That her present situation was not a tenable one, she knew—but a *home*! For that to be the only door left open to her, and to hear it from Inez of all people, who possessed that singular talent for reminding her that the world was a cruel and hard place, which all eldest sisters seem to possess from birth.

She tried to think why this suggestion frightened her so. It was not just the prospect of institutionalization, for she had been living institutionally almost half of her adult life. But at least the Biedermeier was an institution with some claim toward being organized along lines of voluntary, common consent. Neither was it merely the natural, human aversion to hospital corridors and fluorescent lighting and rooms reeking of antiseptic.

It was the sense of being shut away from the rest of life, as if some judge on high had determined that no, she should never be called upon to hold a baby again, could never be needed to look after anyone's children for an afternoon (never mind that she had not done so in years, and was not particularly at ease with children, nor they with her) or help a friend pour tea or plan a party, would not have anything to do with any person younger than herself ever again. She would be entirely and irrevocably cut off from other people, even from simply *watching* the younger lives around her flourish and taking vicarious pleasure in their growth. She who had been young until just a minute ago was to be shut away with not only her oldness, but all the oldness in the world—

Not ten minutes after speaking with her sister, the iron entered Josephine Marbury's soul, and she resolved that from then on, she was going to steal. Not cadge, not borrow, not filch, but commit out-and-honest theft, and not just of goods or food, but cash.

Josephine, it must be admitted, made a marvelous thief, despite never having displayed either talent or inclination in that direction before her seventieth year. Her first attempt was not a success—few first attempts are—but it was merely a failure of nerve. She was not spotted, so she waited a while until hunger and panic honed her nerves to the sharpest possible edge, and she tried again, this time on a park bench where a woman about her own age was reading a magazine and enjoying the light green morning, with her open handbag resting casually beside her. Josephine fiddled with her shoes, removed and shook out her light jacket, lifting the wallet from out of the nearby handbag as she did so, pocketing three of the six dollar bills within, then returning the wallet under the jacket's cover, before rebuttoning it and walking off in quiet, panicked triumph. She walked immediately to a chophouse, waiting patiently outside until they opened at 11:30, and ordered a little entrecôte, cooked medium, and a baked potato almost the size of her own head, which came with its own separate plate, just for sour cream and chives.

She once again ventured out, this time glorying in the shabbiness of her clothes, the uncertainty in her address, the helplessness in her voice as she asked tourists and businessmen for directions, a helplessness that was now guided by a bright and animal cunning, a thrilling and wicked determination not to be displaced, not to be dragged away until she had been finally knocked out once and for all—and she stole. She stole from open coat pockets and unattended shopping bags. She stole from polite young women who asked her to watch their pocketbooks and purses while they ran to the ladies' room. She stole from bathroom attendants, from fountains in the park and in museums. Occasionally she stole from department stores, but she did not do this often; she preferred to do her thieving either outdoors or on a moving target like a bus or a subway car. She stole exclusively from her fellow whites, less out of any racial consciousness than from a sense that she would find it easier to read white faces for signs of suspicion. And she never once stole food.

For the most part no one ever suspected her. Those who did usually managed to talk themselves out of it, given her age and appearance, and on those few occasions when exposure caught her out red-handed, she either changed cars, if she was in transit, or simply walked away, and no one ever followed her. She stole no more than two or three times a week; she was not ambitious. Curiously, she never saw anyone else pickpocketing (for she did not try to call it anything other than what it was) when she went out looking for targets. She might have been the only pickpocket in the world; she might have invented theft itself.

Why steal money, rather than her breakfast? Had she been thinking more clearly after her conversation with Inez, Josephine might have rallied, or sought counsel from someone else in the hotel who could have offered a more sensible plan of action, or possibly appealed to someone for money. But she did not. The circle of her acquaintance had grown ruinously small over the last ten years, and she could not bring herself to call Inez again; the few editors who still looked at her drawings were mostly retired and hardly in a position to give her money if they had wanted to. Inez's casual suggestion had so profoundly unseated Josephine that her problem was no longer "What to do about breakfast" nor even "How am I going to get enough to eat?" but how to defend herself now that the whole world was set against her. That was how she saw things, and why she did not try to justify, even to herself, what she did. She did not limit her theft only to the very rich or the mean tempered—she stole from whomever she thought she could safely and swiftly get money from.

And she did not lie to herself, saying they probably would not miss it; on the contrary, she knew perfectly well how much they would. "That is *their* problem, not mine," she said to herself. "I am solving *my* problem. Let them solve theirs."

But to have started stealing Danishes or hot dogs at her age seemed ridiculous. Besides which, stealing could only postpone the inevitable day when the home became necessary; it could not forestall it. She stole money, in the end, because money was the thing she needed most.

Chapter Eleven

"CHILDE ROLAND TO THE DARK TOWER CAME"

K atherine, it must be admitted, had done nothing to improve her condition after that fatal haircut, and in fact had done a great deal to worsen it. In front of Ruth she had pretended not to mind it, going so far in the other direction that Ruth began to doubt the evidence of her own eyes: she had not at first thought she had done a very good job cutting hair, but Katherine was so sincere and so detailed in her appreciation that she ended up thinking she must have a knack for innovation. Over the next week, Katherine exhausted her own limited supply of hats and scarves, as well as some of Lucianne's, and did her best to forget what was underneath them until even Mrs. Mossler commented on the sudden change in headgear.

Finally, in a panic and entirely on a sudden whim of the moment, she ran into an unfamiliar hairdresser's one afternoon while she was walking down Thompson Street in the Village and asked the young man in the gray coat at the front desk for an appointment. That one was immediately available did not strike her as an auspicious sign. Neither was she cheered by the row of empty chairs or the extremely elderly shampooist who sat in the corner wearing house slippers, the smoke from her cigarette being the only indication that she had not already died and been posed there for effect. But whenever Katherine noticed misgivings or a sense of uneasiness in the middle of a transaction, it was, strangely enough, more likely to convince her to go through with it than otherwise. She could never imagine changing her mind once she started speaking to a clerk or a hairdresser—it would have felt rude, or somehow like going back on her word.

So she unwound the scarf from her head, hoping that the gesture would speak for itself, since she hardly knew what to ask the young man (who seemed to be both receptionist and stylist) to do about it. It was all she could do to demonstrate the problem. Identifying a solution was far beyond her powers.

To his credit, the young man neither laughed nor made a face. He simply looked at her seriously, walking in a half circle around her chair in order to take it all in. "I know I look like Joan of Arc," she said at last.

"It is a difficult hairstyle," he said cheerfully. "Even Ingrid Bergman had trouble with it."

Katherine must have looked blank, because he added, "When she played Joan in forty-eight. Of course she was terrible in it. It's better that you haven't seen it, because the only Joan of Arc, as far as I'm concerned, is Falconetti. What's harder to believe is that Ingrid played Joan again in fifty-four, this time with even worse hair and a face that was starting to show her age. Not that she didn't look good for her age, because of course she did, she's Ingrid Bergman, and she looks better now than I ever will, but nobody looks good playing nineteen when they're forty, especially not in a bright-red crew cut wig. But Joan of Arc doesn't work when you put her in a chipper little pageboy and a suit of armor and make some poor woman recite a lot of stiff speeches; they had the same problem with Mary Martin. That's why the Falconetti works and all the others are flops. Falconetti had a face, that's all, and it doesn't matter what your hair looks like if you have a face." He kept up a steady, comfortable stream of talk along these lines all throughout the haircut, which Katherine appreciated. He was funny and clearly knew a lot about the movies. He didn't try to explain to her what he was going to do, or ask her for her opinion or what she was trying to "go for" (Katherine never knew what she was going for with a haircut, and hated being asked because it meant coming up with an explanation that was almost certainly a lie right on the spot, and she hated having to fake expertise about her own appearance), and the one-sided conversation was actually rather restful. The old woman in the corner never moved, yet neither did she finish her cigarette. Whether she was chain-smoking or simply going through the first at an inhumanly slow pace, Katherine could never be sure.

When he had finished with Katherine's hair the young man seemed pleased, even chipper, and she wondered if what she had at first believed to be a sign of his remarkable equanimity indicated in fact a remarkable lack of taste. Again she stayed calm, and looked directly at the mirror with a steady gaze for five full seconds before turning away. Unbidden, the first few lines of "Childe Roland" came to her mind: "My first thought was, he lied in every word / That hoary cripple, with malicious eye / Askance to watch the working of his lie / On mine." But there was no sign on his face that she was being tested, and nothing hid behind the friendly look in his eye, so Katherine thanked and paid the young man, and walked squarely out

into the street. There was no point in making a scene. How someone who had seemed so sympathetic, who thought so carefully about
faces, whose own gray jacket had been beautifully draped in a manner that suggested a great soul lay beneath it, could have done this
to her head and then had the nerve to charge four dollars for it—but
perhaps he did have taste after all, and this was simply the best that
anyone could have done.

But it was a long walk home to the Biedermeier and the Village,
and like Childe Roland she saw the tattered banners and pennants
of fallen companions and wrecked nobility everywhere she looked.
He must have thought this was what she *wanted* to look like—which
could only mean she had looked to him like the sort of person who
wanted to look like the sort of person she now looked like!

Lucianne might have been able to make something out of a haircut
like this. She had an essentially feline quality that would have made
the crop chic, even feminine; Pauline would have simply looked
handsomer and more like herself than ever, as if a severe but loving
hand had cut away everything that was inessential to beauty. But if
Katherine had looked ridiculous before, she now looked frightening.
This time even Lucianne would not laugh when she saw her, because
Lucianne understood the importance of a person's looks, and Katherine's had been mangled.

Katherine was wrong about one thing, however. Lucianne did
laugh when she saw her, just as readily and as heartily as she had the
first time.

"This one isn't funny," Katherine said. "I *paid* for this one. It's
going to take six months, if not longer, to start looking like myself
again, and—Oh, Lucianne, I look like *Dolly*." She pulled the scarf
out of her purse and started wrapping it around her head once more.
"I don't mean anything against Dolly, either, you know that—"

"And I wouldn't care if you did," Lucianne said. "Who wants

to look like Dolly? I'm sure it's a free country and she's welcome to dress that way if it makes her happy, but my God, if any Village queer tried to give me her haircut, I'd knock him down, myself. Don't say I didn't warn you, but you should know better than to get an emergency haircut from someplace you've never been before."

"You've never said that," Katherine said reproachfully. "No one warned me about that. It was a salon that cut hair, and I needed my hair cut—I didn't know there were any further rules."

"Didn't I?" Lucianne said. "Well, I should have. Although really I thought it was the sort of thing everyone's mother tells her, or she's born knowing, or something, like how homing pigeons always know to fly upstream to spawn, or whatever it is they do. You can keep the scarf, if that would help," she added grandly.

It was only when Lucianne had said "everyone's mother" that Katherine realized the full extent of her distress. It was ridiculous to be so overwrought over a haircut, even a very bad one, and she had been somewhat puzzled by the force and urgency of her own reaction, until that moment. This was the sort of everyday problem you were supposed to be able to take to your own mother, because your own mother was bound to be interested in the boring, everyday details you wouldn't necessarily share with anyone else. She would have something practical and reassuring to say, but she still would feel the sting of disappointment with you, and your sense of being ridiculous would shrink to the size of a pin and disappear. *But I can't call mine*, Katherine thought wildly, *because we've lost our closeness*— and then just as quickly she thought, *But that isn't true at all. I simply haven't called. All I have to do is pick up the phone and speak to her—I know that perfectly well. So why do I want to think of the gulf between us as something fixed and impossible to cross?* For even now there was a hot pricking sensation behind her eyes, and she knew that in another minute she would begin to cry, and not the sort of crying that had to do with looking awful but the sort of crying that came from having nowhere to go. And in that moment the fear of calling and being rejected explicitly seemed so real to her that it felt as though it had already happened. *And she wouldn't know me if she saw me now,* Katherine thought; *the last time she saw me I didn't look like this, and your mother is supposed to know what you look like—*

Come, now! This was only a feeling, and feelings pass. She would find a meeting this evening, and say everything ridiculous she could think of, and everyone in the room would laugh with her, feeling as she had felt, and they would let it pass over them together.

"I'll take every scarf you've got," Katherine said. "And hat, and shower cap, and swimming cap, if you've got one, and Esther's spare hairnets, if she's got any." They sat quietly for another moment. Katherine felt poised right on the edge of regaining her self-possession and sliding back down into morbid reflection.

"You certainly do look terrible," Lucianne said then, and there was such a companionable, friendly sort of honesty in the way she said it that Katherine began to feel better immediately. So much better, in fact, that within a week she abandoned the scarf altogether.

———··———

In the meanwhile Lucianne had not wasted a single opportunity to catch Gia in the hallway. This was not difficult, since aside from the single column she had written for the *Herald-Tribune* about the National Horse Show, Lucianne had not worked since Christmas (unless you counted the weekly letters she wrote to her sister, which Lucianne included in her monthly letter home to her parents), and feeling she could honestly claim to have picked up several hours' worth of temp typing that week, she could easily adjust her schedule with an eye toward accidentally sharing an elevator in the mornings.

"You're Catholic, aren't you?" Lucianne had asked her straight out the first time they had gone down together. "Or something?" Gia eyed her coolly without answering, and Lucianne continued: "It's all right. I'm Catholic, as it happens, and Eye-talian too. I'm not trying to catch you out or anything; I just wanted to know."

"Maronite Catholic," Gia said, which meant absolutely nothing to Lucianne, who had not set foot inside a church aside from her friends' weddings since her confirmation. Besides which, a lot of her friends had gotten married from home, or at the courthouse, and one had even gotten married outdoors in Central Park. (Later that week Giuliana explained that the Maronites were one of several Eastern but not Orthodox churches with their own patriarchs that were still somehow nevertheless in full communion with the West, which sounded like the sort of getting things your own way that Lucianne naturally approved of.)

"I hear you're husband hunting," Lucianne said, and was a little taken aback by the force and suddenness of how this statement transformed Gia. She became radiant. Her face relaxed beautifully, her posture softened; where she had been clipped and resistant she was now beaming and open.

"So Stephen has told you," Gia cried happily. "I am glad. He seemed like such a talker."

Lucianne had in all honesty said it hoping to needle her—but this was even better, all the more so for being unexpected. "Are you in a hurry for anything? Can't you stop for a cup of coffee on your way out and tell me all about it?"

"It's only work," Gia said, further securing Lucianne's good opinion. "I can be late."

"Since you're a working girl, how about standing me the first cup?" Lucianne said, taking Gia by the arm and leading her out the door. "I'll pay you back with a disgustingly expensive wedding present. There's a little place the next block over that won't bother you even if you don't buy anything to eat."

Over coffee Gia elaborated on the version Stephen had already spread throughout the building: how her father had died when she was only six, how her mother had never remarried and hardly ever brought men around the house (besides Gia, there had been three boys and another girl), only going out on occasion with a few old and respectable friends of the family.

"Such as Douglas?" Lucianne asked.

"Such as Douglas," Gia said gravely, "plus a few others. But we didn't see him often. I remember once he hung around while Mother made dinner, but then he didn't stay for dinner with us. Mostly he would appear at the door, say hello, shake our hands, make a little small talk while Mother finished getting ready, and then they'd go out."

"And this mysterious man-at-the-door act—was that when you decided to marry him?"

Gia shook her head. Either she did not know when she was being teased, or she was willing to tolerate being teased but unwilling to enter into it. Lucianne could not be quite sure which was which without Stephen's help. "No. I didn't think about marriage much as a child. Just dancing and looking after my brothers and sister. But I had a feeling that my mother would have liked to marry him, only she didn't do it, and that interested me. My mother almost never lies, but I could always tell when she was hiding something."

"Oh, can you?" Lucianne said. "I can never tell when anyone's lying. It's funny, but I guess if I suspect anything, it's when people claim to always know when someone else is lying. No matter what, as soon as someone says that to me, right away I think, *But how could you possibly know you're right?* Not that I'm trying to argue with you," she added, "and I'm sure you were right in this instance."

Fortunately Gia did not take offense. She treated Lucianne's conversational detours very lightly indeed, so that Lucianne started to feel like they were talking in parallel tracks to one another, rather than together. "I *was* right," Gia said. "She loved him. She told me so herself last year. Douglas's wife was sick—he had moved here years ago, when they got married, and we hardly ever saw them except once at Christmas when they came through town on a road trip to California—and Mother and I came to New York to visit them. Really it was to pay our last respects to her, only no one wanted to say so. He picked us up at the airport in his car. *You* know what a woman is like when she's next to the man she's in love with, don't you?"

Lucianne was torn. On the one hand, she knew exactly what Gia meant, or thought she did; besides which, she thought of herself as a sophisticated person, with real emotional expertise and a knack for recognizing desire when she saw it. On the other hand, she felt a trifle corralled by the cozy certainty of the question, which always put her in a perverse mood. (And besides all this, her own spasmodic affections for Sidney, which seemed to descend on her like sudden lightning and then just as quickly vanish, made her wonder if she knew what a woman in love felt like to begin with.) Deciding she'd rather get the full story than argue the point, she said, "Oh yes, I know just what you mean."

"Everything she did told me she had lied," Gia continued. "The way she got into his car, the way she looked at him as he drove, the way she answered his questions; I knew she had loved him when I was a child, and that she had lied about his being just a friend. I knew that she loved him still, and I even knew that she hoped to marry him after his wife was dead."

"Your family must be an awfully determined bunch," Lucianne said. "Determined and perceptive. I can't tell hardly anything about my mother from the way she sits, except maybe if she wants a cigarette or to turn on the radio. I didn't even know about Stephen until he told me, and he's queerer than a three-dollar bill."

Gia politely ignored this. "I don't say that this is what made me love him. But it did interest me, very much, this man I knew almost nothing about, but who had often turned up on my doorstep when I was a child, who was now almost broken in half by sorrow. I think a very unhappy man is something very rare and very beautiful."

Lucianne did not share this view herself, but decided against further interruption. Youth and beauty and certainty were so charmingly united in Gia; it would be churlish of her to try to separate them. Either life would eventually prize them apart on its own, or else she would remain one of those enchanted few who never live to see their wills thwarted and die miraculously intact, like saints.

"We stayed with Douglas for three days, his wife dying in the next room. My mother cooked eggs and had their laundry sent out and I took their little dog Daisy on a walk through the park every morning and afternoon. He didn't do much, except go into his wife's room to look after her, and sometimes he would sit down at the breakfast table and smoke cigars. And I talked to him, sometimes, or listened to him talk to my mother, and I liked to hear him talk. And I thought there was nothing my mother could do for him that I could not do better. And I think, if I am honest, I was a little disgusted with her for loving him and letting him go when she might have had the chance. Then—but you know this part from Stephen—his wife died. So now I'm here."

"And do you think he feels the same way about you?"

Gia shrugged. "He doesn't. But he will." This was not an unreasonable degree of confidence, Lucianne thought. She was right; he would. Already she had been placed as a typist at a building near his by a temp agency Lucianne had used several times herself.

"So you've given up dancing?" Lucianne said.

"I've danced enough," Gia said. "You dance, and it's your whole life, with nothing left over for anything else. I want to do all the things I've been leaving over. I want to have a job—for a little while, anyway—and get married, and maybe go to college. I can dance at parties."

They lingered a few more minutes over their coffee, and Lucianne picked up a few more stray observations to share later with Stephen: Gia did not like Julie Andrews's voice ("It's perfect, obviously, but there's nothing to hold on to, nothing behind it but perfection. Listening to her makes me feel like a cat sliding down a wall"), she had no idea what her mother would say if she managed to pull off the heist of her ex-lover ("She'll either forgive me or she won't"), and her greatest ambition, outside of changing her last name to Burgess, was to someday stay in a cottage where the front door was cut in half, like in *Snow White* ("just to visit, not to stay. I want to live in New York City with the man I love and meet a lot of interesting people and die in a penthouse at the Plaza Hotel"). Then Gia stood abruptly and said, "It's getting late. I'll have to go now," as if there was a serious difference between getting to the office an hour and a half late instead of only an hour late, "but next time we get coffee you'll tell me all about yourself," and Lucianne went with her to the subway entrance before walking slowly back to the hotel.

————••————

When Stephen had told Lucianne about himself, it was shortly after they had gone to bed together, about six months after Stephen had first come to work at the Biedermeier. Lucianne had been on a particularly dispiriting date with an exceptionally flat man about eight years her senior who had next to nothing to say, despite her best efforts to draw him out, and come home a little drunk, exhausted, and restless, and Stephen had been hanging around in the lobby in his shirtsleeves, as he often did at the end of his shift. He had said something unusually soft to her—unusual because Stephen and Lucianne usually delighted in drawing barbs from one another, although this was almost always done without malice and in real fun—and she asked him upstairs, almost without thinking. And since Stephen was responsible for making sure men didn't go up to the residential floors after hours, he was extremely well situated to approve himself as an exception, and he granted the approval almost immediately. The sex had been fun and companionable between them: a little more like roughhousing than Lucianne would have guessed, but that was the sort of thing she needed just then, and Stephen was very good at guessing just what finishing touches a certain situation called for, which kind of music, which tone of voice, which sort of attitude would suit.

"You might as well know," Stephen said afterward, seeming slightly uncomfortable for the first time that evening, "that I'm predominantly homosexual."

"Then I'm afraid you've made a very embarrassing mistake," Lucianne said, "since I'm predominantly a woman," and he relaxed enough to smile again. On almost any other night, this might have bruised her ego, but as it was she felt extremely sophisticated and still relieved to have exchanged her dull and silent date for something affectionate and active. They might have just played a game of tennis together; she felt fond of him, like they belonged to the same very informal team. "And I've made a very embarrassing mistake, too," she added, "because we didn't use anything, and I ought to have said something."

"I know," said Stephen. "More fools, we."

"I'm not worried," Lucianne said. "Not that I sleep around more than the average, but when I do I tend to be careless, and I've never even had a scare so far, so I keep on being careless. And I probably will until someday I get scared enough."

"And maybe you never will get scared," Stephen said. "Some people don't."

Lucianne had shrugged. It was the sort of problem she knew got other people very excited, but somehow it simply never bothered her. "If we do it again, will you get something?"

"Sure," Stephen said, "but I don't think we will."

"All right," Lucianne agreed. "We won't do it again," and then they shook hands over it.

"The next time you come home from a bad date," Stephen said, "I'll take you out for ice cream."

"What's stopping you from taking me out for ice cream right now?" Lucianne said.

"I haven't got any money," Stephen said.

"I've got a little," Lucianne said. "It's on the dresser. Look, I'll go hunt for my shoes in the corner, and you take the money, and then you can ask me out for ice cream. I'm starved. I could barely eat a thing at dinner, I was so busy coming up with questions because he'd answer them so fast and then just stare at me, like a cat."

"Lucianne," Stephen said after a respectable interval had passed, "you're not going to believe it, but it turns out I've recently come into a little bit of money."

"This calls for a celebration," Lucianne said. "And you've hidden my shoes somewhere. Where in the world can they have got to? This room isn't big enough for anything to go missing in."

"This calls for ice cream," Stephen said. "We can both go barefoot, like Good King Wenceslas and his page, who I think was also called Stephen."

"I think it was the *Feast* of Stephen," Lucianne said, now entirely dressed except for her shoes, "but the page certainly isn't named Stephen."

"Well, *I* am," Stephen said grandly, and tried to pick her up. "Now mark my footsteps, my good page; Tread thou in them boldly." It was only after he dropped her that Lucianne could see her shoes under the dresser, and after a few more moments of hilarity and setting furniture to rights they got dressed and went out for ice cream.

They did not sleep together again, and nothing ever resulted from their carelessness that night except for a shared, childlike glee at having been slightly bad together, although Lucianne was occasionally careless again with other men. That was the night they really began to be friends, Lucianne thought, although by Stephen's reckoning they had been good friends right away.

In that year Stephen had still been a student at Cooper Union, at least by Cooper Union's count and not merely by his own. In 1961 he had been accepted into four colleges, all of them in New York City, and he had sent the same inquiry via registered mail to each of them: "Would you permit a homosexual student to register, if he were otherwise an outstanding candidate?"

For Stephen had concluded, at the age of seventeen, that his homosexuality was inveterate and unlikely to be outgrown, and his interest in women, sporadic at the very best of times, was unlikely ever to get sufficiently up off the ground such that he might expect a normal sex life. He had been more or less kindly expelled from the Boy Scouts, two junior high schools, and Model Congress for his precocious homosexual activity, but was rarely disliked for it, since he was reasonably clever and good at sports and liked talking to girls. (He had also been politely, if formally, invited not to hang around several local naval bases.) His temperament was cheerful, his manner frank; he had light eyes, sandy and slightly curling hair, and better-than-average good looks, and his experience with authority figures had taught him that authority wanted things to work out for him more than he wanted things to work out himself. He had a curious sense that he was likely to turn out something like a failure, and yet he was not bothered by it; on the contrary, it interested him. Like Pauline, he had been raised by his grandparents, who ran a bed-and-breakfast in Cape May, New Jersey; unlike Pauline, they had not exhibited a particular interest in molding his soul in service of a particular cause. They did not know what to do with a polite, normal-looking child who feared neither ostracism nor penury, and they parted from him after graduation with some very real regret that was nevertheless heavily outweighed by a sense of relief.

Two of the colleges had not replied, one had rescinded his acceptance, and three weeks later he received a phone call from someone at the Cooper Union student dean's office. Among the few questions he answered were one about what sort of treatment he had sought (almost none, aside from a pediatrician who had assured him he would grow out of it, so long as he got plenty of exercise and sleep) and another about whether he was willing to see a school psychiatrist twice a week for the duration of his freshman year (he was). He was also willing to take a single room, since he would not promise to keep the news to himself and the school administration was unwilling to put potential roommates in an impossible situation, and he promised not to try to seduce any of his fellow students.

This last promise he had been able to keep without any real difficulty, because New York City was simply alive with interested and willing alternatives. In fact, it had been almost entirely for this reason that he had decided he must go to college there—the other reason had been museums—and he was delighted to find that almost everywhere he looked, so long as he kept his wits about him and never lingered overlong in one place, a young man could get to know any kind of man he wanted, in almost no time at all.

Possibly this was another reason Stephen enjoyed his work at the Biedermeier so much. Aside from Lucianne, he had never slept with any of the residents; he may have found the change of pace restful.

By his sophomore year, Stephen found his engineering classes almost as tedious as his appointments with the psychiatrist, and avoided both roughly as often. He moved into a cheap apartment off school property, so he was less frequently on campus, and since some of his dates liked to give him money, which seriously augmented his income from the Biedermeier, this made everything about school seem less pressing, less real, and less important, even though in high school the thought of college in New York had seemed like the grandest possible fate he could imagine. He did not like to be reminded that he was in trouble, so the more he avoided his psychiatrist, the more he wanted to avoid his psychiatrist, such that by his fourth year manning the elevators at the Biedermeier he was still a student in name only. But the name was nonetheless important to him; he was not quite ready to give up the idea of school, and what it might yet turn into, under the right circumstances—although he could not have said what those circumstances might have been. He spent his days among women, and his evenings with men, and he counted himself very lucky indeed.

Chapter Twelve

A QUICK TRIP DOWNTOWN

Thursday made for a considerable change in routine at the Biedermeier that week, because that was the day Katherine was
arrested. Since she had not planned on being arrested, and
had never been arrested before, she could scarcely have made any
preparatory arrangements ahead of her absence; it was an entirely
unanticipated break in schedule. Her journey to the courthouse on
Kitty's behalf had been simple enough, if slightly daunting. Manhattan's Foley Square Courthouse was constructed upon colossal and
unrelenting lines, and seemed perpetually wreathed in twilight and
cut off from the sun; nine in the morning here felt like four in the
afternoon on a winter's day, with both light and warmth in rapidly
dwindling supply. Katherine had hurried inside the narrow office
tower that sprang out of the granite-pillared facade.

It was only on later reflection that Katherine wished she had
not taken Kitty so immediately at her word about not being in any

real trouble with the United States District Court for the Southern District of New York, aside from having failed to appear for a previous summons. The district court's opinion of the matter would materially and substantially differ from Kitty's—which Katherine only began to suspect after she gave her name, Kitty Milham, to the frowning little clerk in the reception hall.

"No aliases here," the clerk said. "What's it short for?"

"Oh, it's not an alias," Katherine said, a little flustered, "only a nickname. But everybody uses it—"

"No nicknames," the clerk said in the same tone. "I need your full name, as it's written on your birth certificate."

Damn Kitty! Who else would ask someone to temporarily use their name, without giving them the proper name to be used? Was it likelier to be short for Katherine, like herself, or for Kathleen? But she couldn't very well ask the clerk.

"Katherine Milham," she guessed at last. He frowned and looked down at a little bundle of paper in front of him, and did not answer her right away. "Can you see my name? I had a letter saying the date and time I was meant to appear"—this may have been true, but if Kitty ever had such a letter, she had not shown it to Katherine. Katherine hoped she had not guessed the wrong name, but all the same there would be something awful in having shared the same first name this whole time, especially since she had never before guessed the possibility existed—"but I'm afraid I lost it."

"Yes, your name is here all right, missie," the clerk said, at last looking up at her. Did he blench, slightly, when he took in her haircut, or was her imagination still a trifle oversensitive? "You're meant to be in room 113, and quick."

Katherine, now only half lying and bearing her own first name honestly, gratefully fled from the clerk's gaze and followed the signs down the densely carpeted hall into room 113, where she seated herself along the back row next to the door. The room was quite crowded, with an incredible assortment of characters seated in little groups; a few little old ladies with gigantic handbags, a number of fairly tough-looking middle-aged men, a mother and daughter who might have been sisters, a couple of newlyweds, and a few girls, each of them sitting by herself, who might have easily been either students or working girls—Katherine couldn't tell. Toward the front of the room sat a judge, situated high above everyone else, and surrounded by a constellation of bailiffs, reporters, a stenographer, sheriff's deputies, and clerks. These representatives of the law were separated from the general public by a low dividing wall, with a swinging saloon-style half door in the middle for those leaving the spectators' benches and approaching the bench itself.

Katherine leaned over to the middle-aged woman on her right, who was wearing a forest-green cape jacket suit and a dreamy expression, and whispered, "Excuse me, but do you know what we're supposed to do, now that we're here? . . . I mean, will they be calling our names, or anything?"

"Do you know, I haven't the faintest idea," the woman whispered back. "I had a summons with me, at one point or another, but I'm afraid I've lost it. I only just arrived a few minutes ago myself. It certainly doesn't seem like they're in a hurry, does it?" Katherine had to agree. "But we shouldn't keep whispering either. One of those little bailiffs yelled something fierce at that pair over there"—here she indicated the mother-daughter sisters—"for talking while the judge was trying to read something. And I *will* cry if anyone yells at me today."

Katherine, slightly amazed by the frankness of this admission, only nodded and withdrew back into her own seat, and wished she had thought to bring a book with her to pass the time. This was going to be her last favor, she decided fiercely, not just for Kitty but for anybody. Well—not her *last* favor—besides which, the third pillar of Alcoholics Anonymous was meant to be service—but the last favor she ran by herself for Kitty outside the building, anyhow. That much of a resolution she could keep.

The officers of the court seemingly had two modes only: aimless, unconcerned milling and highly intimidating regimentation. Without any warning they switched from one to the other, and the bailiff started barking out people's names from his little podium. A Richard Dorset was called first; he was charged with speeding in a school district, asked if he was willing to pay his fine (he was), whether he was prepared to pay it in full today (he was not, but was prepared to pay it in full by next Thursday), and subsequently dismissed. Next was Kay Buglino, who had run a red light, and Esther and Anna Schultz, who were operating an establishment in violation of the liquor licensing board. Esther and Anna assured the court that they had not, in fact, violated any of the rules outlined by the liquor licensing board, were asked if they had found representation, promised to do so, and were asked to return at a later date, at which point they sailed happily out into the hallway, twin visions of youth and honor. Then it was Katherine Milham's turn.

Katherine jumped up. "Hello, Your Honor," she said, a little taken aback. "I'll be right there." Her neighbor in the green winked ostentatiously.

"I should think so," the judge said, laughing a little as she made her way up to the podium. The walk there was dizzying. It was very much like coming to in the middle of a dream and being asked to deliver a speech, only of course Katherine knew she could not wake up and that speaking extemporaneously in court was frowned upon. (*Why* had she not pressed Kitty for more details?)

The judge did not laugh again. Instead he began to recite a series of absolutely astonishing and preposterous phrases, each one of which made Katherine feel sick: *criminal nuisance, disorderly conduct, loitering in the first degree, petty larceny, prior failure to appear*, and to which she could only stammer out in reply, "Oh, oh, oh no."

"You've got to let me finish," he said sternly, and kept going— she had disobeyed repeated summonses—had been seen to evade official representatives of the law attempting to bring this matter to her attention—

"Oh, *no*, Your Honor," Katherine exclaimed, almost without meaning to. She couldn't possibly tell them *now* that she wasn't Kitty Milham, because the only thing she could imagine that could be worse than this litany of offenses was adding a charge of impersonation under her own name, but what a hideous mistake all the same!

"You mustn't interrupt," the judge said, and then he explained that she was going to have to be arrested now, "so you can't enter a plea just now. You'll have to wait until after you're booked and can find a lawyer. Do you understand?"

"No, not in the least," Katherine said wretchedly, which did not seem to trouble the judge or anyone else in the courtroom, except for her old friend in the back row, who made a commiserating face of despair. She couldn't bring herself to say anything else, only stared dumbly at her shoes, and in another minute one of the deputies came over and led her out of the room through a side door she had not previously noticed. He chained her left arm to an iron ring in the middle of a black bench, and she apologized to him, more out of reflex than anything else.

"Wait here," he said, somewhat unnecessarily, and then he disappeared. Now Katherine could understand why the woman in green had said, "I *will* cry if anyone yells at me today." The idea that anyone would come and speak to her while she was chained to a bench was mortifying past the limits of belief; it was a humiliation unlike all previous encounters with humiliation, abjection beyond abjection.

I've been chained to a chair, she thought in amazement. *A man's just chained me to this chair, and anybody could see me like this—I've never been chained to anything in my life, and here I am—*

This was no good. This was the sort of morbid reflection that could only lead to panic and hysterics. It was a particularly alcoholic reaction: chain an alcoholic to anything and he will find a good reason he ought to have been chained up. *But I haven't done anything* competed in her mind against *I wouldn't be here for no reason. Even if I haven't done—whatever Kitty is supposed to have done—I've lied to a judge, and I've impersonated someone else in a court of law, and now I'm a criminal.*

The bench was at the end of what seemed to be a service hallway, although no one else that Katherine could see either came or went ever since her own bailiff had handcuffed her and walked away. She felt unbearably like a spectacle on display, even though there was no one there to see her. The fact that at any moment someone *might* walk past and see her, and worse, see her by herself, the only person in the hallway and the only person handcuffed to the bench, made it seem somehow worse than if she had been cuffed back in the courtroom, in full view of all the other defendants. At least some of them might have sympathized with her; anyone walking down this hallway was bound to work for the city and would therefore hold her in righteous horror and contempt. When would the door open next? Who would see her, and would they look away or stare?

An hour later, when a second bailiff came and released her from the bench, she could have cried with relief, and even though he was only leading her to the bus that would take her up to the women's prison in the Village, she thanked him, twice.

————··————

It had not been Kitty's intention that Katherine should be arrested in her place. In Kitty's way of looking at things, there was no need for anyone to have been arrested, since she had not committed half of the things she stood accused of, and the city was behaving entirely unreasonably. That she had missed three previous summonses was true; but was it her fault that the City of New York only scheduled court appearances during working hours? She worked from 8:00 a.m. to 5:30 p.m. at a downtown telephone exchange and only got a half hour for lunch, which was nowhere near enough time to get down to the courthouse and back, besides which the courthouse was also closed for lunch at the same time. Was she supposed to quit her job just because some beat cop couldn't do his properly? Was it her fault that teenaged kids sometimes hung around in bars after school and pestered every third patron for a drink, her fault if a bartender over-served someone else, her fault when some drunk broke something? (As the police had it, Kitty had been herself overserved at an Irish bar in Midtown on the evening of February sixth, had threatened the bartender when he asked her drinking companions for proof of age, and had overturned several nearby tables full of drinks in so doing. Where precisely the truth of that evening lay between Kitty's account and the beat cop's is difficult to say; neither was he strictly sober that evening.)

Kitty believed, more than almost anything else, in the power of positive thinking. She *knew* that Katherine would not be arrested if she went in her place, so of course news of the arrest came just as much as a shock to her as it did to everyone else in the building when Mrs. Mossler received a collect call from the Women's House of Detention that evening, just a few minutes after the dinner service.

"I—oh, my goodness—yes, I'll accept the charges—Hello, who's this? Oh, *Katherine*—"

"I'm awfully sorry, Mrs. Mossler," her surprisingly steady voice came over the line, "but as you know I haven't got very much time for this call. Would you mind getting Pauline for me, please?"

"Oh, *Pauline*," Mrs. Mossler said, overwhelmingly relieved that she was not going to be called upon to sort out whatever this was. "Yes, Pauline's a wonderful idea, for this sort of thing. I'll get her at once. Don't you go anywhere. You know, I was worried when I saw you missed dinner. We had corned beef and dumplings, which I wouldn't have thought would really go together. As it happens they didn't go together very well. Is everything all right? But of course it isn't. Yes, I'm going. Don't *you* go anywhere. I'll be right back with Pauline."

Pauline was precisely the sort of person one ought to call from jail, everyone else agreed; no one else would have had the faintest idea what to do in such a situation, even Dolly, Ruth, and Stephen, who had all been arrested before—although neither Dolly, Ruth, nor Stephen mentioned anything about that (and Ruth's arrests had been sealed on her coming of age, so nobody but herself knew about them). Pauline listened carefully (surprisingly carefully, considering that at least six other people were squeezed into Mrs. Mossler's office watching her talk on the phone) as Katherine did her best to discreetly summarize the morning's events without betraying her real name to anyone who might have been listening on *her* end.

"I see what you mean," Pauline said after a minute. "I think you'd better stay just as you are for the present, and I'll send somebody down with the money as soon as I can get it. How much did they set your bail at? Oh, that's nothing. All right, just sit tight and be a good girl." Then she hung up the phone and whistled a little, before turning round to face her audience.

"The thing is," she said, "is you'll all get your money back once Kitty gets sentenced. But I'm going to need as much as you can spare."

Together Pauline and Mrs. Mossler were able to shake down the residents in the building for a collective forty-seven dollars, which was itself something of a miracle. A few gave because they were convinced of Katherine's innocence, whatever the charge could have been, while a few gave because they were impressed that Katherine might have done anything that could have gotten her arrested in the first place. Lucianne was among that second party. Kitty kept careful notes of who gave what, mostly because Pauline had threatened her, but also out of a sincere desire to atone. From her grandparents Pauline was able to secure twenty dollars, who were thrilled to hear someone she knew was in jail, although she lost fifty cents in sending Stephen out to collect it. The rest she managed to secure from a bail fund some friends of hers managed, by heavily implying that the arrest had been politically motivated and that, once released, Katherine would prove an invaluable asset to the movement. The rapidity with which she had been able to secure a significant sum of money surprised and pleased even Pauline. She had seen colleagues and comrades and relatives arrested often enough, but she had never herself been anyone's first call from jail, had never single-handedly organized someone's release, and felt a great swell of optimism and excitement for all the arrests she hoped lay in her future. She knew how to drum up support, when to inspire, when to cajole, and how to get money where money was scarce. She knew how to get things; she would continue to get them for the people who needed them most.

Kitty, who knew herself to be in utter disgrace, kept close to Pauline and Mrs. Mossler throughout the evening, since as long as she had errands to run or notes to keep on their behalf, she could not be lectured by anybody, and she wanted more than anything else to avoid being lectured. To have crashed so abruptly out of the pleasant fiction that had sustained her in the three months since her own arrest was painful enough; she had no desire to let anyone else add to it by asking her what she had been thinking, when her primary resentment about the entire situation was being forced to think about it at all.

When something happened to Kitty that she did not like (and she usually counted the things she did herself as things that happened to her), she would shudder briefly, think, *That didn't really happen*, and then forget it. Quite often this worked, too. Today she thought to herself, *This will only have to be true for a little while longer, just a little while longer, and then it won't be true again anymore*, and in this way she was able to bear it, an hour at a time.

Gia gave them five dollars and then closed her door. She found the entire escapade distasteful, and did not think about it again.

Lucianne enjoyed herself immensely, and stayed as close to the action as she possibly could without ever being forced into usefulness. Stephen was as usual a sport, and Josephine surprised everybody with a loan of twenty dollars. She really did like Katherine, and she felt a private thrill not only for having been in a position to offer spontaneous generosity but also for having stolen so often herself without ever once getting caught. Dolly gave a dollar-fifty and offered to take the bail over herself, "since I'm in the neighborhood so often and know quite a lot of the girls there." This was more or less true; Dolly worked at a bar in the Village near the detention house, and while she was not quite as well known to all the inmates as she might have wanted others to think, it *was* true that Katherine was not the first associate of hers to be locked up.

"Dolly," Pauline said, "you've seen Katherine's haircut, and I know you've seen yourself in at least one mirror. Do you think they're likelier to release her into your care, or pick you up for disorderly conduct?"

Dolly, who it must be admitted was wearing corduroy coveralls and whose hair was held in place with Murray's Superior, laughed and conceded the point. "I'll just keep an eye out in case they pick her up again," she said cheerfully. "Especially if she keeps the haircut."

Ruth was—perhaps surprisingly, given how miserable she had become when she feared she had inconvenienced Katherine with a bad haircut—remarkably unconcerned about the whole affair. She had no money to offer the collection team, but she said, "I'm sure it'll all work out," and calmly closed her door to them. Where Kitty could only pretend to fend off the intrusions of the rest of the world, Ruth could really do it. The law was not real to her; it had no power to either hurt or frighten her in the way that people could. Katherine, whose greatest fear was shame and humiliation, found the experience of being in jail even for a very short time and under the mildest of treatment almost entirely annihilating; Ruth considered jail a place very much like any other, where someone might occasionally be obligated to go, such as the library or a train station. Later that evening, Ruth poked her head into Mrs. Mossler's room and asked, perfectly casually, if the Biedermeier would take her on as a temporary day maid, "since I haven't been able to find a job here yet."

"You told me you worked at a beauty salon when I gave you the room," Mrs. Mossler said in amazement.

"Yes, I did," Ruth said, still casual, "but that didn't work out."

"Yes, you did *tell* me, or yes, you did have the job?" Mrs. Mossler asked. "And we hardly need maids now, when we can barely keep enough tenants living in. Most of the girls keep their own rooms clean, and do their laundry together—and wouldn't it be strange, I mean, living and cleaning in the same place? It's so old-fashioned, I mean. I really do think you'd be better off just getting a job at another salon."

"But I'm absolutely hopeless with hair," Ruth said. "I don't think anyplace else is likely to hire me. And in the meantime, if I'm looking for a job, I won't be able to bring home any money until I get one, and I don't think I'm likely to get one. But I'm already here, and I overheard Stephen telling Carol that the last maid just gave notice on account of her daughter has a baby and she's going to help her raise it, so I know you're short."

"You should talk to Katherine about it," Mrs. Mossler said, although she wasn't sure why—Katherine had never been in charge of either of the maids, when they still had two, and it wasn't as if Mrs. Mossler was in the habit of deferring to her on hotel matters. But there was something very upsetting about the quiet and determined way Ruth argued for the job, something that Mrs. Mossler was too tired and too upset to resist but unwilling to give in to, either. "Go away now, and I'll talk to Katherine about it after she gets back. Not right away, of course, but—I'll talk to her later, and we'll let you know."

"In the meantime I'll start making myself useful," Ruth said, "just in case. And you'll see how good a cleaner I can be."

"You can make yourself useful by closing the door behind you," Mrs. Mossler said. Later she chided herself for being so rude to someone who was obviously in need of care and direction. It was not like her, this antipathy, but it had to be admitted: she did not like Ruth, did not like the sight of that blond, inquisitive head thrust around the corner of her door, and for this reason felt all the more obligation to give her the job: *Most girls don't even want to live here anymore,* she thought angrily to herself, *and here's this one who wants to live and work, if she can, and nobody else is going to cut her a break, if you don't.*

Katherine's afternoon in jail *was* mild, all things being considered equal. She was less than two miles away from home. No one whistled at her or called her names; the medical examination was cursory, brief, and conducted more or less respectfully. It was still early enough in spring that the weather was moderate, so that the building was not overheated, and the holding cells were not too crowded;

she had room enough to stretch her legs and even to lie down, if she wanted to. Nonetheless she had to often wrap her hands around her knees and slowly press her fingernails into the backs of her legs to keep from crying in front of everyone, and she had been distractedly reprimanded by a booking officer for repeatedly apologizing while he signed her in. "I'm sorry," she said before she could think better of it.

"Let that be the last time I hear you say that today," he said. "It gives me the creeps." Katherine had been tempted in that moment to thank him, and felt real disgust with herself for the impulse. There was something humiliating in knowing that she looked like someone who had never been arrested before—which was particularly strange, given how humiliating she had already found the experience of being arrested to begin with. She wanted both to look as if she had done this a dozen times before, and knew exactly what she was doing, and to be immediately recognizable as someone who *could* not be arrested, had no business here, and never could have.

After the first half hour, one of the other women in the cell had asked Katherine if she played bridge; she said she didn't, and the woman did not try to speak to her again. Later it transpired that a few of the others could play canasta, but since nobody had any cards, they could only describe games they had played in the past to the best of their memories, which did not last especially long. After a few more hours, she was led down the hallway and permitted to make a phone call. Then she was directed back to the cell.

It was Tobias, in the end, who came to pick her up sometime shortly before midnight; he was dressed much less shabbily than when she had first met him, and he had his hair pushed back and out of his eyes, as a concession to the law. He wore a serious expression and carried a little envelope with two hundred dollars in it, which he signed over to the jailhouse clerk and then carefully pocketed the receipt. The sight of him made Katherine burst into tears at last.

"Hey," he said, terribly uncomfortable, "hey now, none of that. Anyone would think you'd never been in jail before." She tried to smile and only ended up crying the harder. He reached out and twisted a lock of her remaining hair over her forehead. "Did they do that to your hair in there? Jesus, that ought to be illegal, pretty girl like you. Well, I'll always remember you the way you were, and not like this, if it's any consolation."

This last remark finally took her out of herself long enough to interrupt what had been threatening to become a crying jag. "Don't you know you're never supposed to mention a woman's hair or her shoes when you're bailing her out?"

"My family could never afford the second volume of Emily Post," he said solemnly. "We had to content ourselves with the first half of the book, and guess all the etiquette that came after *O*. To this day I know exactly how to behave correctly at the opera, but if anyone were to invite me to the Philharmonic, there's no telling what I might do."

"Murder and mayhem," she said, which was not especially funny or original, but it was nice, nonetheless, to talk nonsense with a friendly face.

"For a start, and at the very least," he said. "But don't you think I am more to be pitied than censured, never having been taught the right conduct for letters *P* through *Z*?"

"You certainly were cruelly deprived as a child," she said. "But what's stopping you from reading the rest of it now?"

He considered this. "It would be like putting on airs," he said finally. "I never want to learn more than what my poor old mother knows. If she had to stop at *O*—well then, *O*'s good enough for me. I'm hungry. Are you hungry? I'm sure you've had enough pheasant and caviar to last you a lifetime. How about a hot dog?"

"I could eat," Katherine said. "But could we please get out of this neighborhood first? It's not like I think anyone would bother to follow me or anything. Only I'd be embarrassed if anyone noticed us walking from the jail to—"

"Say no more," Tobias said. "I always prefer to eat incognito, too. Let's beat it. And I don't like the looks of this joint," he said, suddenly raising his voice to an extraordinary volume. "They look like they've got rats in there. And I don't like the looks of those customers, either. A bunch of fat-faced businessmen with crumbs on their ties. They all ought to be drowned, and that right soon, for the beautification of the city. I wash my hands of you people!"

"It was the only thing I could think of to cheer her up," he said to Pauline later. "She looked so haunted, like she'd just spent six months doing hard labor, but in my experience you can make anybody laugh by suddenly abusing a bunch of perfectly nice-looking strangers who are minding their own business." And it had worked, too; after they left the Village, Katherine felt much better, and ate three hot dogs in a row, all while standing up. She felt even better, later that evening, after Tobias had dropped her off in the lobby, when she went straight to Kitty's room, opened the door without knocking, and slapped her in the face.

"I'm sorry for that," Katherine said right away, relieved to be able to apologize again without surveillance or recrimination. "I had to do it, but I am sorry, and it was wrong of me, too."

Chapter Thirteen

A MIDNIGHT VISITOR

Arthur, Katherine's sponsor in AA, said that it did not count, apologizing to Kitty just after hitting her. She had called him straightaway the next morning after she woke up with what felt like a hangover and briefly panicked that she'd gotten drunk the night before and somehow forgotten about it before waking up. He laughed more often than she would have liked during the telling of the story, but worse than that, he told her she had to do more to make things right with Kitty.

"If you knew it was wrong right away—fast enough to apologize to her the next minute," he said, "then you knew it was wrong when you did it."

"Yes," Katherine said, knowing full well he was right, but still hoping to delay the inevitable conclusion, "I suppose I did. But I think that day would have tested anybody's patience. And she *did* say she didn't blame me for it. I don't think there's a person in the building who would."

"Well, now," Arthur said. "That may be. But I don't believe any of the people in your building are God. And it's a little funny, to start taking Kitty as an example of reasonable behavior, when just last night you were angry enough at her *un*reasonableness to hit her." The irony of this set him off laughing again.

"It's difficult to take your scolding seriously when you're laughing throughout," Katherine said.

"'We are not a glum lot,' as the saying goes. And it isn't scolding," Arthur said, but he collected himself nonetheless. "I'm not your father or your employer. I can't send you to your room, or make you do anything you don't want to. But what I want to know is why you didn't think to go to a meeting, or give me a call, before you decided to loan a dollar to a person who has already borrowed two, or to go down to the courthouse and give a false name to a *judge*"—here he started to laugh again—"and then act surprised when it gets you into trouble. Did you think you were behaving reasonably?"

Katherine started to laugh too. "When you put it like that, it doesn't sound very smart, does it?"

This set Arthur roaring. "Do you mean—you thought it sounded—like a good idea—when it was just inside your own head?"

"Not *exactly* good," Katherine said. "I guess I thought of it sort of like holding somebody's place in line."

"They don't arrest people for that, dear heart," Arthur said. "Do you think it might be possible that you avoided learning too much about just *what* you were being asked to do because you knew it was wrong to begin with? And that just possibly what *you* were searching for was a genuine reason to be really, truly, thoroughly and completely, at last angry with Kitty, so angry that you'd never feel any pressure to do her a favor ever again?"

This possibility startled Katherine so much that she did not answer.

"I'm taking your silence as an opportunity to read to you a little. You remember step three, don't you? I know you've been avoiding meetings and generally behaving like a maniac, but surely even you can still remember we have something in the neighborhood of twelve steps that guide our conduct: *How persistently we claim the right to decide all by ourselves just what we shall think and just how we shall act. Oh yes, we'll weigh the pros and cons of every problem. We'll listen politely to those who would advise us, but all the decisions are to be ours alone. Nobody is going to meddle with our personal independence in such matters. Besides, we think, there is no one we can surely trust. We are certain that our intelligence, backed by willpower, can rightly control our inner lives and guarantee us success in the world we live in. This brave philosophy, wherein each man plays God, sounds good in the speaking, but it still has to meet the acid test: how well does it actually work? One good look in the mirror ought to be answer enough for any alcoholic.*"

Katherine experienced the sudden cataract of internal relief that always follows the abandonment of a protective lie. "I must have wanted to hit her first—so I looked for sufficient justification, so when I did do it, I felt safe, like nobody would blame me, even at the expense of doing something monumentally stupid, like trying to play a trick on a district judge."

"Attaboy," Arthur said. "Drop the 'must have,' and you've got it. Well, that's it for *Truth or Consequences.* Why don't you come on up for a meeting today? Maybe you'll win a prize for this story; it's a doozy."

"All right," Katherine said. "You win."

"Listen, you're free to suffer as much as you like," Arthur said blandly. "Don't let *me* stop you, sister. I just think it's easier to live sober when you do right by others and don't lie to yourself. But this new method of lying in court and smacking your roommates around might have something to it. What do I know?"

"I resign, I quit, I abdicate," Katherine said. "I've run the show enough for one week. I know when I've had enough. I'm coming uptown and I don't care how much dignity it costs me to make things right with Kitty again. One day of prison and mob violence is enough for me."

———••———

By the end of that week Ruth had gotten her own way again, at least when it came to Mrs. Mossler. So far her tenure in New York had been characterized by the most intermittent and arbitrary displays of determination. In most everyday matters she was meek to the point of self-effacement, but every so often she displayed a truly ferocious ambition toward those people in particular she wanted to serve. She had not made a success of things by anyone's reckoning—but she *had* gotten her own way on the occasions that were really important to her. It may have been possible that Ruth was every bit as tenacious and ambitious as Gia, only her ambition was too thinly spread, too diffused, to have any recognizable effect on the world. There was no identifiable or unifying target for her ambition, only desperation that caused her to periodically thrash in the direction of the nearest safe cover.

Gia had, within a week of her arrival at the Biedermeier, secured a job as an editorial assistant at a publishing house on the same block as Viking. By the end of the second week she had left a message with Douglas Burgess's secretary, who was not at all sure whether it was a social or professional call: on the one hand, Gia had called him "Mr. Burgess" rather than by his Christian name, but on the other hand, she had not left her own number so he could properly return the call, but actually instructed her to *inform* Mr. Burgess that Gia would be getting a drink that evening at Raphael's at 5:30 if he wished to join her. Gia had successfully parlayed drinks into a late dinner, and spent her third weekend in his apartment. It had been perfectly friendly and perfectly chaste. He had ordered for her a lamb chop and for himself only soup—he was not eating much these days. He was delighted to see her, was sorry that she was giving up dance but not at all sorry to hear she was interested in editorial work, would be more than happy to make introductions for her, not that she needed them, was bearing up as well as could be expected under the circumstances, he supposed, and was relieved at least that Audrey was no longer suffering, that was the important thing, and would have loved to bring her up for a nightcap but the place was a wreck—

She would not mind in the least, she told him, for her mother had never been much of a housekeeper so there was hardly anything that she had not seen—a gin rickey, thank you—it's not so bad in here really, she went on, but you haven't even got clean coffee cups for in the morning, you can't possibly have a good day tomorrow if you wake up to a sink full of dirty dishes, everybody knows that—she *really* didn't mind, she didn't even have a sink to put cups in at that funny little hotel, so this was, if anything, a treat, and hadn't he better clear out of the kitchen and finish making those drinks, if he really wanted to be useful?

Douglas made up a bed for her in the guest room, which was just what she had hoped he would do. To invite her into his bed straight off would have been all wrong, would have spoiled the triumph of the eventual accomplishment. The full sweep of his grief was required in order for there to be room sufficient for her purposefulness, her vigor, her intenseness. He was still young enough to be desirable, but old enough to have been crushed by life, to require her in a way no young man could, and Gia wanted, more than she wanted to be admired or appreciated or even adored, to be absolutely, vitally necessary to the man that she loved. Whether she loved him now, or whether she had merely decided that he ought to be the man she would love, and was willing to let the love arrive later, was very nearly beside the point. He was the man of her choosing, and she was proud of having arrived at her decision. This made him interesting, heroic, and worthwhile to her. The fact that he did not want her, that he did not at present want anyone—perhaps it is more strictly correct to say that he did not want to be alone, but neither did he want another woman—only made him more valuable. Good-looking, sophisticated men with exciting jobs who did not want women were rare, and therefore to be prized. That he had loved his wife (Gia already thought of her, not without respect, as his first wife) spoke in his favor; that his not wanting another woman was temporary meant she would have to work fast. And it was more thrilling, somehow, to prove yourself a worthy successor to a dead and beloved woman, than merely to snag some man's affections at random. To inherit a position of such esteem (in Gia's case, to inherit *two* positions, first that of his dead wife and second that of her mother's old place as one of his lovers)—especially when the last woman who had held it had been unfairly struck down almost in the prime of life—would be like winning a race, or winning a war; Gia could hardly understand why any woman would marry someone her own age, some fellow sapling with whom she would be forced to share the privileges of youth, rather than bear the palm alone, and be borne aloft in her turn on a pair of seasoned shoulders. A man who had first made himself strong, then been weakened enough by life to need her—that was the only sort of man worth having.

Besides, this way she could insist on sleeping in his bed a little later on, and he could protest long enough to not feel guilty about it afterward. He was beautiful, catastrophically sad, and was going gray not just at the temples but all across the front, in a perfectly unbroken line, but everywhere else his hair was still dark as ink.

Douglas had been a little concerned when she stayed over the second night. This was another good sign; it meant he was thinking about how things would look to other people, which meant he was feeling a little guilty, which meant he already liked her more than he had intended to. Hadn't she stayed in his apartment before? Yes, but then her mother had been with her. Surely if she had visited him before with her *mother*, she ought to be seen in the light of an old family friend, who did not need to stand on ceremony, and besides which, now that the kitchen was back in working order, somebody ought to cook in it. He wasn't hungry; that was entirely beside the point. Men looked terrible when they got too thin, particularly handsome men, and handsome men owed it to the world to stay in good animal health, and moreover he was sure to be hungry once he tried her cooking. He gave in. She did not overwhelm his appetite with some big slab of meat that would have caught in his throat, but presented him with a series of deceptively light and fragrant tidbits, that felt like he was eating mostly steam and air, and so in the very old manner of things the man was deceived, and he ate.

He was hideously glad to be giving in to someone, especially to someone young and beautiful and generous. After all, he had been very unhappy for a very long time, and suspected almost nothing. And Gia could afford to be generous; she already had everything, and expected to have even more, very soon.

Whereas Ruth could only be said to have scored two victories to her name in roughly the same period: one had been against Katherine's hair, and the other had been against Mrs. Mossler's better judgment, neither of which made for especially impressive opposition.

Mrs. Mossler had not realized that it was possible for anyone to be so bad at cleaning as Ruth was. She had known (and had occasion to fire) plenty of indifferent maids in her career, of course, but their besetting sins had all run along the same familiar lines: they were late to work, or failed to turn up at all, they worked too slowly, they ignored ashtrays and put out their cigarettes on the carpet, they tied up the phones while they were supposed to be making up the beds, they took naps in the laundry room. And of course Mrs. Mossler did some of these things herself from time to time. But Ruth managed to be earnest and hardworking in her near-total ineffectiveness. Several girls stopped by Mrs. Mossler's office to complain that they had come back from the bathroom to find Ruth halfway underneath their beds with a feather duster, completely unannounced, or turning over their wastebaskets in the middle of the floor and picking over the contents like a seagull before taking it to the incinerator. Lucianne found a tiny bite taken out of the corner of three of her lipsticks. "It looked like a doll, or an especially fastidious rat, had been at it. Gave me the creeps. I would have thrown them all away, only I can't afford to, so I just took a piece of dental floss and decapitated them, so now three of my best lipsticks have little flattop haircuts, like the marines."

Patricia even swore up and down that Ruth had stripped the shed strands of hair right out of her hairbrush: "It's a *nude* hairbrush now. It doesn't even look decent. I liked that hair right where it was. I might have wanted to use that hair for something." Had anyone else in the building said that, they would sound petty minded, but with Patricia it really might have been true. If it was possible to use human detritus in a way she could call artistic and others called unsettling, she wanted to do it. "Anyhow, she had no business epilating it."

To which Ruth's reply had been, quite reasonably, "I'm terribly sorry to have cleaned Ms. De Boer's hairbrush. I won't do it again," which made both Patricia and Mrs. Mossler feel a little sick to their stomachs.

But the strangest incident that transpired during Ruth's turn as a housekeeper never even made it to Mrs. Mossler's ears. It was a little more difficult to sneak dates into the eleventh floor than elsewhere, partly because most of that floor's rooms were double- or even triple-occupancy suites and partly because the longer the ride on the elevator, the greater the chances of being interrupted on the intermediary floors, so Carol did not do it often. But Patricia had been kept late at work every night for a week (they were installing radios on the entire fleet of subway trains that month, although why this would have affected the work of a transit authority secretary, Carol neither knew nor cared) and Sadie was visiting friends in New Jersey, and Carol had now been on enough dates with a graduate student named Bryan Kettler that saying good night at the door was beginning to feel like a cruel joke. She had bundled him up through the service elevator, which had slightly disappointed Bryan, who had been hoping for something a little more along the lines of *The Prisoner of Zenda*.

"Can't you take me up the service elevator for the first part, and then I could scale the fire escape for the last few floors?" he asked while she outlined her plan for getting him upstairs over coffee at the diner around the corner. "I'd feel a little stupid being dragged in like Cleopatra, rolled up in a rug. And wouldn't you have a better time, watching me alight on the window then hauling me in like a piece of luggage? I could strike a heroic attitude on the window. I strike a very nice heroic attitude when the situation calls for it. You don't know that about me yet, because the situation has never called for it."

"No, you couldn't come up the fire escape," Carol said after a moment's consideration. "In the winter that's the fridge, and in the summer that's where Patricia hangs all her clean paintbrushes and dress mannequins, so there's no clear passage to the window."

"Hey, wait a minute," Bryan said, in half-comic and half-real alarm. "What does that mean if there's a fire? Suppose the night I finally surrender my virtue to you is the same night somebody else falls asleep playing with matches, and I'm burned alive because the fire escape is being used as an art supply storage facility?"

"If there *was* a fire," Carol said, "you could just kick the mannequins and things out of your way, because they wouldn't matter. But as long as there isn't a fire, those mannequins and things are pretty important to Patricia, and I wouldn't like to be you if she found out you had moved them."

"Kick them out of the way?" Bryan said. "So the building's on fire and now all the concerned citizens watching on the street below are going to get brained by falling debris? I have half a mind to call the fire department on you girls," and here he looked at his watch before settling his arm around her, "in something like sixteen or twenty-four hours."

"But in the meantime, the service elevator," Carol said.

"In the meantime," Bryan said easily, "the service elevator. But if anyone asks, you tell them I scaled the walls from the ground floor with a dagger in my teeth. And one of those black eye patches like the Lone Ranger wears. And I fought off ten or twenty guys before I alighted on your window. No," he interrupted himself, "*hoisted* myself over your window. I think alighting makes me look too much like Peter Pan. Hoisting is what Ronald Colman would do. There, it's decided."

This version of events having been resoundingly approved on both sides, they sprang into action. Once in the Biedermeier lobby, Bryan tried to make himself inconspicuous behind one of the pillars, which hardly mattered, since there was no one else in the lobby, not even Stephen.

"It's the principle of the thing," he stage-whispered at Carol when she motioned for him to join her at the loading bay in front of the service elevator. Then, when she motioned again, this time more insistently, he tried somersaulting over to her, which quickly turned into a sort of exaggerated bear crawl once he realized he no longer knew how to do a somersault.

"Don't hold that against me," he said, still crouched in readiness for a surprise attack even when they were alone in the elevator. Carol only grinned and waited until they reached the eleventh floor before somersaulting six times in succession, standing up triumphantly, if a little dizzily, at her own front door.

It was so lovely, Carol fell asleep wondering why she didn't always have her own room. Their first time having sex had been slightly frenetic, which was not at all unwelcome, and was followed by a midnight feast on the floor, with crackers and olives and coupe glasses of sherry and the contents of a little white paper bag that Bryan had unexpectedly pulled from his jacket pocket—it was full of wine gums, the kind that wrapped around your teeth and made your cheeks hurt, but were delicious just the same—and the second time had been wonderfully lazy, and they finally fell asleep almost at the same time, right in the middle of a nonsensical, meandering conversation about ships.

Several hours later she was suddenly jostled awake by a hand on her shoulder and Bryan's pale face hovering closely over hers. "Either you've got another roommate you forgot to tell me about," he whispered, "or there's a ghost, or you put something in that sherry, because *there's someone standing in the corner and looking at us.*"

Carol bolted upright and very nearly screamed before thinking better of it. Bryan switched on the light—and there was Ruth, looking not at all out of place, blinking as mildly at them as if they'd just bumped into one another at the post office. "Hello," she said. She was stripping the sheets from Patricia's bed and stowing them into a little linen satchel by the corner. She was wearing pajamas and her hair was tucked messily under a knit cap. Her lips moved a little even when she wasn't talking. "Don't mind me. I'm just getting an early start on the laundry."

"Jesus *Christ*," Bryan said. He dove under the covers and shot out a hand to fish around on the floor for his trousers.

"Ruth," Carol said as loudly as she dared, "how on earth did you get into this room?"

"I used a key," Ruth said. "If your friend is looking for his things, they're on the desk over there. But don't get dressed on my account. I don't mind."

Bryan's clothes had been folded into a neat little pile on the desk, with his socks and glasses arranged on top and his wallet just to one side.

"Jesus Christ," he said again. "Carol, I wish you'd warned me about this."

Carol looked meaningfully at him, then tried again with Ruth: "Ruth, I never gave you a key to this room, and I don't want you in here. It's not decent. You've got to get out."

"That's all right with me," Ruth said. "I'm mostly finished anyways. Your crackers and things—"

"Ruth," Carol said, "get the hell out of here."

"—are on the vanity table," Ruth continued. "It was awfully nice to meet you, Bryan. I hope I'll see you around again," and then she threw the little satchel over her shoulder, opened the door noiselessly, and disappeared out into the hall.

"Bryan!" Carol exclaimed after a moment's silence. "You think I wouldn't have *warned* you about her if I'd known she was going to—"

Bryan started laughing, silently and helplessly, until the bed shook. "Of course not. Of course not. I'm sorry. I know you can't have known she would have—only I had just woken up from a dead sleep to find the Flying Dutchman stripping the sheets from the other bed—I don't think I've ever been more frightened of a smaller woman in all my life. She can't be a hundred pounds soaking wet and here I was, afraid she was going to kill me—"

Carol laughed too; it was too difficult not to join Bryan in whatever he was doing, because he made whatever he was doing seem like such fun. And once she was out of the room, Ruth seemed once again harmless, absurd, and pitiable. But there was an insistence to that easy calm that had been disorienting, even frightening—so the next day, after Bryan had left (during normal visiting hours, and by the regular elevator, although with such an enormously pleased and rumpled look on his face that it left no doubt in the minds of all who saw him what must have happened the night before), Carol asked Katherine whether she or Mrs. Mossler gave out keys to the girls' rooms.

"Well, we give them out to the girls who live in them, if that's what you mean," Katherine said.

"No, I mean—like a spare, or a backup key, for emergencies or for housekeeping, or for laundry, or that sort of thing."

"No," Katherine said decisively. "I mean, Mrs. Mossler has a skeleton key that she keeps with her, of course, but as far as I know she's never had to use it except if a girl moves out and forgets to leave her key at the front desk. And the maids, when we have them, just knock, as far as I know—and isn't everyone doing their own laundry these days, anyhow? I know they used to pile up their linens at the end of the hall on second and fourth Wednesdays for pickup a few years ago, but even then nobody came into your room to collect it, and I think it's every girl for herself when it comes to washing, now. Why do you ask?"

"I was just wondering," Carol said slowly, "since Patricia has been working so late lately, and I thought she might want her laundry looked after on nights she can't get back. But I'll just ask her when I see her next." It seemed ridiculous to make a fuss over some-one as oblivious and naive as Ruth, who was only trying to help, so what was the point of getting her into trouble?

Ruth clearly felt bad about it, because she came by to apologize the next day, sounding much less anesthetized and much more rea-sonable. She never went into Carol's room again, and frequently asked after Bryan, saying, "Gosh, I must have terrified him. He must have thought I was a terrific prude, interrupting you two like that," until Carol finally reassured her that he had only been momentarily startled and certainly didn't think she'd done it on purpose—and never thought to wonder how it was Ruth had learned Bryan's name, since neither of them had ever told her.

———••———

After two weeks of this even Mrs. Mossler could not pretend that things could go on as they had been; she informed Ruth that the trial period was finished, and had not been a success, and that she'd better look elsewhere for a job. Ruth took this news in stride; for one rea-son or another, which may have been known only to Ruth, she did not resist it. Possibly even Ruth herself did not know the reason. As a general rule, she fought harder to be given chances than she fought against rejection after the chance had been given.

After Ruth had been fired from her second career, Lucianne and Carol began to refer to her by the equally admiring and mean-spirited nickname of Lily: "Because like the lily of the fields she toils not, neither does she spin, yet even Solomon in all his glory was not ar-ranged so comfortably as she." The nickname stuck, mostly among Lucianne and Carol's particular friends; the people who called her Lily soon forgot she had ever been called anything else, while those who called her Ruth assumed that Lily was an entirely new person they hadn't yet met. She had not made a success of herself, but she had managed to become familiar to the others; her particular, conspicuous style of failure was of a type well known to them, and they felt comfortable with it.

It has been elsewhere argued that infancy does not really happen to anybody, for nobody remembers it. We are born sleeping, are periodically roused by thirst or intolerable discomfort, and if all goes as it should, if our caretakers are affectionate and attentive and well disposed toward us, we sleep again. Babies can only ever manage to look cunning or stupefied, with very little in between; a successful infancy is an unconscious one, and only gradually, inscrutably, does anyone much later wake into real life. Our earliest impressions are doubtful and sporadic: a certain hair ribbon, a snatch of a song, a distorted expression on a mother's face, a party we may have attended or may have simply heard described so many times in later life that we believe we must have been there. With Ruth it seemed as if the process of waking up had never quite taken.

———··———

Katherine's anger at Kitty was pretty thoroughly swept away after her conversation with Arthur. She thought the lion's share of that anger belonged by rights toward herself, for going out of her way to "give in" to Kitty, even at the expense of her own patience and pocketbook, and made up with her squarely. It was not the first, nor was it the last, time that somebody had slapped Kitty, so Kitty was perfectly happy to make up, too. She also thought that she had gotten off pretty lightly, as she would much rather be struck than spend a whole day in jail or be handcuffed to a bench down at the courthouse. As it happened the beat cop who had arrested her in the first place failed to show at her next court appointment, and the Irish bartender could no longer identify with real certainty just who had taken the first swing at him, and so the charges were reduced to public disorderliness and a fine. But as Kitty could *not* pay the fine, she ended up spending six weeks in jail all the same, later that year in August, at the absolute peak of the summer heat, and nearly stifled to death.

The next disruption to the Biedermeier's routine came from the eleventh floor: toward the end of May, less than a month after Moving Day, Sadie Waldvogel announced to her suitemates that she was not only engaged (they had not even known she was seeing anyone in particular) but also married, and in fact had been married for almost a week already, and would be gone by the end of the month to live with her husband's family in Throgs Neck.

"If this is a joke, it's a very sad one," Patricia said first.

"Married?" Carol said. "To a man, you mean?"

Sadie nodded miserably. "I'm sorry not to have told you sooner," she said.

"You could hardly have told us any *later*," Patricia said. "What's his name? Or don't you know it?"

"Please don't be hateful," Sadie said.

"I haven't had time to be anything yet," Patricia said. "We've only been talking about it for ten seconds." But her ire was quickly spent. She softened almost immediately and said, if still a little begrudgingly, "Congratulations, of course."

"You don't *congratulate* a bride, ass," Carol said, and then rose to embrace Sadie, telling her, "I'm sure you'll both be *very* happy, and you won't hold it against Patricia that she was raised by laboratory monkeys. They did their best with the tools they had available. My very best wishes to you both—and Pat's, too."

"You Easterners," Patricia said, "make politeness seem like a bunch of encrypted codes. Isn't it enough to congratulate a person on happiness? And they weren't monkeys, they were circus elephants," she corrected Carol as she got up to embrace Sadie, too.

"I would have told you about it sooner," Sadie said, still a little tearful, "only I didn't know anything sooner, and I didn't want to tell you anything I might have to take back."

"Of course you didn't," Carol said soothingly, still sending off the occasional protective spark in Patricia's direction, although she was just as worried herself about what this meant for the rest of them. "You haven't done a thing wrong. Getting married's the nicest and most natural thing in the world, and we went and practically bit your head off, first thing. I don't blame you for wanting to give up living with a couple of abnormals."

"It's not like I'm marrying a stockbroker or anything like that," Sadie said, relapsing into tears. "It's not like there's been any work downtown lately—but oh, he's an artist too, and that's why we're going to be living with—his mother-r-r, who's really very kind—but oh, girls, I'm going to be able to have *breakfast* every morning again—she's a wonderful cook—and Jasper's awfully nice—and I'm going to have things to do again. And I've been looking everywhere to find a replacement so you won't be on the hook for my share of the rent, I want you to know that."

"You shouldn't worry yourself about that," Carol said. "Let me and Pat worry about that. You should only worry about telling us every single detail of the wedding. What's he look like? What did you wear? You know how to make a happy marriage, don't you? *Have no illusions and feed the brute.* What's his mother's cooking taste like?"

Privately, though, she felt struck to the heart. Sadie had lived there for almost six years, longer than either Patricia or Carol, and they'd never had any idea that she was worried about money or thinking of getting married. They were all worried about money, of course, and from time to time almost everyone in the hotel had thought about getting married, but it seemed to Carol like thinking about getting married was the same as thinking about being a Rockette or moving to Montana and taking up fly-fishing—something you *thought* about so you'd never really have to *do* it—but here was direct evidence to the contrary. And where were they going to find someone to take Sadie's place? But that was a problem for another day; the job now was to take the news graciously and keep Sadie from starting her married life feeling as if she'd betrayed her friends. She hadn't asked their advice about handling a proposal; she was gone and married already, and there was no point trying to argue the point with her now.

Just then Patricia started whistling "Wedding Bells (Are Breaking Up That Old Gang of Mine)," and it was all Carol could do to keep from crying, too. "Whistle something *cheerful*," Carol demanded, "you jackass." Patricia obligingly switched to "The March of the Soviet Tankman."

Chapter Fourteen

WEDDING SEASON

Things for the most part quieted down in the days following Katherine's abbreviated stint downtown. Five days later Sadie decamped for the Bronx, having been first fêted with a little supper party in the Quaker suite.

"This will have to count for your bridal shower and honeymoon both, I'm afraid," Patricia said, handing over a little silver-plated tray with what she had been jokingly referring to as Sadie's "trousseau." It contained one highball glass, three Triscuits, each with a half slice of canned pineapple, a new lipstick that would never have suited Sadie by even the most generous of assessments, a buffalo nickel that Carol had assured her was counterfeit, three of Lucianne's dummy subway tokens, an empty canister of Quaker Oats, a pincushion, and twenty dollars' worth of traveler's checks belonging to a former resident named Molly Haskett, whom nobody could remember. There was also a copy of *Seven Days in May* that was missing the better part of its cover and a funny little sketch from Josephine of the new-lyweds where Rex Harrison's face stood in for Jasper's, since she had never met him and had no idea what he looked like. It was not a very good collection, largely because everyone had already given so much for Katherine's bail.

"It's perfect," Sadie cried in all sincerity. "If he ever tries to beat me or hide my pocket money, I'll use this to escape, and come right back here." But she would not come back, they knew; the Bieder-meier was not the kind of place where people came back. You either stayed on longer than you had ever intended to, or you left for good; it never hosted reunions. They had not come there on purpose, and they left it as often as they could. Perhaps this was why they had all tried so hard to make the party seem gay, as if they were all a bunch of great friends from childhood, who got married and got promoted at work and threw each other parties in turn, instead of a collection of mostly strangers who didn't know what to do with themselves.

Sadie had been close with Patricia and Carol, of course, but she didn't know Kitty or Lucianne except in passing, and mostly only spoke to Katherine about the laundry and the library; she had never even met Gia and had to be introduced in the middle of going away.

"Dream a little bigger, Sadie," Carol said. "You go right ahead and beat him on the first day, so he knows you're not kidding around."

They had quite a lot to drink; as far as refreshments were concerned it was an excellent party, although there had been nothing to eat but the Triscuits. Sadie sometimes called Carol during the first year of married life, but those calls dropped off eventually, as they so often do; when there is only the memory of affectionate yet mild proximity to sustain a friendship, it tends to wilt and eventually droop to the ground slowly enough that it gives nobody any cause for alarm. Perhaps this was why Patricia and Carol made as big a fuss as they possibly could about her going away—they knew, and felt a premonition of future guilt, that as sorry as they were at present, they would scarcely miss her at all in a year's time.

Dolly ended up missing a great deal of the excitement, first around Katherine's arrest and later about Sadie's going-away party, because she worked from early in the afternoon until pretty late in the evening, which were usually the hours of the Biedermeier's greatest activity. There was a little further uptown a much more glamorous hotel, which resembled the Biedermeier only conceptually, set back in rose-pink brick, like a wedding cake, and brimming with models, actresses, novelists of promise, typists who worked for huge, successful companies where the secretarial pools worked in rooms the size of airplane hangars, with sleek matching covers that went over the machines at the end of the day—in this hotel, men were barred from going any higher than the lobby, and this prohibition was strictly kept, and the busiest hours came in the early morning, when the hotel resembled an immaculate beehive, and again during the cocktail hour, when the hotel resembled a slightly more glamorous beehive. Perhaps it is more correct to say this other hotel was full of people who often found themselves in the orbit of important people—and let us say that everyone at the Biedermeier was at least three or four circles (or in some cases, two or three generations) removed from anyone important, such that many of them did not really get going until ten or eleven in the morning, which meant news had very little time to circulate before Dolly had already left for the day.

Lucianne was not the only one who noticed the profound difference between Dolly and Pauline, although either of them could have been described as gentlemanly. But Pauline was gentlemanly in a way that gentlemen often liked, and Dolly was gentlemanly in a way that they generally didn't.

In truth, Dolly was more mannish than gentlemanly, because men are sometimes called gentlemanly, but never mannish, and a man cannot be mannish any more than a woman càn be effeminate. In Pauline's gentlemanliness, many men saw something of themselves that they already liked, profusely and distinctively arranged in a face and figure that were beautifully feminine. If she had been a few inches shorter, or skinny rather than vigorous, she might have been called gamine; as it was, she wasn't. Pauline, who was already a success as a woman, had some of the better elements of maleness layered on top—it struck most people almost as an indicator of prosperity and good health. A generation earlier this sort of strapping androgyny had been a recognizable, even sometimes a very popular, type. Garbo and Hepburn and Dietrich were certainly the most well-known and recognizable members of this type, but it was not just a famous few, either: turn through your mother or grandmother's old issues of *Harper's* or *Vogue* and you will see page after page of woolen and flannel suits with broad lapels and broader shoulders, trousers of stout fabric with deep cuffs and straight-cut pockets, and a dozen snub-nosed models dressed like sailors, clubmen, and English schoolboys. Ask your mother and your grandmother to show you some of their old photo albums, and see how many of them *you* can spot. For a certain period—perhaps ten years after adolescence, perhaps fifteen—the world beams on girls like this. They are almost invariably and startlingly active, like schools of minnows; they sail and play tennis from sunup to sundown without flagging, if they live in the city; they tramp across country with Girl Guides; and they whittle and ride horses if they live in the country. (But they must always have money.) In later years they become either handsome matrons in long tweeds, or they retire gracefully, vanishing entirely into a sea of unremarkable-looking womanhood.

But Dolly did not look androgynous, or like an already-successful woman whom the angels had granted some supernumerary, ineffable quality. Dolly was a little short, a little round, and she looked more than a little indeterminate, like an overgrown leprechaun or a satyr in disguise. Lucianne thought she also looked a little bit like Mickey Rooney, but Lucianne could be more than a little cruel about how people looked. Katherine thought she looked a little bit like Spencer Tracy or a present-day Jimmy Cagney, but she was trying to be kind. There were certain elements of truth in both comparisons: Dolly *was* hopelessly Irish-looking, with a face as broad and as cheerful as a milk truck, small, beaming eyes, a low, squared-off hairline, and a squashed nose that smeared her profile. She wore stiff and heavily starched waistcoats over what must have been shockingly tenacious foundation garments and either one of two suits, a brown one in winter and a light brown one in summer. People sometimes had to get a second look before they felt confident in knowing whether to address her as "Sir" or "Miss," which did not often endear her to them. This meant a lot of her interactions with strangers were kicked off with an inaugural sense of impatience on the side of the strangers, as if she were backward or was withholding crucial information from them. And in Dolly's mannishness, men saw very little of themselves, and a great deal of something else, something they neither understood nor wished for. As a general rule, they did their best to politely ignore her.

But those who fell outside the general rule adored her, and she had what seemed to the rest of the Biedermeier girls an absolutely shocking number of men friends. There was scarcely a milkman or a doorman or a mailman on the entire East Side of Manhattan who did not seem to know her, or who would not specially hail her during his rounds for a smoke and a jaw session (Dolly was a more habitual nicotine fiend than almost anyone in the building apart from Stephen and "bummed" cigarettes from friends and acquaintances—whom she chose to call her "associates"—even oftener than he). For Dolly was as stately and as cheerful as a tugboat, and wore her squat ugliness with such unconcerned pleasure that it rested delightfully on her shoulders.

That is not to say that the people who loved her ever forgot that she was ugly. She remained ugly from the day of her birth right up until the last; she had been an ugly baby, and she made a wonderfully ugly old woman later on. Nor was she incessantly good natured; she had an Irish temper, and was very often just as catty toward Lucianne as Lucianne was toward her. But she was terribly fun, and she was never angry for long, and once people stopped being strangers to her, they were usually her devoted friends. And like many unusual-looking people, she was tremendously thick skinned. If people looked surprised or even angry at her appearance, she would plunge her hands into her pockets, thrust out her lower jaw, and aim a waterfall-wide smile at her audience until they smiled back despite themselves. And if they did not smile back, she simply sailed on her magnificent, boisterous little way.

Dolly was a bartender and she looked exactly like how a bartender ought to, especially to Katherine, who had encountered very few bartenders in her drinking career outside of her mother, and whose mental picture of the profession was derived chiefly from old Westerns. She could have been nothing but a bartender, and seemed as though she had been sent over straight from Central Casting already wiping down the inside of a clean glass with a rag. She worked at an old bar in the Village called Vernon's, which was less than two blocks away from the House of Detention and saw its fair share of the recently sprung and hard up.

Vernon's had a terrifically contentious relationship with this specific portion of its clientele, and nearly equally as contentious a relationship with Dolly. It had been operating in that neighborhood since the 1870s, when a significant portion of the local populace was either Prussian or Hanoverian, and Avenue B was known as "German

Broadway." In those days it had been a beer hall and racing parlor, and managed to undercut most of its competitors on the lunchtime sale of oysters, until by 1905 it was the only remaining bar on the block. It became a popular gathering spot for Hearst journalists and vaudeville actors in the first decades of the new century, when it also briefly featured a nightly burlesque show, but it was only now, in its ninth decade of operation, that Vernon's management suddenly began to take intermittent exception to the seediness which had always been its stock-in-trade.

Depending on the time of day, which manager, and how many bartenders were on duty, Vernon's was either a fairly comfortable (and no more than ordinarily discreet) gay bar or an ordinary, respectable, long-standing bar for the sexually normal that had to be regularly rescued from homosexual invasion by police. And depending on the same factors, either Dolly was a perfectly ordinary bartender whose cross-dressing was so erotically neutralizing, so unobtrusive, and a habit of such long standing that it was practically a local monument, and no more morally dangerous than the statue of the Marquis de Lafayette in Union Square Park, or she was a pimp, a procurer, and a magnet for deviants. Dolly for the most part did not mind this, as she expected her employer to be her enemy, and considered it their job to try to strong-arm her back into women's clothing, and her job to be too slippery to catch. Whereas no one considered Pauline (or Garbo, or Dietrich, or Hepburn before her) to be doing anything like cross-dressing; they were doing something glamorous, fashionable, and even alluring, itself a titillating drag of what transgression might have looked like, if transgression could somehow also be cosmopolitan.

Whether there really were more open homosexuals in the neighborhood now than ten years previous, or whether the management had become more paranoid over the same period, was not a question Dolly could answer with satisfaction. Possibly it was a little bit of both. Certainly the homosexuals did not stop coming to drink there—or, if they were briefly scared away, it was only in the same manner as pigeons in the park, who at most might flutter a few scattered feet away at the sound of impending human steps, then sail directly back to their former places, emboldened by their own numbers and habits. And just like with pigeons, the more seriously anyone tried to drive them off for good, the more foolish that person came to look.

But did Dolly think of herself as having something in common with Pauline? Insofar as Pauline was a woman—and Dolly liked women—she liked Pauline, but she did not think of Pauline as a creature like herself. She was a charming girl who looked as though she had borrowed her brother's school uniform for the afternoon: a little daring, a little jaunty, and thoroughly feminine. *Feminine* was not a word anyone else used for Pauline, but from where Dolly was situated, Pauline was about as masculine as Little Lord Fauntleroy. She felt indulgent toward her, as she might have felt toward a younger brother recovering from a bad fever. Pauline thought of Dolly as a natural comrade, admired and encouraged her healthy hatred of bosses, and if she was ever made uneasy at the wolfish pace Dolly went through girlfriends, she was wise enough to consider it an acquired case of middle-class prudishness, and did her best to strangle it.

This particular night in early June was more tortured than usual, since Dolly was the only one tending bar, but she had been paired with Roscoe Almer, the most interfering and poison-minded shift manager on the schedule, who practically turned out people's pockets if they came in for a drink and he hadn't seen them before. Of course he could be worse than that to someone he'd seen before and decided was a fairy. Sometimes he'd come by moments after she had served a customer and say, "Cut him off and get him out of here." Sometimes he'd do it himself, often waiting to interrupt until she was halfway through mixing the guy's drink, just to make things as uncomfortable as possible for everyone involved. This effectively dampened most of the regulars' spirits, so the greater portion bolted down their drinks and walked back out the door within twenty minutes, hoping for better luck a little later on, but it nettled others— who grew waspish in return, asking loudly for the most sibilantly named cocktails on offer, and drawing out each *S* until the whole room sounded carbonated. Dolly only made it worse. She'd get rid of anyone Roscoe told her so fast the man never got the chance to pay his bill. "We don't want that kind of money, boss," she'd say if he objected to the shortness of her register. "When you say they're out, they're out. Who knows where that kind of money's come from. Anyone else need bumping, you just say the word. I don't care how much it costs us."

Sometimes Dolly and the regulars would "go into business together": they would pick up a pair of the most outrageous fairies they could find and order a round of the most expensive cocktails on the menu, Brandies Alexander or Planter's Punches, and after she'd mixed the drinks but before they'd settled the bill, Dolly would realize her error and throw them out herself. If Roscoe seemed really agitated, she'd go to the back room to "call the cops," which usually meant calling Nicola, unless Nicola was at work, in which case she'd call Katherine, who was almost always within shouting distance of the Biedermeier's telephone, tying up the line for at least fifteen minutes before telling Roscoe: "Well, they had me waiting a while—I guess there's been a pretty nasty accident on Mott Street that's kept most of the officers busy a while. They needed a circular saw to open the car up and cut free a woman that was nearly crushed to death by her own roof, if you can believe it. But they're sending somebody around to take a look, soon as they can. No promises, though. I told them I guessed we could take care of a couple of fairies without the fire department." And a hundred other little tactics designed to wear Roscoe down to a nub. He was a very weathered-looking man when he at last retired in 1972.

Sometimes, of course, it was not fairies but new releases from the House of Detention who came to Vernon's, also against Vernon's express wishes. But there were only so many fronts that Vernon's could fight at once, and any bar that successfully gets rid of all low-lifes is a bar that is not very long for this world, since lowlifes are their very existence in the final tally. These customers were often sent there in particular by a recommendation to look for Dolly, who was usually good for putting them in touch with like-minded and sympathetic people, helping them find more or less legal employ-ment and, after her own shift was over, finding even more poorly lit and disreputable bars than Vernon's.

Nicola often came down to Vernon's at the end of the workday to keep Dolly company until it was time for her to go home too. She worked in the back room at a Loehmann's on Seventh Avenue, and almost nothing ever happened to her there. There was the Back Room, which customers saw, where women picked over discounted clothes and tried them on in a big communal dressing room, which was a pretty exciting place, especially when someone's shoes went missing and it turned into a sort of impromptu dinner theater, but Nicola never worked in that part of the store. She was in the back room, not the Back Room, and she spent most shifts refolding unsold and out-of-season and duplicate items that nobody much wanted, and double-checking stock against the inventory list. Things really only ever happened to Nicola when she was with Dolly, which was one of the reasons they made such good friends. Another reason was that they both enjoyed carrying on roughly the same argument, on a stop-and-start basis, without ever deciding on a victor. Nicola wanted to go home at the end of Dolly's shift, and Dolly thought that Nicola ought to go home at the end of Nicola's shift while she, Dolly, ought to go out and have a good time for another four or five hours, with at least one pretty girl.

"Come on, let's go home. There's nobody left in this bar you haven't tried it on with. Get some beauty sleep and try again tomorrow when you look a little bit less like Boris Karloff than usual. I'm tired."

"What else is new? You know, I don't think you're queer at all. I think you're just tired. Besides, some of these girls aren't old enough to know what Boris Karloff looks like. Why don't *you* go home, and lend me a dollar?"

"A dollar? You've lost your mind. If any of these gold diggers ever dreamed you had that kind of money on you, they'd cut your throat and leave you to die in the street. Better let them think you've only got a nickel or two; it might be just enough to keep them hanging around, but not worth the risk of sticking you up."

They would continue this until one of them either got too drunk to continue or they finally gave up and started walking home. There was some sort of informal point-scoring arrangement that Nicola was meant to be in charge of, although neither really knew who was up or down at any given moment; the real fun lay in finding new ways to call one another old or hideous and to see who was left at the end of the night, when they finally had enough of horrifying one another.

——··——

"It's the damnedest thing," Bryan said to Carol one afternoon, as they sat on a blanket together in St. Gabriel's Park, a few blocks away from the Biedermeier. "You're sure Ruth hasn't been back in your room since that night?"

"I'm sure," Carol said. "Believe you me, I don't relish the thought of seeing that face in the dark again. I've checked with Katherine and Mrs. Mossler both, and all the keys have been accounted for, besides which she got fired from that maid job, thank heavens, so she doesn't have that excuse anymore for breaking in. And—look, I feel sorry for the poor kid, too, you know I do, so I haven't exactly gone around telling everyone, but I *did* feel like I ought to tell Pat, and she's agreed that we'll both use the dead bolt when we go to sleep, as well as whenever we leave the room empty."

"I think that's a good idea," Bryan said. "Not that I don't think you could take her in a fight, if it came to that—although I don't really think she's the fighting type—but it's not healthy for her to be doing that kind of thing. I agree there's no reason to make her look foolish in front of everybody, but all the same, I'm glad you're both keeping the door locked. I can't figure her. She's a funny-looking thing—she looks like if Olive Oyl had a kid sister—and I don't think she ever washes her hair, but it's like she was born without embarrassment. The last three times I've come by looking for you, she's found me in the elevator or the hallway and cornered me with a lot of questions about my work and my commute and where I get my shirts and how many brothers and sisters I have, like she's a census taker. And it doesn't matter what I say or how many times I tell her I'm looking for you—as long as she's asking a question and I have to answer it, even though I'm just being polite, that seems to make her as happy as anything. And then she keeps asking if I'll take her to the movies or on the ferry or to the zoo, and I'll say, 'I don't think that's a very good idea, Ruth,' which in my experience is a pretty crushing thing for a girl to hear—I'm sorry, I hope I don't sound stuck up, because believe you me it's not as if girls are constantly stopping me on the street to ask me out. I'm not saying I've had to let any more girls down gently than the next guy—"

"I know what you mean," Carol said. "Don't worry about it. You're a nice guy, and you're a nice-looking guy, that's all."

Bryan looked uncomfortable. "I don't want you thinking that I think I'm some kind of Casanova, that's all."

"I think you look like the Phantom of the Opera," Carol said. "Does that help?"

"Thank you," he said in mock seriousness, but she could tell that this was helping to lighten his mood a little. "But I mean, if a girl asks a guy out, and he says he doesn't think that's a good idea, she usually feels a little—well, mortified, and that's the end of it. But with Ruth it's like it doesn't bother her in the least, that I don't want to go with her. She'll just ask *Why*, like I've told her we can't take the Brooklyn Bridge because there's been an accident, and all we have to do is come up with an alternate route."

"Well, what have you said to her?"

"Well, at first I told her I couldn't go out with her because I was going out with you. You know what she said to that?"

"No—what?"

"She said, 'But you're not going out with her every night?'"

"She *didn't*."

"She certainly did. So I said no, not every night, but that other nights I have my work, and other friends to see, so *she* suggested that I save time and take her out sometime *after I brought you home from one of our dates*. It would save time, she said; I could go out with you both on the same night, since I'd be in the same area. It was like she was asking me to pick up milk for her, since I was already going to the store, anyway. I was half-afraid she was going to suggest she start tagging along on our dates—I'm pretty sure she'd say yes, if I suggested it."

"Oh, you poor thing," Carol groaned.

"I don't know what to do about it," Bryan said, "aside from meeting you in the park more often, and maybe start coming up to see you by way of the fire escape. But there's something you don't know about me; I'm actually a real coward when it comes to heights, and I think you'd have to send the fire department after me before I reached the fifth floor, even." There was no question of meeting at Bryan's; he shared his apartment with five other students, with bunk beds in the master bedroom and a makeshift bed made up on the couch in the living room for the odd man out. "Plus, I'm half-afraid she'll figure it out, and start hanging off the window ledge to make sure she runs into me there, too. I've never met someone who didn't know what it means to feel embarrassed, or who can't take no for an answer. It makes me feel mean as hell, I don't mind telling you."

"I'm awfully sorry," Carol said. "I'll try talking to her myself, and see if I can't help."

"Go easy on her if you can," Bryan said. "She's like a babe in the woods. I don't want to hurt her feelings. But the last time I had to answer 'Why?' so many times in a row, I was babysitting my cousin's kid, and he's three years old."

"I'll be as nice as I can," Carol promised. "But you've probably been too easy on her, which is probably the right thing to do, in your position. I can afford to be a little more straight with her, girl to girl."

Older women were married, or widowed, or lived with their grown sons in New Jersey and Queens and Brooklyn, or they lived in lavender pairs uptown and ran cozy little boutiques together. A few of them even opened tea shops of the kind that had been popular forty years ago, and were now old-fashioned enough to be popular again, which would have shocked Mrs. Mossler, had she heard about it. Katherine's family had not visited once from Ohio, and she was afraid to call home even on Christmas. Lucianne, who had a real

236 OF DANIEL M. LAVERY

pedigree, had never even been engaged, and none of her sorority sisters (most of whom had finished college before getting married, while Lucianne did neither) ever did more than write a few times a year. Pauline's friends tended toward the septuagenarian, and most of Dolly's friends looked like extras from *Marty*; Nicola's only friend was Dolly; Josephine stole from tired young mothers and tourists in Central Park; and Stephen's friends were sometimes as old as Pauline's and all of them were perverts, so why should Ruth stand out as a misfit among misfits?

But these were not questions that Ruth asked herself. She did not think of herself as a particularly difficult or even unpopular person. She understood that making people like you was often very challenging, but she thought there was bound to be a trick to it that could be learned and mastered and later replicated with others until you had all the friends that you wanted. She did not seem to realize that making frequent repeat attempts on the same person diminished your chances of ever pulling "the trick" off in the first place. Trying over and over again, often in the face of unrelenting defeat, was widely considered admirable in sport and in business, so why should it be any different with people?

Other people did not always know *why* it was different. They only knew that they did not like Ruth, as decisively and instinctively as the family dog decides to take against the mailman. Her inability to attract friends was immediately and incredibly obvious to everyone but herself, which made them dislike her all the more. When it comes to friendship, many people are more magically minded than they ever realize; success does not always breed success, but failure always breeds more failure. The tool Ruth relied upon most faithfully to win friends—relentless, dogged determination—was the very quality that drove people from her. So she tried again, a little harder the next time, sure of her eventual reward, until people finally reacted to her with violence or by running away. She could not come up with a satisfactory explanation for this behavior—all she could think was that people were strange, and sometimes brutal, and there was no telling when or where violence might erupt between them. Then she would try again.

Chapter Fifteen

BELLING THE CAT

B y now it was practically August. Spring had been folded easily into summer, and the days were getting very, very hot. The nights were almost as hot now, too, so that most of the girls slept with their windows open, and Katherine took to running her dress shields under the cold-water faucet first thing in the morning, so they were still damp and cool when she got dressed for the day.

Katherine and Tobias had gone on a date together back in June. It had been her first date in quite some time, and at first she was not quite sure if either one of them really wanted to go, or if they merely felt like they'd already been on one together, and were making a second date out of force of habit. It seemed only natural that bailing someone out of jail would make you feel as if you knew them, or even as if you were very close with them. It was a fairly intimate, or at least an *unusually* intimate, act. And Katherine had thought, when they first met, that he seemed just as interested, if not more so, in talking to Pauline and Lucianne than he had been in talking to her; one of Katherine's particularly bad habits was that, whenever she suspected that she did not rank first in someone's attentions, she always retreated from them socially—sometimes just as sharply as if she had been rejected or insulted, even when no such thing had taken place. Katherine had enjoyed herself very much at dinner, and still found Tobias as easy to talk to as ever, but after they had kissed for a while on a bench in the park, he suddenly drew back from her before saying, "Look, I'm not bothering you, am I?"

Katherine had been so startled by the question she could only laugh a little.

"I suppose that's my answer," he said, and if his manner was a little sulky as he said it, it was only a very *little* sulkiness, and he mastered it almost as quickly as it had crept into his voice.

"I'm sorry," Katherine said, "I didn't mean to laugh at you. I've just never been asked that question in quite that sort of moment before."

"I like you," Tobias said, "but if you'd rather just be pals who go to the movies once in a while, you've only got to say so. I don't want to bark up the wrong tree, so to speak."

Katherine almost corrected him, thinking he had gotten the wrong idea, first about Pauline for dressing like Squire Allworthy, and then about *her* for the botched haircut (which, now that it had been grown out about a month, actually suited her better than she might have guessed). But correct him in what sense, exactly? There wasn't an answer she could give him that could have satisfactorily explained things, or why she had missed out on so many things that most girls her age took for granted, or what kept her from calling her mother, or what she wanted from a man on a date, or even what she didn't want. She wasn't like Dolly, she knew that much, but she wasn't much like a girl on a date was supposed to be, either.

She shook his hand. It was an odd sort of thing to do, but it also struck her as an honest, comradely sort of thing to do, too, and he seemed to appreciate it, because he shook her hand back with real warmth and enthusiasm, and even laughed a little. "Okay," he said, as if she had answered whatever question he had not quite asked. "Fair enough. They're playing *Gold Diggers of 1933* at the revival house next Saturday. Let's get a little group together and go see it, or something. That'll give me enough time to recover my wounded pride. I'm not made of steel, you know." Then he had walked her home, still talking lightly about nothing in particular to show there were no hard feelings, and the next week they had seen *Gold Diggers*, exactly as he had outlined.

William Rufus's whereabouts during the day were still unknown, but every evening, about an hour before sunset, he would put in a sudden appearance on the fire escape just outside J.D.'s window, chirping mournfully and thrusting the side of his head against the window frame two or three times before dropping onto her desk and hunting for olives. It was her greatest delight—J.D. had never had so much as a parakeet or a goldfish in all her life, and having spent so many years in a hotel with a lot of singletons who came and went every few months, knew next to nothing about animals, so that his every little movement amazed and delighted her, as if he had been the only cat ever to enter the world. She began leaving her desk at unusual hours, departing from her faithful schedule for the first time in living memory, calling down the hallway and sometimes even venturing down to the first floor if an audience was not to be found on her own:

"Katherine" (or Posey, or Pauline, or Josephine, or sometimes even Ruth, if no one better was available), "you've just got to come and see what William Rufus has just done. It's the most incredible thing—" and there would be so much eagerness in her voice it nearly shook, as if she were terrified by the extent of such a creature's ability to excite joy and astonishment. And because it was J.D., whose own mental whereabouts were so often mysterious to them, and because she was herself wonderfully strange-looking, such that her joy was marvelous and weird and a pleasure to behold, they went, and always confessed themselves amazed, whether he repeated the action or simply sat there ("But the *way* he sits there, so primly, when only a moment ago he was doing it!" "I know just what you mean. He looks pleased as punch!"). She began to chirp back at him, which only led him to chirp more, and sometimes the fourth-floor hallway sounded like *The Undersea World of Jacques Cousteau*. This violated no rules of the hotel, since William Rufus did not technically live with J.D. Like an old lover who will never propose but whose routine affections have become comfortably entrenched, he took his meals elsewhere, made no promises, and vanished promptly in the morning, which suited her to no end, since J.D. could only adore him, but had no idea what he might have needed to live or how to care for him. He produced astonishment and she provided it, and so they got on beautifully together.

Ruth had not worked in over three months, not since Mrs. Mossler had released her from her trial as a hotel maid. For a while she had gone on leaving her name and number at a haphazard assortment of nearby beauty salons, cafés, gas stations, and movie theaters, but nothing ever came of it. She looked at newspapers a day late, because they were cheaper that way, and kept all the classifieds in a little pile in the corner of her bedroom, just in case she had missed something that might later be important. She also saved movie stubs, her own and other people's, and any food that wasn't too perishable, in case she got hungry later; she found the longer that summer went on, the less hungry she got, because there was so much to do, and she was having to work so hard to figure out how to do it.

She tried to make friends with other girls in the building, but they were always rushing off someplace and never sure when they would be back again; she tried to make friends with some of the young people she saw talking or playing music in the park, but this did not work either, and some of them even took to throwing things at her when they saw her coming. They never threw anything heavy, that might have hurt her—just balled-up napkins and old leaves and beer cans, so she didn't think they really meant it, and waited patiently until they ran out of ammunition; then they usually got up and left. Some days she would walk down to Whitehall Street just to ride the ferry, which still cost only a nickel and was cheaper than either the bus or the subway, back and forth between Lower Manhattan and Staten Island; she got very suntanned that way. And she thought about Bryan.

Bryan was the nicest person she had met in New York City—possibly the only really nice person she had met in New York City, or anywhere else, and he was a very important person, too. He always stopped to talk to her on his way in and out of the building, no matter what else he was doing or how late he was running. And he was very smart. He was in a master's program for translation and interpretation, and he hoped after graduation to get a job at the United Nations, which Ruth thought was a very good idea because the UN headquarters were so close to the Biedermeier, much closer than Hunter College was, which she knew because she had carefully timed her walks there, and even twice seen him studying in the library. He hadn't seen her because she hadn't wanted to disturb him, not when he was working, but he was never working when he was at the Biedermeier, those were just social calls, so it was perfectly safe to talk to him then, as much as she wanted to. Carol had once or twice talked about Bryan with Ruth, which had been very nice because Carol liked Bryan almost as much as Ruth did—Carol understood about Bryan, and how important he was, and how busy, too. Carol was almost a friend, in her own way, but Bryan was really and properly Ruth's friend. She had been able to tell Gia about him once, although she hardly ever saw Gia nowadays.

Gia had become engaged to her older man and spent most nights at his apartment, only coming back to the hotel every couple of days to change suitcases and refresh her wardrobe. Weddings did not especially interest Ruth, although she was broadly happy for Gia, since Gia had wanted to be married so badly. The strange thing about weddings was that they were as public a thing as you could possibly imagine, but they always and invariably marked the beginning of an immediate and resounding retreat into privacy for the newlyweds. There was something hypocritical, almost deceitful, Ruth thought, about a wedding. People made a lot of drunken speeches afterward, sometimes about how they had introduced the happy couple, or about what fun they hoped to have with the happy couple now that they could all be a bunch of married friends together, but afterward, she had noticed, the married couple almost always vanished off the face of the earth together. She hoped Bryan and Carol wouldn't get married, although she was perfectly happy for them to continue sleeping with each other, since they both seemed to like it so much. *That* was all right, as long as they didn't get married. What right would he and Carol have to shut other people out of their happiness? Happiness wasn't supposed to be private, but people were always shutting Ruth out of theirs.

Gia and Douglas were married quietly in early July out of the courthouse. None of his friends came, and from the hotel only Ruth and Lucianne were invited, because they needed witnesses and Douglas didn't like to ask anyone who had known his late wife. He wanted to let them get used to the idea slowly, he said to Lucianne, and then after another moment added, "You see, I don't want them to see me like this yet—I'm so happy, and it's much too soon to be so happy, and I wouldn't like to hurt anybody with my happiness—*she* understands," and Gia looked very demure and closed her eyes for a moment. Lucianne thought she had never liked another woman quite so much in all her life, and Ruth was faintly bored. Gia wore a bouquet of gardenias at her wrist and a peach-colored Givenchy suit with a slender, pale-blue sash at the waist. Ruth had never seen a bride out of white before, but Gia said Douglas couldn't bear the idea of a white wedding and she didn't want anything Douglas didn't want. She looked beautiful, and even more suntanned than Ruth. The four of them got cocktails afterward, but nothing to eat besides bar nuts, and as soon as they had ordered a second round Douglas said they had to go, and they vanished almost immediately, so Ruth and Lucianne finished their drinks for them.

Gia sent Douglas's secretary down to the hotel for the rest of her things, which once again required the service of two cabs; then she was gone. Lucianne never heard how her mother had taken the news, although Gia had promised she would write when she could—but that was not the sort of promise that Lucianne expected any woman to keep after getting married, Lucianne taking almost exactly the opposite views on weddings that Ruth did.

It was about a week after Gia's wedding, on a day when the temperature at LaGuardia Airport set a new record at 107 degrees, that J.D. noticed that William Rufus was missing. He had failed their usual nightly rendezvous for the third evening in a row, which she had never known him to do before in all the months he had been visiting her. She went to every floor asking if anyone had seen him, and spent the next three days driven nearly to distraction hunting for him, both inside and outside the hotel, nearly bent over from the heat. On the third day Pauline saw her calling for him behind the garbage cans, still in all black, and nearly as warmly dressed as if it had been October, and forced her back inside the building, taking her to her own room on the second floor to lie down, when suddenly J.D. blazed up and said:

"I hear him! I hear him! He's on this floor somewhere—*listen!*"

And Pauline had stood there, holding J.D. up in the middle of the hallway, and listened as carefully as she could for several minutes, but hearing nothing herself. "I'm sure you're right, J.D., but you're probably just better tuned in to his sounds than I am. At least come sit down and let me bring you a glass of water first, and I'll try to see if I can figure out where it's coming from. You're burning up. I'm worried you've gotten a little heat sick." It took nearly all Pauline's strength to get J.D. to agree to this much, but when she reentered the hall a few moments later, she *did* think she might have heard something—a terribly faint chirp, scarcely distinguishable from the chirping the birds did in the trees in the courtyard, and yet not the same as a bird, so that she was able to return in something like triumph and tell J.D. it was surely just a matter of time now—

But a few minutes later, the sound had vanished again. Pauline and J.D. managed to recruit Katherine, Stephen, Carol, and Bryan from the lobby, but none of them heard anything more, and J.D., being sure he had somehow gotten himself trapped inside the walls of the building and was starving to death even that very minute, was almost hysterical, so they spent most of their time trying to convince her to go back up to her own room.

At last, having put J.D. to bed while promising to try again in the morning, Pauline held a brief conference with the others in her room. "I didn't like to say so in front of J.D.," Pauline began slowly, "because she was already so upset, and I couldn't be quite sure. But I'm fairly certain that when I *did* hear him calling, it sounded like it was coming from somewhere in Ruth's room." She looked a little guilty, then continued: "Maybe I've made a mistake, of course. And

I don't like to go through someone's room when they're not home, or to assume someone's done something wrong just because she's a little—but maybe she didn't know about William Rufus and J.D., if that is him in there. It may be that he got in there by accident—"

But Carol and Bryan were both looking white and anxious, and Pauline had the uncomfortable feeling that she *wasn't* wrong, despite wishing to be so.

"I've found Ruth in my room before," Carol said slowly. "When she was trying out a job here, I mean. It was a while ago now, but she used one of the housekeeping keys to come into the room while I was asleep—Bryan was there, too," she said, since there was no one in the room who would have needed them to pretend otherwise; Katherine was the closest thing to an authority figure among them, and she certainly wouldn't care.

"I think we'd better go and see," Katherine said. "I don't like it either, Pauline, and I'm not saying Ruth's done anything she shouldn't have. But if you heard something, and it's this hot out, we'd better check. I won't pretend it's not snooping, because it is. But we're not going to turn over her dressers or read her diary, either. We'll just see if he's in there, and afterward we'll tell her what we did, so nobody will have to lie about it."

Katherine retreated to Mrs. Mossler's office for a key, and Stephen went with her for moral support. They came back a few minutes later, Mrs. Mossler now in tow, and walked over to Ruth's room as a group. Mrs. Mossler produced the key, and in another second they had the door open—

At least at first glance, there was no sign of a cat anywhere. But on a green baize-covered chair, standing right in the middle of the room, was a neatly arranged pile of Katherine's hair, now several months old.

After the initial shock had made its way through the group,

they settled down to a more thorough search of the room, except for Carol, who had said only, "Oh, no *thank* you, I'll wait outside," before stepping back out into the hallway. It had been so remarkably filled with detritus of every imaginable variety that it looked as though someone had been living there—and not very happily—for years rather than months. They were confronted with an absolutely shocking number of shoes. Hardly any of them could have been Ruth's, and many of them were unwearable, or in singles instead of pairs; quite a lot of them were ancient-looking men's shoes, too. Lucianne recognized the chewed-off tips from her defaced lipsticks in a stubby little Stonehenge arrangement on top of the dresser, next to a lot of loose theater tickets and cigarette butts.

"She must have been emptying ashtrays into her purse or something," Lucianne said, "because they're all different brands, and some of them have lipstick on the filters. She can't have smoked all these herself; I mean, she had to have been bringing these into the building, but what I can't understand is *why*," and she felt so utterly bewildered, so genuinely sorry at the idea of Ruth smuggling garbage into her bedroom at night, that she started to cry—and not just for herself, standing as she was in the middle of a truly filthy, baffling room, but for Ruth, whom she had neither liked nor treated especially kindly but was living in such a state practically underneath her.

"I can't understand it, either," Bryan said to Katherine. "I just can't understand it. She was always so clean when I saw her. She looked a little tired, but she was always clean."

"The bathroom's at the end of the hall," Pauline said. "Nobody leaves anything in there, and we all would have noticed if—the bathroom's at the end of the hall, is why, I think." She sounded a little dazed.

"But does anyone hear anything?" Mrs. Mossler asked. "I know this is a terrible surprise, and I know we're all worried about Ruth, but does anyone hear anything, or see any signs that a cat might have gotten in here?"

There were shopping bags from Gia's room filled with old apple cores and cheese rinds and soda cans; there were nail clippings from what must have been a dozen different people in little heaps on nearly every surface; there were dead moths arranged in circles and semicircles and once in the initial *B*, and everywhere, there were shoes, all limp and toppled over one another. What was most distressing about the room—aside from the dirtiness—was the undifferentiated way the useful and the filthy were jumbled together. It was absolutely and deliberately mad. The room seemed full of half-assembled traps and charms and magic spells arranged in no particular logic other than the impulse of each moment. It was all accretion, all acquisition, and there was no room for a human being to stay clean or sane within it. Her own clothes had no more important pride of place than other people's cutoff hair and fingernails, or a pile of wet cardboard, or pillowcases full of something hard and lumpy—there was a terrifying degree of *love* in the room, as if its inhabitant was so profoundly attached to everything she came into contact with, whether it was bright and new and useful or dead and discarded and turning into slime, that she loved it all equally, because you cannot love something and throw it away at the same time. And it smelled dark-brown and rotten and *wet*, and the rotted smell clung to the inside of everyone's mouth and nose, and Pauline wondered how it was that she'd never smelled it out in the hallway, or noticed it on any of Ruth's clothes—but no one ever stood close to Ruth if they could help it. And still there was no cat.

Katherine got down on her hands and knees to look underneath the sofa, then suddenly leapt up with a little scream. Bryan was by her side in an instant, and Carol ran back in from the hallway. Katherine swept her hands around in a tense little circle and whispered intently: "*Ruth is still in the room. She's lying under the bed.*"

Mrs. Mossler got down on her hands and knees to see—there was Ruth, flat on the floor, looking back at her.

"Hello, Ruth," she said, a little shakily. "We didn't know you were in, or we would have knocked."

"I heard you at the door," Ruth said, climbing out from under the bed and causing Mrs. Mossler to beetle so rapidly backward to avoid her that she fell over a bag of what Carol recognized as the dirty sheets stripped from Patricia's bed back in May. "And I could hear that everyone was talking about me, so I got scared and hid." It was strange, to think there could be a person like this, who could hide so much but cheerfully tell the truth.

There was beginning to be a crowd in the hallway; Katherine's little scream must have carried, and every few minutes somebody new joined them, and sometimes the newcomers shouted a bit when they first saw Ruth's room. Apparently J.D. was also drawn down by all the commotion, because at last she wandered in, too, and looked around with a heartbreaking expression of confusion, unable to understand just what it was she saw: "Is somebody hurt?" Nobody answered her.

"We came in here," Katherine said to Ruth, and the skin around her mouth and eyes felt very tight, "because we thought we heard J.D.'s cat making sounds from in here. Have you seen him?"

Suddenly Ruth's eyes narrowed, and her usual facial expression, slightly plaintive and pop-eyed, became cunning and thoughtful and drawn into itself—it was hateful. "He's not J.D.'s cat," she said. "He's not anyone's cat, and he can go wherever he likes."

There was a little basket out on Ruth's part of the fire escape—Bryan could just spot the lid past the window frame, which was partly covered by an old-fashioned folding screen—and just as quickly as he spotted it, he knew what it must have been put there for. In another moment he had crossed the room and thrown the window open, and in the next he had the basket in his hands, and inside the basket was a little red body, which had been shut up inside it for who knows how long, and was now gone very limp and very hot and very still—

"Oh, not *him*," J.D. cried, and she rushed to the window, took the basket out of Bryan's hands, and very carefully pulled William Rufus out of it. He nearly slid out of her hands. She could not keep ahold of his body, and she sank down to the floor, bracing him against her lap, crying over and over, "Oh, what an awful thing—what an awful thing—why awful—awful, awful, awful!"

Ruth's eyes were wide and awful. Without saying another word, she dashed over to the corner of the room, and before he could think to move or speak or get ahold of her, she shoved Bryan as hard as she could, right in his midsection. He doubled over, and she kept charging forward, and then they both went quietly and entirely out the window and over the fire escape. And all Katherine could think was, *The second floor was still too high. I ought to have put her on the first floor.*

———··———

It has been said before that the Biedermeier Hotel was a second-rate institution. The second-rate cannot accommodate tragedy; neither can the second floor. Bryan survived the drop; so did Ruth. They fell, yes, but they did not fall a *tragic* distance, only a little more than twenty feet, which had been further broken up at the halfway point by scaffolding. Even William Rufus was very ungracefully revived under the cold water faucet in the bathroom by Pauline and J.D., although his recovery was understandably missed by most in the excitement of an impromptu ride to the hospital in two ambulances and a fire truck. (The uninjured residents were not permitted to ride in either the ambulances or the fire truck but had to content themselves with running alongside both, although Pauline got very close at one point to making it up onto the fire truck's running board.)

Rufus's revival was not missed by J.D., of course, for whom the survival of the small red cat was the only meaningful episode, not only of the entire evening but of practically that entire year, although she was very relieved when she heard that both Ruth and Bryan were expected to eventually recover, although not at the same rate or to the same extent.

In her youth Mrs. Mossler had been an enthusiastic reader of the biologist J. B. S. Haldane, who in 1928 wrote the following in an essay on gravity called *On Being the Right Size*:

> To the mouse and any smaller animal gravity presents practically no dangers. You can drop a mouse down a thousand-yard mine shift; and, on arriving at the bottom, it gets a slight shock and walks away, provided that the ground is fairly soft. A rat is killed, a man is broken, a horse splashes.

She always thought of that anecdotal mouse whenever someone mentioned Ruth; she could not help it. By the end of that summer, after Kitty had been sent to jail for six weeks and Ruth to a state-run institution for a much longer period, Mrs. Mossler decided she was ready to retire. She did not want to stick around long enough to find out what happened to the next generation. She remained optimistic about the future of working women; she had only lost faith in her own ability to superintend them, and was grateful to leave their well-being in Katherine's hands, and Katherine's remit was expanded from the first, second, third, eighth, and eleventh floors to the entirety of the building.

Ruth's room was treated by a professional cleaning team and, after a decent interval, rented out to someone else. The next year the Biedermeier ceased to operate as a women's hotel and became, instead, a reasonably clean, reasonably priced residential hotel for all paying customers, which arrested its financial slide for a little while and staved off demolition for perhaps another decade, perhaps two. Carol and Patricia invited Posey to take Sadie's place in their little art collective on the eleventh floor; she accepted, and they lived together well into the next decade—and quite happily, too. Josephine suffered a broken hip from a fall in her room in 1969 and was eventually moved into a nursing home—but several years later than she would have been moved into a home otherwise. She, too, had arrested the slide for a gallant little while. Lucianne married and moved away. The *Herald-Tribune*, the *Journal-American*, *Freie Arbeiter Stimme*, and *L'Adunata Dei Refrattari* all folded, the latter two without ever learning they had for more than twelve years shared a typesetter between them. Pauline brought innumerable hippies into the hotel, many of whom turned into squatters in its latter days. Lucianne got divorced and moved back in. Stephen got a job with the city commission for the Department of Buildings, and was once picked up for solicitation. Bryan had a steel plate put in his hip.

Gia Burgess lived with the man she loved for twenty-seven years and, after he died, took a room at the Plaza Hotel. Her mother never forgave her. Katherine's mother never forgave her, either; the only difference between the two was that Gia's mother could admit it. Katherine remained an AA member in good standing her whole life long. She tried very hard to take responsibility so that whenever anyone, anywhere, reached out for help, the hand of AA was always ready to meet them; as her old sponsor Arthur had often told her, "There was a room full of sober people the first time *you* came to a meeting. Why should the next alcoholic who needs help have to face an empty room just because you like to sleep in on Saturday mornings?"

The Biedermeier never served its residents another breakfast. All the Automats in the city closed. When Ruth was released from state care a little more than a decade later, there was nowhere left in the city where she could afford to live, so she was forced to go and live elsewhere. Whatever else might be said about her, she never again pushed anyone else out a window, and she never stole another cat.

As for the others, they lived as long as they could, and many of them went on to be useful to each other. The odd and inadequate establishment that for so many decades had housed them was itself broken up shortly thereafter. Its remnants can be found almost anywhere one cares to look. The building itself remains standing, and has survived more than one attempted remodeling. As Mrs. Mossler said to herself by way of consolation, "It's a pity the Automats are gone, but after all people still eat meals all over the city."

ACKNOWLEDGMENTS

I'm tremendously grateful to my agent Kate McKean for saying to me a few years ago, "Why not write a book about a women's hotel? And why don't we meet at the library to discuss it?" In the twelve years we have worked together, she has been the source of a number of excellent ideas, of which these two are merely the latest in a long line. I owe a great deal to her equanimity, curiosity, and patience, and could not have written this book without her.

I'm also indebted to my editor Rakesh Satyal and his careful eye, which is ever-bent on ventilation and motion, who often guided me out of stuffy rooms and into the open air.

I'm grateful to the library staff at the General Research Division at the Stephen A. Schwarzman Building in New York, which enabled me to research, among other things, subway posters, newspapers, restaurant menus, and advertisements for women's hotels of the mid-twentieth century. This book owes a great deal to the public library system.

I'd like to thank The Mastheads in Pittsfield, Massachusetts, for granting me the residency that enabled me to finish this book, and in particular for the bracing and invigorating support of my cohort there: Auyon Mukharji, Elisa Gonzalez, Julia Mounsey, Kristina Gaddy. What a gift it has been to come to know you marvelous strangers.

And to my partners, Grace Lavery and Lily Woodruff: Women are such a pleasure to live with and to think about. I am very lucky it has been granted to me to live with and think about you.

ABOUT THE AUTHOR

Daniel M. Lavery is a former "Dear Prudence" advice columnist at *SLATE*, the cofounder of *The Toast*, and the *New York Times* bestselling author of *Texts from Jane Eyre*, *The Merry Spinster*, and *Something That May Shock and Discredit You*. He also writes the popular newsletter *The Chatner*.

A NOTE FROM THE COVER DESIGNER

"The poster for *The Grand Budapest Hotel* comes to mind." This line from the *Women's Hotel* cover design brief resonated with me most. I loved the idea of creating a cover design as memorable as a Wes Anderson film poster.

I wanted to visualize the layers (or floors?) in Lavery's writing in a unique way and commissioned French illustrator Thibaud Herem to illustrate the cover art. Herem is known for his distinct signature style; working with pencil and Indian inks, he specializes in creating architectural drawings with an incredible level of hand-drawn detail.

Herem's art perfectly captures the essence of The Biedermeier, its walls cracking and windows opened just enough to get a glimpse of the daily lives of the hotel's many eclectic residents.

—Stephen Brayda

Here ends Daniel M. Lavery's
Women's Hotel.

The first edition of this book was printed
and bound at Lakeside Book Company
in Harrisonburg, Virginia, in September 2024.

A NOTE ON THE TYPE

The text of this novel was set in Fournier, a serif type-face released by Monotype Corporation in 1924. It was based on the typeface of the same name created by French typefounder and typographic theoretician Pierre-Simon Fournier around 1742. With its strong contrast between thin and thick strokes and sparse serif bracketing, Fournier was a "transitional" style of typeface, and anticipated the more severe modern fonts that would debut later in the eighteenth century. Its light, clean design presents well on the page, making it a popular choice for printed matter.

HARPERVIA

An imprint dedicated to publishing international voices,
offering readers a chance to encounter other lives and other
points of view via the language of the imagination.